LETHAL JUSTICE

Also by Fern Michaels . . .

Sweet Revenge
Fool Me Once
The Jury
Vendetta
Payback
Picture Perfect
Weekend Warriors
About Face
The Future Scrolls
Kentucky Rich
Kentucky Heat
Kentucky Sunrise
Plain Jane
Charming Lily
What You Wish For
The Guest List
Listen to Your Heart
Celebration
Yesterday
Finders Keepers
Annie's Rainbow
Sara's Song
Vegas Sunrise
Vegas Heat
Vegas Rich
Whitefire
Wish List
Dear Emily

FERN MICHAELS

LETHAL JUSTICE

ZEBRA BOOKS
KENSINGTON PUBLISHING CORP.
http://www.kensingtonbooks.com

Except where actual historical events and characters are being described for the storyline of this novel, all situations in this publication are fictitious and any resemblance to living persons is purely coincidental.

ZEBRA BOOKS are published by

Kensington Publishing Corp.
850 Third Avenue
New York, NY 10022

All Kensington titles, imprints and distributed lines are available at special quantity discounts for bulk purchases for sales promotion, premiums, fund-raising, educational or institutional use.

Special book excerpts or customized printings can also be created to fit specific needs. For details, write or phone the office of the Kensington Special Sales Manager: Kensington Publishing Corp., 850 Third Avenue, New York, NY 10022. Attn. Special Sales Department. Phone: 1-800-221-2647.

First Printing: January 2007
10 9 8 7 6 5 4 3 2 1

Printed in the United States of America

LETHAL JUSTICE

Prologue

Alexis Thorne slipped out of bed and walked over to the window. She loved watching the sun creep over the horizon, loved that a new day was beginning. She was mindful that today was the first day of spring. Finally, finally, she was going to get the justice she deserved. Today, she was ready. She curled up on the window seat with its flowered pillows and hugged her knees to her chest. Excitement rippled through every inch of her.

Once before she'd been in this same emotional state but it hadn't worked out, because back then she wasn't ready to exact her revenge against the two people who had ruined her life and sent her to prison. Now, though, she was *soooo* ready to take them on! Her body just screamed with vengeance.

"Woof."

Alexis untangled herself and rushed over to her beloved dog Grady, the dog she had thought she would never see again. But here he was and her life was better for it. "Want to go out, huh? Okay, but be quiet, everyone is still asleep."

The golden retriever dipped his head and it looked as if he understood, which he probably did.

There was nothing fashionable about the flannel robe Alexis slipped into or the fuzzy, worn slippers. Once, a long time ago, before prison or BP, as she referred to that ugly time, she'd had fine things and a fine life. These days, thanks to Nikki Quinn, her attorney, she earned a living as a personal shopper for some of Washington's elderly residents. It paid the rent, her car payment, and her living expenses. Somehow or other, she managed to save a few dollars each month. It was a far cry from the high salary she used to earn as a securities broker but she'd gotten used to a frugal lifestyle.

Alexis opened the kitchen door to let Grady romp the grounds of Pinewood. She was startled to see Charles Martin on the terrace, surrounded by clay pots of brilliant spring flowers and drinking a cup of coffee.

"Good morning, luv. Can I get you some coffee?" he asked.

"I'll get it if you don't mind me joining you. It looks like it's going to be a beautiful day. I've always loved the first day of spring with its promise of warm breezes, gentle rains, and golden sunshine." Alexis was back within seconds, a cup of coffee in her hands. She sat down on one of the terrace chairs. "A penny for your thoughts, Charles."

"Right now, my dear, my thoughts aren't worth a penny. My mind is clear. It's rare that this happens so I'm trying to enjoy these few minutes."

"How do you do it, Charles?" Alexis asked. "Keeping it all straight, staying on top of everything, even while you may be missing your homeland? I would never be able to do that. I obsess. I can't move on and I can't seem to do two things at one time. Sometimes I think I'm caught in a time warp."

"Training. I can compartmentalize. Fifteen minute power naps. Protein. I love what I'm doing. It's part of my life," Charles replied.

"I envy you," Alexis said. "When do you expect the others?"

"Myra said by noon. We'll have lunch before we get down to work. Are you ready, luv?"

"I'm ready, Charles. I think I feel like Myra did when it was finally her turn to seek revenge against the man who killed her daughter. Like Myra, I thought this day would never get here. I am so grateful—we all are—that Myra formed the Sisterhood for all of us to do what the law failed to do for us. Sometimes, especially late at night, I have a hard time believing someone as good and kind as Myra would use her vast fortune to help all of us get our lives back. I don't know what I'm trying to say here, Charles. Help me out."

Charles smiled. "You're grateful. Sometimes

the law . . . doesn't quite work. Myra wanted to pick up the pieces, to try and make things right for all of you. As you said, her vast fortune allows her to do this." Charles looked down at his watch. "It's time to start breakfast. I promised Myra I would make waffles this morning. Is there anything in particular that you would like, Alexis?"

Alexis sighed as she finished the last of her coffee. "Waffles sound delicious. I'm going to run upstairs to take a shower. This was nice," she said, waving her arms about to indicate the early morning sunshine, the beginning of a new day, and their conversation. "The flowers are so beautiful. I didn't see them when I got here last night."

Charles laughed. "Myra will be so pleased to hear you say that. She and I worked all day in the greenhouses potting all those gorgeous flowers. She wanted the terrace to look beautiful as a welcome for all of you. Run along, dear. I'll give Grady his breakfast."

As Alexis ran up the back stairway, 63-year-old Myra Rutledge was descending the front staircase. Grady ran to greet her. Myra was always good for a brisk belly rub. She sat down on the stairs and obliged the golden retriever until Charles called that breakfast was ready. Grady ran ahead of her, his tail swishing in anticipation of a tidbit of bacon and maybe a bit of waffle in addition to the dog food he usually got.

Myra walked over to the stove where she kissed the love of her life soundly. So soundly,

Charles groaned. "I missed you when I woke up. What time did you get up, dear?"

"A little after three. I had some work to do, calls to make around the globe. Would you like strawberries or blueberries with your waffles?"

"Blueberries and two slices of bacon. It smells wonderful, but then everything you cook tastes and smells wonderful. I thought I heard Alexis earlier. Has she been downstairs?"

"We had coffee on the terrace while Grady romped in the yard. Before you can ask, she said the flowers are beautiful. She also told me she's ready for her mission. She is, Myra. Our girl won't back away this time. She's more confident these days and I do think Grady might have something to do with that newfound confidence."

Myra found herself smiling as she watched the man she loved with all her heart. He hadn't skipped a beat when she'd told him she wanted to form a *little club* to help certain women who fell through the cracks of the judicial system. Charles had jumped in with both feet, both arms swinging to help make it all happen. With her money and his expertise, they'd taken on the *bad guys*, as she thought of them, and got the justice the women deserved. These days, no one questioned Charles. If he said it could be done, then it could be done. It was that simple.

With the Queen of his homeland on his speed dial, who would dare question him? His personal Rolodex would be the envy of the White House if they knew it existed.

Myra beamed with happiness. "The best thing that ever happened to me was when your cover was blown and the Queen spirited you away to our shores. I cannot imagine what my life would have been without you beside me."

Charles raised his eyebrows. "Are we feeling sentimental this morning, Myra?"

"A little. It is the first day of spring. I always expect wonderful things to happen on this day. I don't know why that is. Do you know, Charles?"

Charles thought about the question. "Everything comes alive in the spring. The long cold winter goes back to sleep and the sun comes out. It's just a beautiful time of year. Alexis was saying the same thing earlier. She's equating this day with her mission. Do you want to get married, Myra?" Charles chuckled. "This is proposal number 4,756 if you're counting."

"I would love to marry you, Charles. One of these days. I don't want you stewing and fretting about . . . you know . . . getting caught. I know husbands and wives cannot be forced to testify against each other. They can stick needles under my toenails and I would never mention your name nor the names of our girls to anyone in authority. I am prepared to take the sole blame for our . . . our little endeavors. We've discussed this many times, Charles. Perhaps when all our missions are complete, we can revisit your marriage proposal. In the meantime, isn't it enough to know I love you body and soul? It's so boring being made an honest woman."

Charles laughed. "Point taken, my dear."

Myra leaned across the table and whispered.

"Do you remember the time you fashioned a maypole in the back yard and we danced *naked* in the moonlight?" Myra burst out laughing when she saw her companion of many years flush a bright pink.

"It's one of my finest and fondest memories. Now that I know how to make a maypole complete with streaming ribbons, I'm up for another dance. Just say the word."

It was Myra's turn to blush. "I'll let you know. Go! I can see you're getting antsy. I'll clean up. I think I hear Alexis on the stairs."

"Her waffles are in the warming oven. Call me when the others arrive."

Myra nodded.

Alexis, dressed in a bright turquoise pantsuit, leaned over to give Myra a morning hug. "It's a wonderful day, isn't it? The terrace looks absolutely delicious. It's like looking at a rainbow. You must be so happy living here all year long. I can't even begin to imagine what that would be like. I mean, the permanence." Alexis's voice turned wistful. "Living here with the man you love has to be a wonderful feeling. It doesn't get any better than that, does it, Myra?"

Myra bit down on her lower lip. "For a time, it was like you said. I was the happiest woman in the world. I had it all, my cup runneth over, that kind of feeling. Then my world turned upside down when that Chinese diplomat's son killed my daughter. Now, Pinewood is simply a place to live. A place where we all conduct our business. If I had to leave here, I could do it. Your day will come, dear. You'll find the happiness you deserve, you'll be vindicated, and then you can get back into the world you were forced to leave because of those hateful greedy people."

Alexis picked up a blueberry, wondering where it came from at this time of year. "One can't go home again, Myra. I think I'm a little nervous about what will happen to me after . . . after I've been vindicated. How do you go back to your old life, pick up the pieces and . . . ?" Alexis threw up her hands in frustration at her inability to finish her thought.

"You aren't going to go home again, dear. You're going to go forward to a new life that isn't ugly and controlled by greedy, manipulative people. Once you get your reputation back, you may well decide you don't want that kind of life anymore. When you're whole again, then it will be time to make decisions. Whatever those decisions turn out to be, all of us will be behind you. Is there something else bothering you? I'm a good listener, Alexis."

Alexis picked up another blueberry and bit into it. "I have this fear that we'll get caught and I'll have to go to prison again. I can't go back there again, Myra. I just can't. I have awful dreams, night after night. Even in the bright daylight, I hear that cell door clanging shut. In my dreams my hands and feet are raw and bleeding from kicking and hitting the bars. I sleep with the lights on and my bedroom door wide open. I thought about going to therapy but what good would it do? It happened. I can't change that. The fear is real. More real because of what we're doing. You'd think I would have run long and hard instead of opening myself up to the possibility of going to prison again when Nikki invited me to join the Sisterhood. Is there something wrong with me? When I've been vindicated, will I feel differently? Will the past go away?"

Myra knew she was in the tall grass and that the young woman sitting across from her needed answers she wasn't sure she had. Still, she had to try. "The short answer is, I don't know, Alexis. When I was vindicated, so to speak, I thought . . . I hoped . . . the pain would go away. It didn't. There is nothing worse in the whole world than losing a child; especially painful is losing your only child. I had to accept the fact that no matter what we did to that horrible man it wasn't going to bring my daughter back to me. Did I get personal satisfaction out of caning and skinning him? Yes. I know he will never, ever, kill anyone again. No other mother will have to go through what I went through at his hands. I still dream of my daughter. I hope that never stops. When I wake in the morning, my pillow is wet.

"I am well aware that if we get caught, which I don't think will happen, I will go to prison. I'm prepared for that because I know that with my help, your help, Charles's help, the others were vindicated. Whatever happens, you'll be able to handle it. You will, Alexis. Did that help at all?"

Always truthful, Alexis grimaced. "Yes and no. It's one of those wait and see things. I wish I were as tough as Kathryn, as gentle as Isabelle, as smart as Nikki, and had the inner peace that Yoko has. I wish. . . I wish. . ."

Myra laughed. "Charles always says, be careful

what you wish for because you might get it." This brought a smile to Alexis's face.

"I think I can handle it. No, that's not right. I *know* I can handle it."

Myra nodded sagely. She wanted to say "you have no other choice" but she held her tongue. Alexis would prevail, just the way she and the others had.

It was a given.

Chapter 1

Maggie Spritzer sat at her desk staring at her blank computer screen. She'd been sitting there ever since she returned from Pinewood at two o'clock. She looked at her watch, stunned that a whole hour had gone by. She was aware of Ted's eyes at full bore on her back. Sometimes Ted could be tiresome. She thought about all the promises she'd made to Ted about sharing, about maybe getting married. Her stomach started to churn. She didn't want to share. That was her bottom line. Her motto had always been "what's mine is mine and what's yours is *ours.*" Ted didn't see it that way. Right now, she realized, she had enough *togetherness* to last her into the next century. How she was going to break it to Ted was something she didn't want to think about right now.

Ever since that night in the cemetery when they had the ladies of Pinewood in their cross hairs, only to be rendered useless by some guy's Taser, things had been different between them. Ted blamed her for getting *tasered*, if there was such a word, and she blamed him.

No one, and that included Ted, would ever convince her that the man at the cemetery who felled them wasn't Jack Emery. Ted said it was impossible. Said he knew where Emery was that night and it wasn't at the cemetery. Guys always stuck together. It had to be Emery and not Bobby Harcourt, as Ted suggested.

Maggie drummed nervous fingers on the desk top. She needed to do something and she needed to do it quickly before Ted got an edge on her. Her gut told her she had the inside track on a Pulitzer if she could get something concrete on those upscale ladies. Maybe it was time to be bold and brazen and head out to Pinewood again and confront the ladies. Woman to woman.

Her fingers continued their mad dance on the scarred desk top. Better yet, maybe a one-on-one. But the only one she could get close to would be Isabelle Flanders. The truck driver and the personal shopper were too elusive. She had a chance with the Asian woman if she went to her nursery but she hadn't been at the cemetery that night. Any one-on-one meeting had to be with one of the women who had actually been there. Then again, maybe she should schedule an appointment with Nikki Quinn at her law office.

She really wanted a Pulitzer.

Right now, though, she had to figure out a way to outwit Ted. She wondered if he'd lied to her when he said that after the ladies of Pinewood did their dirty work, they took a hiatus and didn't regroup again for several months. He said they took time off to rest on their laurels. Fact or fiction? What she did know was that the women had all met up at noon. Her gut instinct told her they were gearing up for another caper. She felt a little envious, almost wishing she were part of that team. Almost.

Maggie thought she would feel guilty at not sharing everything with Ted but surprisingly, it didn't bother her at all. She must not be a nice person even though Ted thought she was the best thing since sliced bread. She remembered when she'd first started to work at the *Post* and thirty-year veteran curmudgeon Adele Matthews had given her some sage advice: never trust a male reporter; never go with a dual by-line, especially with a male; and always look out for number one because no one else will. And, whatever you do, never forget that your ultimate goal is a Pulitzer.

Maggie got up from her desk, slipped into her light spring jacket, her thoughts on her really big secret, the small handheld recorder she'd used that night at the cemetery. She knew Ted had one, too, but at the last second, when he was occupied with something else, she'd removed the miniature cassette. She'd never told him she had one, too, in her pocket. She had the goods on the gals but she couldn't use it. Not yet.

Maggie tried to work some animation into her facial features. Her voice was short of a trill when she reached Ted's desk. "Hello there, sweet cheeks. How's it going today?"

Ted's eyes narrowed. She was up to something. He could smell her deviousness. He felt like giving her a good swat. He decided to be cagey. The only problem was, Jack Emery never got around to telling him how to do that. Being cagey was probably an addendum to Getting to Know and Understand Women 101.

"Well, it's going. Slow day in the world. I just got in about an hour ago. Gotta take the last shuttle to New York tonight. Big doings at the UN tomorrow. What's the local gossip?" If this was being cagey, he needed a refresher course. Maggie just looked smug. The urge to swat her was so strong he had to fight with himself not to pop her square on her cute little nose. *Cute my ass.* She was a barracuda out for a kill and he knew he was in her sights. He struggled for nonchalance by tilting back in his swivel chair. There was no way in hell he was going to ask her if she wanted to grab a quick bite.

"Want to get some early dinner? I'm free," Maggie said.

Ted couldn't believe his own ears when he said, "No thanks."

Maggie's eyes narrowed. This was a first. He'd actually turned her down. "I'm buying," she smiled.

"Sorry, no can do."

Maggie huffed and puffed and made a production out of buttoning her jacket. "Okay, guess I'll see you when you get back. When will that be?"

Jack Emery's words about "play hard to get once in a while" rang in his ears. He shrugged. "Not sure. I have a job interview at the *Times*. I'm there so why the hell not."

Maggie gaped, her jaw dropping. "You're leaving! Why? You never said a word to me about that. I thought we were a team. If I hadn't asked you, when were you going to tell me?"

Ted shrugged again. Maybe old Jack was onto something. Maggie looked . . . pissed. He wondered exactly what that meant. That maybe she really did care? Or, she was just pissed at being left out of the loop. More likely the latter. "Where is it written that I have to tell you *everything?* We both know you don't tell me *everything.* I suppose I would have gotten around to telling you when and if I got the job, which is unlikely. I don't like jinxing myself."

Maggie switched gears. She decided sweet was the way to go. "If it's what you want, I hope you get it. I'll keep my fingers crossed for you. Remember now, I have first dibs on you, so don't go getting cozy with any of those glitzy New York reporters."

Ted let the chair hit the floor. He swiveled around, his eyes cold and hard. "You took the tape out of my recorder that night at the cemetery, didn't you?"

Maggie did her best to look outraged. "Is that what this is all about? How dare you accuse me of such a dastardly thing, Ted! How dare you! It's not my fault that you get sloppy sometimes.

I'm not your keeper, I can't oversee your every movement. You forgot in the excitement of the evening. Admit it."

"You know what, Maggie, I knew you'd say what you just said. You aren't the person I thought you were. I think we should go our separate ways. I'd like my key back. Since you never saw fit to give me a key to your pad, I have nothing to give back."

She didn't hear what she just heard, did she? Suddenly she felt sick to her stomach. "You're dumping me! Because you forgot to put a cassette in your recorder! Well, here you go, hot shot," Maggie said as she ripped his key off her key ring. She tossed it on the metal desk. "You know what else, you aren't the person I thought you were either. From now on, get your own coffee and doughnuts in the morning. Don't call me either."

Maggie's eyes were filling with tears. She turned and ran from the newsroom. God, what if that old curmudgeon, Adele, was wrong?

Outside in the late afternoon sunshine, Maggie let the tears flow. "He dumped me! He just . . . he just cast me aside like an old shoe." She climbed into her car when she realized she'd been screaming and people were staring at her. "Well, screw you, Ted Robinson."

Inside the newsroom, Ted opened his backpack and fished around until he found what he was looking for. Two days ago he'd picked the lock on Maggie's apartment so he could search it. He'd found the tiny cassette in her tampon box. He'd felt like a thief, which he was, when he copied the tape before he stuck the cassette in his pocket. The tape was very poor quality, the voices indistinguishable.

Ted felt like he was a hundred years old when he trudged his way to his boss's office. "Can you put this in your safe for now?" He tossed a small sealed yellow envelope across the desk. His step was a little lighter when he walked back to his desk, grabbed his backpack, slipped it on, and left the newsroom.

Sometimes life was a bitch.

Maggie let herself into her apartment and was immediately welcomed with sharp barks and wet kisses from Daisy. She reached for the leash, hooked it onto the dog's collar and took the stairs back down to the first floor. She walked the dog for a full hour before she headed out to the boulevard to pick up some Chinese food for her dinner.

Back in the apartment, Maggie made a production out of changing her clothes, feeding Daisy, going through her mail, making coffee before she tackled the dinner she really didn't want. Dumped. Ted had told her to get out of his life. Well, what did she expect. She'd betrayed her partner, the man who'd asked her to marry him. Tears dripped into her shrimp chow mein. Finally, she shoved the cardboard container across the table.

Swiping at her tears, Maggie headed for the bathroom and her tampon box. Her fingers fumbled around at the bottom until she was able to grasp the tiny cassette. She carried it into the bedroom and slipped it into the mini recorder. She hit Play and waited. And waited. All she could hear were smatterings of words, lots of static, the rain and more static. She opened the recorder and turned the tape over to the other side. All she could hear was a soft whirring sound. Ted had outsmarted her.

"You bastard! You stinking bastard! You stole my tape!"

Ted arrived home in a foul mood. Even Mickey and Minnie couldn't make him smile. He headed straight for the kitchen where he picked up the phone, hit the speed dial, popped a Michelob and said, "Espinosa, Ted Robinson. Look, I need you to take my place tonight. You're taking the last shuttle to New York to cover the UN thing in the morning. I'm going to fax you the itinerary right now. Just sign in at the ticket counter. Your name is on the roster. What do you mean, why are you going? You're going because I said you're going. The old man doesn't care who goes as long as the story gets covered. I'm senior to your junior. No, no, I don't owe you anything. It's your job. Wait for the fax."

Ted slugged at his beer as he trooped down the hall to his computer room. He yanked the itinerary out of his backpack and faxed it off to Jesus Espinosa.

Back in the kitchen, Ted opened the refrigerator, knowing there was nothing in it but orange juice, milk, and three wilted apples. No magic fairy had done the grocery shopping while he was at work. He did, however, have boxed macaroni and cheese. He made two boxes, chowed down, and then fed the hissing, snarling cats. So what if he missed a few food groups. Then he watched the early evening news as he waited for it to get dark.

At seven-thirty, Ted changed his clothes to an all-black outfit, got in his car and headed for Pinewood. His reporter's nose had been twitching for two days now. He had to pay attention. The nose twitch, he told himself over and over, had nothing to do with Maggie Spritzer. He wondered if Jack Emery would be proud of him. Jack had warned him early on, dump them before they dump you. That way you get to keep your ego. You get to see her cry. Better she should cry than you, a grown man. Jack just didn't say how much the betrayal was going to hurt. Smart ass Jack Emery. "I hate your fucking guts, you district attorney. Another thing, you asshole, don't think for one minute you fooled me out there at that cemetery. I know that was you. You aided and abetted those women. I got you on tape, you son of a bitch."

Ted hated it when he talked out loud to himself. What he hated even more was when he answered himself. He continued talking to himself as his car ate up the miles. Before he knew it, he was a mile from the entrance to Pinewood. He parked his car on a wide shoulder of the road, got out and hiked the rest of the way to the security gates that led to the private compound. He was pulling out his night binoculars when he felt the fine hairs on the back of his neck move. He didn't stop to think; he made a mad dive into the bushes, clamped his hand over his mouth and lay still. Maggie? Charles Martin's private cops, the ones with the special gold shields? Jack? Maybe a wild animal and maybe none of the above. He lay quietly until he felt something crawl up his leg. A rat? He shook his leg and felt rather than saw something fly to the side. Yes, a rat. God, how he hated vermin.

Ted listened to the quiet spring night as he crept forward, the binoculars at his eyes. Aha! His twitching nose was right on target. All the ladies appeared to be in residence; even the big rig was there.

So, the ladies of Pinewood were getting ready to kick some ass. Yee haw!

Chapter 2

The ladies of Pinewood were having cocktails on the terrace, much to Myra's delight. She truly enjoyed seeing "her girls" and watching them interact with one another. These days they were like an extended family. It wasn't that way in the beginning, though. Back when she'd formed the Sisterhood the young women had been hostile, suspicious, afraid to open up to one another. She hoped she was at least a small part of their blossoming, as she liked to call it.

The girls were doing what Charles called kibitzing. Myra let her mind drift as she listened to them, to the birds singing in the trees, to Kathryn's dog Murphy and Alexis's dog Grady barking and chasing each other around the yard.

"I bought this racy-looking dress," Yoko said. "I have nowhere to wear it."

Frugal, ever practical Kathryn said, "Then why did you buy it? How much was it? What color?"

"In case. I'm not telling you how much it was because you'll say I should have put the money in the bank for a rainy day. I never go anywhere on rainy days. The dress will get ruined in the rain because it's silk. It's sky blue."

Kathryn grinned. "Forget it. We have a language problem here. You wouldn't wear the dress on a rainy day because you wouldn't have bought the dress. Instead of buying the dress you would have put the money in the bank."

Yoko looked perplexed. "Then I would have no dress, in case."

Alexis jumped into the fray. "Hold on here. Is there a man somewhere in regard to this dress?"

Yoko tried to look demure. "In a manner of speaking. I was shopping in the Asian market and met a . . . person there. This person was buying some of the same things I was buying. He looked at me with . . . with . . ."

"Lust?" Isabelle laughed.

"Perhaps."

"Did you get a name, a phone number?"

Yoko turned pink. "No, but he wanted mine. I didn't give it up." She eyed Kathryn and said, "I'm not easy. But . . ." Her eyes grew round. "The clerk called me when I got home and told me the man asked for my address. She gave me his name. She said he was an important man.

She gave it up because she said it was time for me to . . . you know . . ."

"Hop in the sack," Isabelle said, finishing Yoko's sentence for a second time. The women burst out laughing, even Myra and Yoko herself.

"So, who is he?" Nikki asked.

"He's not . . . pretty."

"You mean handsome. Men are handsome, women are pretty," Kathryn said.

"Okay, hand-some. His name is Harry Wong. He teaches martial arts to police officers."

Nikki was glad there was nothing in her hands because she would have dropped it. Harry Wong was Jack's friend. Unless there were two Harry Wongs who taught martial arts to police officers.

Kathryn leaned forward. "And this clerk at the Asian market just gave you all this info . . . because . . ."

"I grilled her," Yoko said smartly. "I could probably teach him a thing or two. He has a *dojo* downtown."

"This is so exciting," Myra said. "Let me guess. You are going to go to the *dojo* and pretend you want to take lessons. It will be a chance encounter, that kind of thing. I think that's what I would do."

Kathryn burst out laughing. "You little devil, Myra." Myra accepted the statement as a compliment.

"Is that what you're going to do?" Alexis demanded.

"Yes. I scheduled an appointment. It will be

very difficult to play stupid. I do not know how to do that."

"Dumb, not stupid. There's a difference. Don't worry, we'll teach you. Well, this certainly has been an interesting discussion. When is your first lesson?" Kathryn asked.

"Tomorrow, but I plan to cancel it. I want him to get wet."

The women went off into peals of laughter. "You mean sweat."

"Yes, sweat. I will reschedule. I may never go. I will schedule and reschedule."

Charles appeared in the doorway leading to the terrace. "What's so funny?"

"You don't want to know, dear. Are you ready for us?"

Charles backed up a step. He blinked. Many thoughts flew through his mind. They were so united. So in tune with one another. So together. He wondered how he would fare if they ever turned on him. He shuddered. He took a second to look across at his lady love. Somewhere along the way, Myra had definitely become a Sister. He had no other choice but to believe it was a good thing.

Charles led the procession to a solid wall of bookshelves. The women waited while he counted down the various carvings on the intricate molding that ran the length of the bookshelves. The moment his fingers touched the lowest carving, the wall moved slowly and silently to reveal a set of stairs and a large room with wall-to-wall computers that blinked and flashed, as well as a mind-boggling, eye-level closed-circuit television screen that showed the outside security gates. Each wall seemed to be made up of television screens, their sound muted. MSNBC was playing on the south wall, CNN on the north wall, FOX on the east wall. Overhead, fans whirred softly, the only sound in the room, and there were no windows to be seen.

This underground room was the Sisterhood's command center. Charles was the one responsible for installing the cutting-edge, solar-powered electrical system. Stored power could last a full month, Charles was proud to announce.

All the women knew the story of the tunnels underneath Pinewood. Myra had told them at their first meeting that in the old days her ancestors helped the slaves reach safety via the tunnels. Now, a modern day ventilation system had been installed but Myra was the one responsible for hanging bells at each entrance. She was fond of saying, "Just in case."

While Charles referred to this special place as the command center, the women called it the war room. They took their seats at a round table just as Charles pressed a button. The plasma TV screens momentarily darkened to be replaced with Lady Justice towering above them. It was always a sobering moment for the women, a reminder of why they were all sitting in a top-secret room no one knew about.

There was no chitchat now, no laughter, not even a smile. Taking the law into one's hands was a sobering experience.

Myra called the meeting to order. "Before we get down to the business of today, is there any old business that needs to be discussed?"

"Anything on the Barringtons?" Nikki asked.

Charles stepped forward. "No, Nikki, nothing. I have not given up but there are just so many hours in the day. Finding the Barringtons is still a top priority. We'll have to leave it at that for the moment."

Nikki leaned back in her chair, her thoughts turning toward Jack and what Yoko had said out on the terrace. Should she tell Jack about Harry Wong? Should she keep Yoko's news to herself? She decided on the latter, having no wish to betray a sister. She didn't have to confide *everything* to Jack. A woman needed to keep some things secret. She wondered how many secrets Jack kept from her. She couldn't help but wonder if trust would ever be total. She rather doubted it.

"If there's no other news then I suggest we move on," Myra said. "If you'll open your folders you can all read Alexis's history. Our sister was a very successful securities broker at one point in her life. As they say in the business, she was up and coming. Then she took a month-long vacation, her first in six years. When she returned, she was arrested for a securities fraud she did not commit. Her employers, a man and a woman, framed Alexis and she served a year in prison. She's a convicted felon. She lost everything, much the way Isabelle lost everything when Rosemary Hershey snatched it all away from her.

Unfortunately, Alexis had to serve a year in prison. She can never get that year of her life back. As we all know, prison is not a nice place.

"In addition to Alexis's incarceration, more tragedy followed. An elderly couple who were bilked by her employers committed suicide when they were stripped of their life savings. That monstrous pair targeted the elderly, many of whom were reduced to the poverty level. Alexis was made out to be an ogre who hated old people and showed no compassion when swindling them.

"When Alexis got out of prison, she went to see Nikki to ask if anything could be done, as Nikki's firm does a lot of pro bono work. The best Nikki could do was get Alexis a new identity and a job outside her field. That pretty much brings us up to date. Now, it's time for Alexis to tell us what she wants us to do by way of punishment for her previous employers."

Alexis cleared her throat. "The first thing I want to say is, I had very poor legal representation. While I was in prison, and Myra is right, it is not a nice place, I plotted their deaths every single night. It was the only way I could go to sleep. I imagined slitting their throats, carving out their hearts, watching them drown, setting them on fire. Nothing would satisfy me. I don't know why I thought killing them would make me feel better. I'm not a murderer but like I said, thinking like that got me through that year. Even now, the best thing I can come up with is that I want them in prison; behind bars. I want them to hear the door clang shut and know they can't get out. I want them to suffer the way I suffered."

Myra turned to Charles. "Tell us what you've come up with in regard to Alexis's previous employers."

Charles turned on one of the television monitors. "This," he said, using his pointer, "is Arden Gillespie." A picture of a beautiful woman dressed in designer wear and an elegant hairdo was smiling up at a tall, handsome, distinguished gentleman. "The man at her side is her partner, Roland Sullivan. Mr. Sullivan is married and has a son in college and a daughter who will graduate from high school in the spring. Mrs. Sullivan is a schoolteacher with a sterling reputation. From the information I was able to gather, she's a wonderful caring mother and a good wife but she does have her own career.

"Mr. Sullivan came from humble beginnings. In his rush to get to the top of his game he's stepped on quite a few people along the way. With no apologies. Miss Gillespie joined his firm three years before Alexis was sent to prison. Eighteen months after she was hired, Mr. Sullivan made her a full partner. At the same time, he began an affair with Miss Gillespie that is still going on. Both partners have very expensive tastes. Both like to take expensive vacations. They drive outrageously expensive cars. Miss Gillespie has a passion for diamonds. She has a high-end apartment at the Watergate that is filled with priceless antiques.

"Mrs. Sullivan is a plain woman, not into frills and jewels. According to my information, she likes to cook and bake, loves her special-needs students, adores her children, and also likes to work in the garden. She prefers family vacations and usually ends up going alone with her two children. At this point in time I think it's safe to say that Mr. and Mrs. Sullivan have a marriage of convenience. I wasn't able to find any evidence that Mrs. Sullivan is aware of her husband's infidelity. She stood at his side during Alexis's problems with the SEC when they hauled her off in handcuffs for swindling all her wealthy elderly clients. It was Gillespie and Sullivan who raped the dormant accounts, forged buy and sell orders, and covered it all up by framing Alexis. Mrs. Sullivan never offered any comments before, during, or after the trial. She distanced herself as much as she could in regard to the media."

"How much money did they dupe their investors out of?" Isabelle asked.

"Tens and tens of millions. I was able to find properties all over the globe. There's a beautiful ten room house in Hawaii right on the Pacific Ocean. There is a high-end chalet in Telluride, Colorado; a working ranch in Wyoming. Mr. Sullivan has a yacht named Rachel, after his daughter, I suppose. Mrs. Sullivan doesn't like going out on the water but Miss Gillespie loves the water. She goes on cruises with Mr. Sullivan quite often. I haven't located all the properties abroad as yet. Monies have been scattered all over the globe. We pretty much have a lock on a lot of it.

"According to some sources, Miss Gillespie put pressure on Mr. Sullivan to leave his wife and marry her. It seems he agreed and would actually have followed through but after Alexis went to prison, he backed out. The firm of Sullivan and Gillespie appears to be in a bit of disarray these days. The affair may be waning but I have no actual proof of that. Mr. Sullivan seems to be spending more time at home these days."

"If Mr. Sullivan is staying home, where is Miss Gillespie staying?" Nikki asked.

"At her pricey Watergate apartment. My personal opinion, for whatever it's worth, is that the two of them are blackmailing each other. All the offshore accounts carry two names so they're tied to one another," Charles said.

Alexis squirmed in her chair. "How are we going to get them?"

Charles smiled and the women relaxed. "Myra and I have come up with a plan. Myra has an old dear friend who lives from time to time on a large estate in Manassas. Her name is Anna Ryland de Silva."

"Not *the* reclusive Anna Ryland de Silva!" Nikki said.

"The one and only. She's in Barcelona right now living in an exquisite villa. Myra and I visited her a few years ago. She's reclusive, a tad dotty and very opinionated. She never gives interviews and no one has actually seen her in years. She travels—when she travels, which is rare—with an entourage. She stays in contact with only a few people: Judge Easter, Myra, and a gentleman friend named Donald something or other. Donald lives in an assisted living facility that Anna pays for. She's incredibly wealthy. Her daddy was in railroads and then automobiles. It's impossible to gauge her late husband's wealth. Old Spanish aristocracy, that kind of thing. Billions with a capital B," Charles said.

"How does all that help us?" Yoko queried.

"Think, ladies. With a little makeup from Alexis's Red Bag of Tricks, Myra can pose as Anna Ryland de Silva. If she suddenly calls the firm of Gillespie and Sullivan and says she's interested in switching brokerage houses, what do you think will happen? I think Miss Gillespie and Mr. Sullivan will pull out all the stops to get such a robust account. They'll both lie awake nights trying to figure ways to plunder it."

"Charles, you are just too clever," Kathryn squealed. "That's perfect! We scam the scammers. I love it! Alexis, what do you think?"

"I . . . I don't . . . I guess I must be stupid. How can all this help me get my revenge?"

"We're going to allow them to plunder the account, allow them to forge papers, allow them to do pretty much what they want, and then we'll . . . we'll nail them. Is that the right term, Charles?" Myra asked.

"More or less. Myra and I are flying to Barcelona at first light to . . . ah, nail it all down. We'll be back the day after tomorrow. While we're gone, you can plot any additional revenge you can think of. Whatever you come up with, we'll manage to fit it in."

"Why don't you just call her up instead of flying all the way to Spain?" Kathryn asked.

"Annie doesn't like to speak on the phone. She's a little paranoid about things like that. She doesn't believe in email either. Unless she's changed her habits, she looks at her mail only every couple of months. Going to Barcelona is our only option if we want to enlist her help," Myra said.

"Do any of you see a problem with what I've told you so far?" Charles asked.

The women said they didn't.

"Then, ladies, we're adjourned. We'll meet up here the day after tomorrow."

In the kitchen, the women declined the offer of drinks and headed out to their cars. Standing in the doorway, Myra reached for Charles's hand. They both laughed when the girls started ribbing Yoko about Harry Wong.

"Oh, I hope she manages to find happiness, don't you, Charles?"

"With Harry Wong?" Charles teased.

"Why not? She's come a long way since joining us. Remember how shy and frightened she was. Now, she's . . . she's her own person. I hope it works out. Oh, Charles, this is such a fantastic idea. I mean going to Barcelona. We have so much to talk to Annie about. I do so hope she agrees."

"My dear, I have never yet met the person who can refuse you anything."

"Charles, you are just too sweet for your own good."

"Sweet, is it? Well, old gal, we're alone. Do you want to see how really sweet I can be?"

Myra giggled. "I thought you would never ask. Lead the way, my dear."

Chapter 3

Myra walked out of the airport into the warm sunshine. She looked around at the busy passengers who were waiting for friends or relatives to take them to their destinations. She reached for Charles's hand and squeezed it. "I do so love traveling. We should do it more often, but just for a few days at a time."

Charles smiled as his eyes scanned the long line of waiting cars, hoping to pick out the one that would take them to Anna Ryland's home. "We don't travel, Myra, because you get homesick after three days. Ah, there's our car. Come along, dear."

The uniformed driver held up a placard that said "Rutledge" in bright red letters. Charles held up his hand in greeting. A moment later, their sparse luggage was settled in the trunk and they were inching their way into the moving airport traffic. Myra and Charles settled back for the long drive to Anna Ryland de Silva's mountaintop retreat.

"I think Barcelona is beautiful but I don't think I could live here. Anna loves it, though. It's so hard for me to believe she doesn't want to live in the United States. I thought . . . hoped . . . once Anna stopped grieving she would want to return to her homeland. Nellie and I miss her. This reclusiveness of hers is not healthy. It's gone on way too long. I'm the living proof. Nellie . . . Nellie . . ." Myra threw her hands in the air when she couldn't finish what she was trying to say.

"It's tragic, Myra, that each of you lost your family. It's almost bizarre. First Anna losing her husband and two children in that boating accident years ago, followed by Barbara's death, then Nellie's daughter Jenny killed in that awful accident. Grief is a terrible thing."

"I know, Charles, but Anna carried it to the extreme. You know how many times Nellie and I tried to get her to come back to the land of the living. She literally told us to mind our own business. Nellie gave up and simply told Anna she was hopeless and she deserved to wallow in her misery. Maybe this time . . . I hope she doesn't kick us out when we show up at her door. Good grief, whatever will we do if that happens?"

Charles reached for Myra's hand. "Anna would never do that, Myra. She adores you. I guarantee she will be happy to see you."

"Do you think she'll be happy enough to give

up watching the weather channel or whatever they call it over here, to spend some time with us?"

"Of course she will. When we were here three years ago she entertained us royally. The three of you were like sisters. You and Nellie are all she has left. The people she surrounds herself with here in Spain are employees and servants. You're the closest thing to family Anna has. I don't want you to give it another thought."

"I've always wondered if the people she has around her are taking care of her financial affairs. I've been tempted to ask but never did. She used to use some of the same financial people Nellie and I use back in the States. I hope that hasn't changed. Armand left her a fortune equal only to that of the late Aristotle Onassis. With the fortune her parents left her as well, Anna is probably one of the wealthiest women in the world. I'm going to have a real heart to heart talk with her on this visit. I don't care if she shows me the door. Someone has to get through to her. Nellie seems to think I can do it.

"The girls gave me a lot of suggestions. I . . . ah . . . might use some of them if things get . . . sticky. I know how to be forceful, Charles. I know when to back off if I hit a nerve. I should have done it a long time ago. Why didn't I, Charles?"

Charles squeezed Myra's hand. "Because you said you didn't want to stomp on Anna's grief. You said it was all she had left. You said you had to respect that grief because you remembered only too well how difficult it was."

"It's been fifteen years. That's way beyond the time one lives in a shell. Maybe I'm too late. Maybe she won't be able to . . . get past that line she's drawn. What will I do then, Charles?"

Charles stared out the tinted window at the brilliant scarlet bougainvillea that seemed to be everywhere. He searched his mind for a response that would satisfy Myra. The best he could come up with was, "I don't know, dear. I think it's best if you think positive and hope for the best. For whatever it's worth, I think, if nothing else, you will pique her interest. If you can do that, I think the rest will fall into place."

Myra leaned back and closed her eyes. She didn't let go of Charles's hand. From time to time, she squeezed it. She smiled to herself when he returned the slight pressure. Eventually, she slept.

A long time later, Charles woke Myra with a gentle kiss on her cheek. "We're almost there, Myra. We're halfway up the mountain."

Myra's eyes snapped open. Her hands started to shake. Charles reached for her hands and held them tightly. "It's all right, Myra. If things don't work out, it won't be the end of the world. We'll just have to fall back and regroup. If you get uptight, if you're nervous, Anna will pick up on it. You have to be calm and serene. Later, you can be the feisty Myra whom I love and adore." Myra laughed.

When the car finally came to a stop, Myra stepped out before the driver could open the door for her. Charles followed her as they stood looking at the refurbished old monastery that was now Anna Ryland de Silva's home. "It's so beautiful it takes my breath away. I think I can understand why Anna doesn't want to leave here. It's like a magical place with all the flowers, the landscaping, the view of the Mediterranean from all sides. It's so blue. I don't think I noticed that before. Well, maybe I did, but I wasn't in the mood back then that I'm in now. The breeze is heavenly, isn't it?"

"It's wonderful. Very peaceful. Yoko would love all these flowers," Charles said. "I wonder how long it took to turn the old monastery into this lovely place."

"Three long years. Anna lived in one of the outer buildings while the work was going on. In the beginning they brought all the materials up the mountain road, and then Anna had the supplies helicoptered in when she saw how long it was taking. There's a helicopter pad in the back somewhere."

"How many people live here?"

"I have no idea. There are at least a dozen gardeners but I think they go home in the evening. Anna is not a demanding kind of person. I'm sure she has a cook and a housekeeper. I never asked. Is it important, Charles?"

"It might be. When it's time to leave, we'll know everything. Should we announce ourselves?"

"I'm sure Anna is in the back in one of the open rooms. Let's just walk around. She'll find us." Charles shrugged but he fell into step next to Myra. "Oh, Yoko would dearly love this place.

I think all the girls would. Do you like it, Charles?"

"It's certainly interesting. I have been here before, dear. Nothing much seems to have changed. Ah, I think I see our hostess."

Myra waved as she ran forward. "Annie!"

"Myra! How nice to see you! You should have told me you were coming." They hugged, kissed, and then hugged again.

"I would have if you'd answer your phone or read your mail. How are you, Annie? Nellie sends her regards. She said to tell you she'll come over for a visit later in the year."

Anna Ryland de Silva was tall and thin. Her long gray hair was braided and twisted in a coronet around her head, making her seem taller than she was. Round, lightly tinted glasses covered her blue eyes. She wore a long flowing dress and sandals. Myra thought Annie looked like a sixties flower child. Her eyes behind the tinted glasses were still vague and basically unfocused. It was as if one part of her was here but the rest of her was somewhere else.

So, nothing had changed since her last visit. Myra tried for a cheerful tone. "I'd like to shower and change. And then, Annie, I'd like to take a nice walk if you're up to it."

"But of course, Myra. Run along. You know where your room is. Charles, you look in need of a nap."

"How astute of you, Annie. Myra slept on the plane and on the ride up the mountain. If you'll excuse me, I'll see you later." Annie waved both of them off as she made her way back to one of the outdoor rooms where she spent most of her time.

It was a beautiful room with a Mediterranean flavor. The furniture was dark, the tile and mosaics so interesting one could carry on a conversation for an hour pointing out the intricacies of each tile. Anna no longer noticed the tiles or the works of art on the walls. She settled herself in a chaise with brilliant colored cushions before she turned up the volume on the plasma TV attached to the wall. Sheer organza hanging from the long open windows billowed in the soft mountain breeze. A moment later she was engrossed in the weather conditions of her adopted country, forgetting that she had guests from her homeland.

Down the hall, Myra stepped out of the shower to see Charles stretched out on the bed sound asleep. She tiptoed around as she dressed and then unpacked both their bags. She brushed out her gray hair, clasped the pearls she was never without, and left the room. At Anna's doorway, she drew a deep breath and then let it out slowly.

"I'm ready, Annie. For heaven's sake, are you still watching the weather station? Whatever do you get out of watching it?"

"Myra! You look wonderful! You must be happy. It shows. Are you ever going to marry that wonderful man?"

Myra perched on a chaise opposite Annie's. "Look at me, Annie. I want you to really look at me. I need to talk to you and I want your undivided attention. But to answer your questions, yes, I am happy. I'm glad it shows. And maybe one of these days I will marry Charles."

"That's nice. How is Nellie?"

Myra decided it was time to take a page out of Kathryn Lucas's book. "A hell of a lot better than you are, that's for sure." She reached over for the remote lying on a marble table next to where Annie was sitting. She looked at it and then stood up and tossed it as far as she could, but not before she turned off the weather channel. Annie looked on in horror. "Watch this, you weather junkie." In the blink of an eye, Myra picked up the marble table and pitched it at the plasma TV. She clapped her hands when the screen shattered. "No more weather!" she said.

"Now get off your skinny ass because we're going for a walk. I didn't come all this way to watch the weather channel. I need your help."

Annie started to cry.

Myra turned another page from the Kathryn Lucas book. "Cut the crap, Annie. All you do is cry and whine. I'm sick of it. Nellie is sick of it. Annie, look at me. We've been friends since that first day at Miss Ambrose's dance studio. The three of us huddled together because there was nothing graceful about any of us. Remember how scared we were when we had to go out on the dance floor with *a boy*. You started to cry. Nellie kicked Miss Ambrose and I turned off the Victrola. She kicked us out and we walked home swearing allegiance to each other. We've been friends for almost sixty years. That allows me to do what I'm doing."

"And you think busting up my television and throwing away my remote will make me want to help you!"

Myra turned to page three in Kathryn's playbook and said, "I don't give a good rat's ass if you help me or not. I want you to get over *it*. And you know what *it* is. It's fifteen years since you lost your family. You can't bring them back. Not ever. They're gone, Annie. I know what you went through. Nellie knows, too. I wanted to die when I lost Barbara, and I might have if Nikki and Charles hadn't stepped in to help me. I wallowed in my grief just the way Nellie did. I'm proud of the fact that I was able to help her get over the worst of it. You wouldn't let us help you, Annie. You shut us out. I'm going to help you whether you like it or not. I'm not going to give up this time."

"Because you need my help." Annie's voice held a tinge of sarcasm.

Page four of Kathryn's playbook. "Screw the help. Nellie will help me. I can't count on you anymore. You're useless, worthless. You exist. That's all you do. You take up air other people need to breathe. Why haven't you ended it all, jumped off that mountain? Because you don't have the guts, right? I'm going to help you do that. That's the main reason I came over here."

Annie leaned forward, her eyes frantic behind the tinted glasses. "Are you insane, Myra? You came here to kill me! Why?"

Page five of Kathryn's playbook. "See! See! You don't listen worth shit! I didn't come here to kill you. I came here to help you do it yourself. So, let's get with the program here."

Panic filled Annie's voice. "You're crazy!"

Myra moved on to page six. "How in the hell would you know if someone is crazy or not? You live in la-la land. If you don't like going over the mountain, Charles can power up that yacht of yours that sits down there in the marina and we can push you overboard the way your family died. Yes, yes, that would be more fitting. I can see it now. The mountain isn't a good idea. You'd be too broken up when they found you."

Annie was still crying, wiping at her eyes with the hem of her long flowing gown. "What happened to you? You sound like a street person. I thought you were my friend and now you want to drown me. Oh, God! Why?"

Myra wasn't sure but she suspected that Kathryn's playbook was working. She pressed on and turned to page seven. "Because." She shrugged. "Give me one thing you've done for someone else in the last fifteen years. Just one, Annie."

"What business is it of yours what I do or don't do?" Annie continued to cry.

"I want you to come back home, Annie. I want to help you. We're coming down the home stretch now. I hate it that you're here alone while Nellie and I are back in the States. We still have each other. I don't want to see that slip away. I want to tell you something, and take it as gospel. After . . . after Barbara died, I went into a very deep depression. I didn't care if I lived or died. What was there to live for? My daughter was gone, I couldn't bring her back. When I came back to join the living—that's how I thought of it at the time—and got involved . . . in . . . other things, Barbara started talking to me. I swear it, Annie. I can be having a cup of tea and she'll start talking to me. I could be in a tizzy over something or other and there she is. I can't see her, but I can talk to her. I want you to open yourself to the possibility that maybe your family will do the same thing for you. I'm not saying it will happen. I'm not crazy, Annie. I know it sounds far-fetched but it does happen. She comes to me when I need her the most. She said she's proud of me. God, Annie, do you have any idea what that means to me? Well, do you?"

"I . . . I can't imagine. I would give anything . . ."

Myra relented and tossed away Kathryn's playbook. "Let me help you, Annie. Then if you want to help me, we'll work on that. Let's go for that walk, okay?"

"Will you tell me what she said to you? You wouldn't lie to me, would you, Myra?"

"I would never lie to an old friend. Yes, I will tell you everything my daughter said to me. It's all part and parcel of me coming here to enlist your help. Do you want to change your clothes before we go for that walk?"

Annie looked down at the white gown. She frowned. "It's so easy to pull it on in the morning. I think I have hiking boots." She looked up at the shattered plasma TV and said, "I'm going to have to get a new television set."

Myra shook her head. "That's the one thing

you are not going to buy. Hurry up, I'm not as patient as I used to be. Shake it, sister!"

Annie allowed herself a small smile. "Your vocabulary is certainly different these days. You must be leading a very interesting life back in the States."

"Annie, you have no idea."

Chapter 4

Myra did her best not to look shocked at Annie's appearance when she walked through the doorway dressed in shorts and hiking boots. She looked like a broom handle draped in cloth. All Myra could think of to say was, "We need to fatten you up." Then she asked, "Do you need a walking stick, a cane or something? You don't look like you have much stamina."

Annie looked off in the distance. "I'm fine, Myra. I don't need a walking stick or a cane. Stop fretting over me. Let's go. Do you need me to point out the perfect place to push me off the mountain or do you have a place in mind?"

Myra yanked page eight out of Kathryn's playbook. "Cut the shit, Annie. I came here because

I need your help. All I want is a yes or no. You want to go over the mountain, go ahead, I won't stop you. Personally, I don't think you have the guts to do something like that. My daughter would have called you a *wuss.* She'd say you're trying to be a martyr. Martyrs are passé, you know."

Annie dug her heels into the path. "Tell me what you want," she said. "Spit it out, stop dancing around what you perceive to be my condition. That means cut the bullshit."

Myra whirled around and blinked. She was delighted to see a spark of something in Annie's eyes. Maybe this was going to work after all. "Miss Boudreau would put soap in both our mouths if she could hear us. I want you to give me the keys to your house in Manassas. I need to . . . we need to use your place to exact a revenge on some very nasty people. I want to pretend to be you. That means I will need access to your financial records, your signature on documents, that kind of thing. If you agree to help me, you are going to have to start answering your phone, reading your mail and learn how to use a computer so we can send emails. Will you do it? That means you have to join the world and stop watching it whirl by you. You have to become active again. Maybe you need to start taking vitamins."

Annie started to laugh and couldn't stop. "You don't want much, do you, Myra?"

"Actually, Annie, I'm asking a lot and I know it. I came to you because I thought we could help each other. Let's find a place to sit down so I can bring you up to date. God, you are bony. Do you eat *anything*?"

"I take a lot of vitamins. I eat when I'm hungry. Let's sit on this log. I hope this story you're about to tell me is interesting or you might be the one sliding down the mountain. After I push you."

Myra turned around and sat down. She was almost giddy at the way Annie now focused on her. Her eyes appeared less glazed. She seemed to be completely aware of her surroundings and she also appeared to be interested in what Myra had to say.

Annie picked up a thick twig and started to dig in the dirt at her feet. "Well? I'm listening, Myra."

"I hope you can handle this, Annie. Nellie always said you were the toughest of the three of us, but I'm not sure anymore. Before I tell you what I came here to say, I want you to promise you won't ever breathe a word of this to anyone if you decide not to help. Can you do that?"

"Of course I can do that. Who would I tell? As you can see, I live here, cut off from the world. I've been an island unto myself for so long, I wouldn't know how to . . . whatever it is you think I might do. That's a yes," she said firmly.

Myra talked for a long time. When she was finished, the hole at Annie's feet was so deep she could have stuck both feet into it.

Annie turned sideways on the log to stare at her friend. "You did all *that*? You . . . you're a criminal! Charles helped you! Amazing! And you never got caught! You of all people, Myra! This is so unbelievable! Why aren't you a nervous wreck? Of course you can use my house in Manassas. I'll do whatever you want me to do." Annie leaned forward, so close their noses almost touched. "Tell me again how you got even with the man who killed your daughter. I didn't know you could skin a person alive. I know the Indians used to do it but I thought that was just in the movies."

Annie's eyes were completely focused now, bright and alert. Myra retold her story, embellishing it a little more for Annie's benefit. When she finished, Annie clapped her hands.

"You're afraid you're going to get caught, is that it?"

"Yes. We need to have a plan in place if that happens. I want you to sell me this place on the mountain. I want to see the construction plans and Charles and I want a tour of the catacombs. I want you to return to the States as soon as the Barrington farm is completed. Even though they're working on it round the clock it won't be finished much before the end of the year. Maybe next year. A lot depends on the weather conditions. When I bought it, I put your name and Nellie's on the deed."

Annie continued digging at the hole. "I can't sell this place to you. Something about Spanish law. Because . . . I think it has something to do with the right of sanctuary. No one in authority can take you away if you are inside the wall. When we . . . I was renovating it all, I wanted to take down the wall but the law said it had to remain intact. The laws of sanctuary, and they are ancient, are somewhere among my husband's papers. He told me about it once, but . . . I didn't want to think about things like that back then. I will, however, deed this place to you or Charles or whomever you designate. That much I do know I can do. Very distant relatives deeded it to Armand when he was only six years old. Myra, are you asking me to join the Sisterhood?"

Myra turned to page nine of Kathryn's playbook. "Well, hell, yes, Annie. And we're going to need a good portion of your fortune. Like me, Annie, you have no family to leave anything to so don't think too hard on the matter. Can you think of a better way to use all that money? Nellie doesn't have a fortune but she's indispensable because she's a judge." Myra flipped to page ten, her face flaming. "A fucking judge, Annie. Think about it!"

Annie reared back to stare at Myra. "Can you teach me to talk like you do these days? Why don't you blink when you use dirty words?"

Myra fingered the pearls around her neck. "Absolutely not. Ladies do not talk like that. I was . . . I was trying to make my points, to shock you so you would listen. Kathryn at times is rather . . . *spirited* and extremely verbal. I picked the lingo up from her. So, are you in or not?"

Annie stared across the mountain and then down at the sparkling blue sea. "Will I fit in, Myra? It's been a . . . I don't know if I can leave here. There is something so comforting about sanctuary. My family . . . died in those waters down below. I stayed because it made me feel closer to them. I don't have a grave to visit like you and Nellie have. That's what's kept me here all these years. How can I leave here? Tell me how, Myra."

Myra's voice was soft, gentle. She wrapped her arms around Annie's bony shoulders. "I can't tell you something like that. You have to find the way, the need, and do it yourself. You can come back here anytime you want. No one can ever take your memories away from you. What's in your heart will always be there, Annie. Always.

"I know this is a lot to throw at you at one time. I want you to think about it and give me your decision before Charles and I leave. If you opt to stay here and rot away, I'll have to make other plans."

A veil dropped over Annie's eyes. "When did you become so cruel, Myra?"

"When I finally opened my eyes to the justice system. Plus, Nellie tells me stories of what goes on in those courthouses. We, the Sisterhood, just want to make things a little better. With my money—and I don't care one little bit if I use the whole amount—and Charles's expertise, we are making a bit of a difference. Unfortunately, there are a few people out there who would like to see us fail. At the moment, we're on top of it, or at least one step ahead. That could change at any time. We could use you, Annie. You have to want to do this. There's nothing else for me to say."

Annie's head jerked forward. "Yes, there is one more thing. Tell me about Barbara talking to you. I want to hear every word. Tell me how you feel when that happens. That's if you don't mind sharing your daughter with me."

Tears gathered in Myra's eyes. "Oh, Annie, I don't mind at all. It all started with Nikki. She and Barbara were so close. She told me that Barbara visited her, talked to her. Always when she was stressed, at her wits' end. She comes to her old room and rocks on her chair with Willie. You remember Willie, her stuffed bear?"

"I remember, Myra."

"One day I was standing by the sink, worrying. It wasn't that I didn't trust Charles or the girls; I did. I guess I'm just a natural born worrier. I heard this voice saying, 'Go for it, Mom.' I whirled around and no one was there. Then she started to talk to me. All I could do was cry. I was so happy. It was almost like I had her back for just a few seconds. It doesn't happen often, Annie. I can't summon her. She seems to know when I need her the most. That's when it happens. Maybe it won't happen for you. Maybe it won't happen for Nellie either. It might, though."

Then Myra told a lie, something she wasn't proud of, but she did it anyway. She knew Barbara would forgive her. "Annie, before I came here, I had . . . I wasn't sure if I should or not. It seemed like such a monstrous thing to ask of you. In the end, I decided to come because I thought I could help you. Barbara said I should give you a kiss and a hug and I should tell you things on the other side are fine. So, here is the kiss and hug."

The two women hugged one another, tears

rolling down their cheeks. It was just a small lie and if it helped Annie, then it was worth it.

"Mom, you are something else. I guess I can't make a liar out of you. You told her the truth when you said things were fine on this side. Give her another kiss and hug."

Myra leaped to her feet and looked around. Her eyes were wild and yet full of hope. "I will, I will," she whispered.

"Okay, enjoy your vacation. By the way, one of those tunnels goes all the way down to a cave at the bottom and on out to the sea. There's only one, Mom. Perfect getaway. Nikki and I found it when we came here the summer after graduation. Ask her about it. Aunt Annie knows about it, too. Talk to you later."

"What? What's wrong with you, Myra?" Annie asked. "Are you all right? Are you having a heart attack?"

Myra sat down on the fallen log. "No, no, nothing like that. It was an attack of the heart. It was Barbara. She said I was to give you another hug and kiss. Let me do that, Annie. I can't deny that child anything. She said . . . she said when she was here with Nikki after graduation they found the tunnel in the catacombs that leads down to a cave and out to the sea. She said it was a perfect getaway. She said that, Annie. You know how the girls used to like to play in the tunnels at Pinewood and how I hung bells at the different entrances so they wouldn't get lost. She said to ask Nikki about it. She said you knew about it, too. I'm not crazy, Annie. Oh, this is so wonderful. Do you realize what it means? It means no matter where I go, my daughter is with me. I truly, truly believe she watches over me."

Annie held out her skinny arms to embrace her friend. They cried together for their losses.

It was Annie who broke the spell. "Okay, I'm all yours."

Myra opened her own playbook to page one to make her first entry. "Well, hot damn!"

Annie started to laugh.

"Oh, Annie, how good it is to hear you laugh. When was the last time you laughed? Really laughed?" Annie just shook her head and kept on laughing.

Arms linked together, the women started back up the mountain.

"You're sure, Annie?"

Annie's head bobbed up and down. "Just tell me what to do. I'll get you the keys to the house in Manassas."

When they approached the converted monastery, Myra asked, "How big is this piece of property?"

Annie shrugged. "Big enough to have its own helicopter pad, an Olympic size pool, tennis courts, seven outbuildings and acres of lawn. Perhaps Charles will know. Is it important, Myra?"

"I think so. We'll leave it up to Charles. We've done our part."

Charles stood at the window looking at the two women. He smiled. His sigh was so loud, it startled him. He didn't realize how tense he was until he watched the two women start to laugh about something.

His heartbeat returned to normal.

Charles joined the women on the terrace outside Annie's television room. He eyed the smashed television but didn't say a word. He knew what had happened: His lady love had expressed her displeasure with her friend.

"I was wondering, ladies, if you'd like me to prepare dinner?"

"Oh, Annie, take him up on it. Charles is a wonderful cook."

"Something American, Charles," Annie smiled. "Something from soup to nuts."

Charles laughed. "I think I can whip something up for your American palate. Are we going to dress for dinner?"

"Do people still do that?" Annie asked curiously. "Let's not."

"You're the hostess. I prefer casual myself. I'll see you ladies later."

Annie squeezed Myra's arm. "You are so blessed."

Myra turned to page two in her new playbook. "Damn straight." Both women went off into peals of laughter.

On his way down the long hall to the kitchen, Charles smiled to himself. The situation was in good hands. And all he had to do was cook.

Chapter 5

Jack Emery walked out into the bright spring sunshine. He looked upward to see that most of the trees on the street were almost in full leaf. He could see a smattering of daffodils and pots of other early flowers on the different stoops. He loved spring. Nikki always filled the house with lilacs from the backyard when they bloomed because she knew they were his favorite flower. Nikki loved autumn. In the past, he'd always managed to find a bale of straw and a huge pumpkin to put on the stoop. They both loved winter because they liked to ski and snowboard. Summer in D.C. was something they tolerated but didn't particularly like.

As he walked to his car Jack could feel his thoughts start to drift. Nikki had seemed tense when she left the house earlier to greet Myra and Charles on their return to Pinewood. When he'd asked where they had gone, Nikki had turned surly and asked him why he wanted to know. At the time he'd thought he was simply making conversation. Now, he really wanted to know where the couple had been. He'd bet his next paycheck their trip had something to do with the Sisterhood.

Jack unlocked his car and settled himself behind the wheel. Before he turned the key in the ignition, he finished the coffee in his travel mug. Nikki had smiled at him when she handed him the cup. He remembered how he'd returned her smile and then kissed her. Shit, he was acting like a sophomoric fool. Maybe that was because he *was* a sophomoric fool. He'd sold his soul, maybe not to the devil, but to a bunch of women, his fiancée included, who deliberately doled out vigilante justice. He just looked the other way and pretended it didn't bother him. Hell, he even had a plaque on his side of the bathroom saying he was an honorary member of the Sisterhood.

As he cruised along, Jack asked himself the same question he asked himself every day. Did Nikki just tell him what she wanted him to know or did she tell him *everything*? Myra and Charles's trip was the perfect example of *everything*. On the other hand, maybe it really was none of his business where the couple went. Being a district attorney made him suspicious of everything these days.

The ladies of Pinewood were gearing up to exact Alexis Thorne's revenge. Nikki had told him that much. She just hadn't shared the details with him. If he had asked pointed questions, she would have answered them. If he didn't ask, she didn't volunteer details. Don't ask, don't tell. It worked for them. The truth was, they both tried to protect each other.

Jack longed to scratch the itch between his shoulder blades, the itch that told him to stay alert and pay attention to details and what was going on around him. He parked his car, reached for his briefcase and headed toward his office building. He dreaded today. Not because he had to spend it in court but because he had to go to the retirement dinner for his boss, Seymour Ridley, who was stepping down to spend more time with his family. Only Jack and a few other close friends knew the truth; Ridley was going out of state for treatment for bladder cancer and didn't want anyone to know. Jack couldn't blame him a bit, knowing the way the District's politics worked.

His new boss, Lionel Ambrose, was hated and feared by everyone in the office. In Jack's opinion, he was a mean-eyed snake. He was also a publicity hound, numbering Ted Robinson and Ted's boss among his best friends. Ambrose came from a long line of politicians. He had one goal in mind and that was to become Police Commissioner. "Not on my back, he isn't," Jack mumbled under his breath.

The itch between his shoulder blades made Jack wiggle his shoulders inside his jacket as he made his way to his office. He sincerely hoped that Ted wasn't going to spill his guts to Ambrose. He didn't worry about Maggie Spritzer because Maggie was a gossip reporter, and since the alliance she'd formed with Ted had disintegrated, the two reporters were at each other's throats all the time. Ted was bitter. Maggie was pissed. Jack knew there was nothing worse than a pissed-off woman.

Jack threw his briefcase on the desk, hung up his suit jacket and rolled up his sleeves. Court was dark today. That was good because he had paperwork coming out his ears. He dived into it, working steadily until he heard a ping announcing he had new email coming in. He leaned back, cupping his head in the palms of his hands as he read the short email from Maggie Spritzer.

Jack read it six times as he tried to figure out what it meant. Maggie wanted him to meet her at the Rusty Nail for lunch at 12:30, thirty minutes from now. And she was buying. That alone made the hairs on the back of his neck stand on end. Should he meet her? He looked at the pile of paperwork on his desk. His plan had been to order in but it was such a nice day, one of those exceptional spring days that made everyone want to be outdoors. He argued with himself for a good five minutes before he typed "Okay," signed his name, and pressed "send."

Jack tidied up his desk, rolled down his sleeves, secured his tie and slipped into his jacket. He headed for the men's room, washed his hands, combed his hair and left the building, his mind whirling and twirling.

He liked Maggie Spritzer as a person but he didn't trust her. Just the way he liked Ted Robinson, whom he didn't trust either. What the hell did she want? Why would she go over Ted's head, so to speak, to talk with him? Even though they were no longer a couple, Ted could have put her up to it. On the other hand, Maggie was a sharp-nosed woman so that meant it wasn't a level playing field. Poor Ted, she was so far ahead of him, he could never catch up. Ted had a certain amount of ethics; Maggie hadn't. *I should talk,* Jack reminded himself, aware that his own ethics left a lot to be desired.

The spring breeze whipped him from behind, literally pushing him along as he walked the five long blocks to the Rusty Nail.

The moment Jack opened the door to the restaurant, he got an immediate headache from the noise and the crowd. He looked around for Maggie. He spotted her in the back in a booth. Her lips were moving but he couldn't hear what she was saying. He fought his way to the booth, stopping here and there to clap one or two of his friends or colleagues on the back. He felt like he'd just done forty yards on the football field when he slid into the booth. "How's it going, Maggie? What's up?"

"I took the liberty of ordering for you as I didn't know how much time you'd have even though court is dark today. Tuna melt and a salad, and iced tea. It should be here any second now. How are you, Jack?"

"I asked you first."

"Fine. Guess you're fine because you look fine. I know I look fine, too. Guess we should cut to the chase here. I want you to introduce me to those ladies out there at Pinewood. I want to join up."

Whatever he was expecting, this sure as hell wasn't it. All Jack could do was stare at the reporter. "Are you crazy?"

"Yeah, crazy like a fox. Listen, I know it was you at the cemetery that night those women went after Rosemary Hershey. I know you let them get away. I know you were the one who shot Ted and me with the Taser. Ask me how I know all this, Jack."

"What the hell are you talking about, Maggie?"

Maggie wiggled her eyebrows and then rolled her eyes as their food arrived. She watched as Jack picked up half of the sandwich and took a bite.

"Well, I guess I can't say I blame you for not answering. It was your cologne. I have a keen sense of smell. You're the only one I know who wears Gray Flannel cologne. Keep eating, Jack. I can do two things at one time." To prove her point, Maggie dug around in a large leather bag and pulled out a small recorder. She pressed the play button before she picked up her own sandwich.

Jack continued to chew, his heart racing as he heard a voice—his voice—ordering the women to leave. The rain interfered with the true sound but if anyone wanted to pay for a voice analysis there would be no doubt it was his voice. Then he heard himself say, "Charles sent me." How the hell was he going to get out of this with his skin intact? "Interesting. The voice isn't clear. Is that rain or what? What makes you think that's my voice on there? Sure as hell doesn't sound like me to me." Jack guffawed at his wit.

Maggie bit down on a pickle sphere. "I guess you can see I'm not laughing here."

"Everyone knows you don't have a sense of humor, Maggie. By the way, where did you get that thing?" Jack tried to work up a proper amount of outrage for his next comment. "You're trying to set me up, aren't you, Maggie? Jesus, is there nothing you reporters won't do to get a story?"

Maggie crunched on the pickle, her gaze boring into Jack. "Your outrage is duly noted. I always travel with backup. Ted had one of these, too, that night," she said pointing to the mini recorder. "Something happened to his, though. Either he forgot to put a tape in it or he lost it. In this business you need to stay on your toes. As you know, I am always on my toes."

Jack gulped at his iced tea. The damn tuna sandwich was sticking in his throat. It was his turn to speak. "I wasn't near the cemetery that night. I have an alibi, Maggie. I sure as hell hope you aren't letting yourself and your paper open for a libel suit. You might want to rethink all of this. Listen, nice as it is talking with you, I have to get back to the office. I have two tons of paperwork to get done since court is dark today. You did say you were buying, right?"

Maggie's eyes narrowed. "Let's hear your alibi."

Jack turned and laughed. "Pursue it and you'll find out so quick your head will spin. First rule of law, Maggie, never ask a question you don't already know the answer to. See you. Tell Ted to call me."

"Screw you, Mister District Attorney. You aren't dealing with Ted now, you're dealing with me." When Maggie realized Jack was already gone and couldn't hear her, she swore under her breath.

On the off chance Jack was telling her the truth, which she doubted, she was back at square one. If Ted didn't trust Jack, then she sure as hell wasn't going to trust him either.

Maggie sat quietly even though there were other people waiting for her booth. She didn't leave until she'd finished all the chips on Jack's plate plus her own. She debated a second before she reached for the last half of Jack's pickle. She finished her tea, wiped her lips, left exactly a ten percent tip and left the Rusty Nail.

Jack headed for the underground garage where his car was parked. He whipped out his cell phone and called Nikki. He smiled when he heard her voice. "Hi. Miss you. Great day for a picnic," he said lightly. "Listen, that's not why I called. Just listen to me, okay? I got an email from Maggie Spritzer inviting me to lunch at the Rusty Nail. I went and you aren't going to believe what she wanted. She said she wants to join up with you ladies at Pinewood. I did my best to play stupid but she has me on tape out at the cemetery. She damn well played the tape while she ate a tuna fish sandwich. I tried to slough it off but she wasn't buying. There's static and rain but a voice analysis will prove it's my voice on that tape. I gave her the alibi bit, but . . . Maggie has that female streak in her that won't allow her to give up. She said Ted had a recorder, too, but somewhere along the way he either lost the tape or it fell out. Probably with a little help from her. Like she said, she always carries backup. We have to get that tape back. I can't do it, Nikki.

"I don't think Maggie is sharing with Ted. She's working on her own. Like Ted, though, she carries everything in a backpack. She's never without it. I hate to dump this on you but there's nothing I can do."

"How's this for off the top of my head," Nikki said. "I call her and tell her you said she wanted to meet up with someone from Pinewood. We meet for a drink. I'll have one of the girls waylay her and snatch the backpack and take it to my office. However, if she's as sharp as you say she is, she might have made copies. Do you think we should do a little breaking and entering?"

"She wouldn't keep something like that at home. If she had a spare, I'm thinking she'd keep it at the paper. At least that's what I would do if I were her. It's your call, Nik. Look, I'm in the underground garage and reception isn't the greatest down here. Call me this evening and we can beat this to death. I'm thinking Ridley's dinner will be over by nine. I should be home by ten. Love you."

"Love you, too, Jack."

Chapter 6

The ladies of Pinewood milled around the command center chattering among themselves before Myra motioned them to their seats. She called the meeting to order and asked if there was any pending business to take care of before they settled down to map out Alexis's revenge.

Nikki cleared her throat. "There is something. A source of mine whom I cannot name, called last night to tell me Maggie Spritzer, the Beltway gossip columnist at the *Post*, has a tape of our activities at the cemetery the night we exacted Isabelle's revenge. My source isn't sure but thinks Miss Spritzer carries the tape in her backpack. My source doesn't know if there are any copies. I would assume so. The question is, if there are copies, are they in her home or at the *Post*? In addition, Miss Spritzer made a request. She wants, as she put it, to join up with the ladies out here at Pinewood." Nikki sat back after she delivered her bombshell and waited for what she thought would be an explosion of sound.

The silence around the table was total. Charles looked up from his battery of computers and clicked some buttons before he walked down the two steps to join the ladies at the table.

"I see that as a potential problem," Charles said quietly. "There's nothing we can do if she's hidden a tape at the *Post*. Her home is another matter. I think, Nikki, a face-to-face meeting with the woman might be a good thing. Draw her out. You're a lawyer and good at such things. It saddens me greatly that you ladies were so careless as to allow this to happen. You should have been more alert, less crazed. I warned you time and again that you have to be prepared for everything and anything at a moment's notice. A mistake is one thing, carelessness is something else. Because of your carelessness you almost got caught and you left your own recorder behind. Without the aid of a good Samaritan, you'd all be languishing in jail right now."

The women looked like naughty pets chastised for peeing on the carpet. They hung their heads in shame for having disappointed Charles and risking their own safety.

"That's behind us now. I don't want to see anything like that happen again. So, let me get back to my work while you all decide what to do."

Myra looked as shamed as the others. "Let's decide, ladies."

"I don't have a problem meeting with Miss Spritzer. I can pick a place of my choosing. My office would be my choice and I'll be on my own turf. While I'm meeting with her, the others can search her apartment. If she carries the tape with her, perhaps she could be waylaid and mugged, for want of a better word, after our meeting. A night meeting would be best for something like this. She and I will leave together and we can both be accosted. My parking lot isn't lit up all that well. Sometimes I spook myself when I leave late at night. It will have to look real, though," Nikki said.

A natural-born worrier, Isabelle frowned. "What do we do about a copy, if there is a copy, at the *Post*?"

"Since we're the ones who screwed up, it's up to us to find a way to get it. Now, let's put our heads together and come up with something that isn't . . . *sloppy and careless*," Alexis said. There was such anger in her voice that the others could only look at her and nod.

"I suggest we tend to our immediate problem before we set up Alexis's revenge. Unless, of course, you want to continue since we're all here," Myra said.

Alexis was still angry. "Obviously, we need to redeem ourselves in Charles's eyes. I suggest we get with the program and do what we have to do before we get to my revenge. I don't want to be shortchanged and I don't want any . . . carelessness or sloppiness when it comes to me."

Kathryn bristled. "What's your problem, Alexis? Things go wrong. We aren't perfect. And, there are some things that are beyond our control. You'll get a hundred percent from all of us when it's your turn. If there's something else bugging you, spit it out right now. Before you do, though, let me remind you that your turn came up a while back and you passed on it because you weren't ready."

Alexis's dark eyes filled with tears. "You're always so damn glib, Kathryn. Look at it from my point of view. I've been in prison and it is not a nice place. Sloppiness and carelessness is not why I want to end up there again. I want to know I can count on all of you. You screwed up. Admit it!"

Kathryn stood up, her eyes blazing. Murphy reared back and howled. "Damn it, Alexis, I never denied it. I take full responsibility for not realizing we were being followed. Now, does that make you feel better? Does it change one damn thing? The answer is, no! If you want me to feel like a failure, you've succeeded. If I could go back to that night, have eyes in the back of my head, I'd do it. I fucked up, okay? I'm sorry."

Alexis licked her lips. "I'm sorry, Kathryn. I don't know what got into me. You don't owe me an apology. Can we just forget it?"

Kathryn stomped about the room. "You know what, I don't know if I want to forget it. Isabelle says I'm mean. Yoko thinks I'm some kind of ogre. You think I let you down. Nikki . . . straddles the fence. Don't look so pained, Nikki. I see the way you look at me. I don't quite fit your genteel group of friends. I'm rough around the edges, I say what I think. I have a very unladylike job, I drive a fucking eighteen-wheeler and I swear. Guess what, that's who I am. I never judged any of you. I resent . . . I resent this . . . this discussion. That goes for you, too, Charles!" Kathryn bellowed. "Wait a minute! As long as I'm venting here, I'd like to know who Nikki's *mysterious source,* her *convenient* mysterious source is. I thought we didn't have secrets when it came to the Sisterhood. What makes her different from the rest of us? I'm not buying that crap anymore. I'm outa here! Come on, Murphy!"

Myra and Charles could only watch as the others jumped to their feet to follow Kathryn and her barking dog.

"Oh dear," Myra said.

"It was bound to happen sooner or later, Myra. I've always found that women are too emotional. Kathryn did make a point when she said she wanted to know who Nikki's mysterious source is. She's a very angry lady right now. They'll work it out among themselves."

"Maybe we should intervene," Myra said.

"That's the one thing we *shouldn't* do, dear."

"You were quite stern, Charles."

"Myra, I had to be stern. I wanted to be rip-roaring mad but because they were women, I held my tongue. They were sloppy, they were careless. There is absolutely no excuse for that. It's the difference between all of us sitting here or sitting in individual jail cells.

"If you recall, I warned all of you back in the beginning that things you wouldn't like would happen and also things you wouldn't agree with. All of you agreed to let me run this show. That's what I've been trying to do with the best interests of all of you as my top priority. If you're hoping for an apology, old girl, it isn't going to happen."

Myra nodded. "Since I have to sit here, do you think you could put on some silly show so I can laugh? If you don't, I'm going to cry. Anything but the news will do just fine."

"Let's take this out on the terrace," Nikki said, opening the kitchen door.

"Kiss my ass, Nikki Quinn. Don't ever make the mistake of telling me what to do again. I said I'm leaving and I'm leaving. You go sit on the terrace with all the pretty flowers. Maybe someone will bring you a glass of champagne. Now, get out of my way."

"This is ridiculous! Why are we fighting like this? What's wrong with us?" Isabelle demanded.

"I said I was sorry, Kathryn. I can't seem to get past that horror of prison. I didn't mean to snap and snarl," Alexis said.

Yoko laid a tiny hand on Kathryn's arm.

"Please, let's sit down among the flowers and talk this out. We need you, Kathryn. I need you. I do not know how it happened but you became my role model. You're the reason I found the courage to change my life. If you leave I will feel like I lost another dear member of my family. We already lost Julia. I would like you to think about that, Kathryn."

Kathryn allowed herself to be guided to the terrace, Murphy hugging her knees. The women gathered round in a circle, Kathryn in the middle. A protective circle.

"This isn't about us, is it, Kathryn?" Nikki asked softly. "Today is the anniversary of your husband's death, isn't it?"

Kathryn nodded miserably. "I go berserk every year on this date. I owe all of you an apology. Except you, Nikki. I still want to know who your source is. I think we all have a right to know. If you really are one of us, you're not special. Myra cuts you slack because you're her adopted daughter. It's not fair, though. Take a vote, see how the others feel."

Nikki looked at the faces staring at her own. She didn't need to take a vote. Before she spoke, she looked toward the kitchen door. "My source is Jack Emery."

No one said a word.

"I don't blame you for being speechless. Sometimes I can't believe it myself. I don't want Charles or Myra to know. I'm sorry I didn't tell you sooner but I was hoping you would never need to know. I see now that I was wrong."

"Why? How can you trust him?" Isabelle asked softly.

"I love him. He loves me. When you love someone, you trust them. Who do you think intervened when we went after the National Security Advisor? It was Jack. It was Jack at the cemetery on Isabelle's mission. We would all be in jail if it wasn't for Jack. If anyone should leave this organization, it should be me, not Kathryn. I want you to know one thing and I want you to believe me when I tell you, if I had even one little doubt, one suspicion, that he'd turn on us, set us up, I would have acted immediately. He has agreed to continue to help us. We need him.

"Last night was a perfect example. Maggie Spritzer called him and asked him point blank if he was at the cemetery. Jack has a distinctive voice. She knows what she has on that tape so she needs to be taken care of. We need to get that tape. Without Jack, she would have taken that tape . . . to God only knows where.

"I'm trusting you with the love of my life. You, my sisters. This is the time to ask questions if you have any," Nikki said.

"Do you really trust this man?" Yoko asked quietly.

"With my life. With all your lives," Nikki smiled.

"Why don't you want Charles and Myra to know?" Alexis asked.

Nikki lowered her voice. "Because those operatives of Charles' almost killed Jack and Ted

Robinson. I want this to be our secret. Think of Jack as an added security blanket."

"Did you tell him everything?" Kathryn asked.

"Every single little thing. I didn't leave anything out. He's on our side."

"You must love him very much," Alexis said.

"So much that I ache when I'm not with him. Some people love only once in their life. I'm one of those people. So is Jack. I can't explain it any better than that. You, Kathryn, should understand what I'm saying." Kathryn nodded, her eyes misty.

"I want to give all of you Jack's private cell phone number. You can call him anytime if you're on a mission and get stuck for whatever reason. Contrary to what some of you might believe, I've been trying to find a way to tell you about Jack."

The women moved closer together, their hands reaching out to each other.

"Do you want us to go with you, Kathryn?"

Kathryn didn't pretend not to understand. "You know what, I think I'd like that. I'd like to introduce you to Alan. I have to stop for some flowers."

"Awk!" protested Yoko. "Kathryn, shame on you. We will stop at my nursery. I would be honored to bring the flowers to your husband's grave site. Let's go in your truck. I love riding in that big monster."

"Okay, let's go," Kathryn said.

In the kitchen, Charles and Myra watched the women as they headed toward Kathryn's rig, Murphy and Grady racing ahead.

"Where do you suppose they're going?" Myra asked.

"This is just a guess on my part, Myra, but I think they're going to the cemetery. With a stop at Yoko's nursery for flowers."

"How do you know that?"

Charles laughed. "My hearing is better than yours and the window is open. I think our little rebellion has been squashed. The air has been cleared for now. It's a good thing, dear."

"Whatever would I do without you and your wisdom?"

Charles chucked his lady love under the chin. "Let's hope you never have to find out."

It was almost closing time when Kathryn pulled her rig into the parking lot behind Nikki's offices. All the women and the two dogs scrambled out. "Follow me, we'll go in the back way and walk up the stairs to my office. We'll hatch our plan right now and go for it before this thing with Maggie Spritzer grows legs and takes off," Nikki said.

The women trooped inside, taking the back entrance off the parking lot rather than the elevator in the lobby of the front entrance. They followed Nikki up the two flights of stairs to her office. Inside, with the door closed, fresh coffee supplied by Maddie, the office manager, in their hands, they got down to business. "This is how I see it. If any of you have a better idea, feel free to chime in. I'm going to call Maggie right now. Jack gave me her cell phone number. I will invite her here to the office. If she balks at the short notice, I'll tell her to take a hike. I'll tell her to be here at seven. It will be dark by 7:30. Alexis, you and Isabelle will break into her apartment. Get in and out as quick as you can. Kathryn, park your rig out of sight. Stake out here in the parking lot. When I turn off the office light that means we'll be coming down the back stairs. I'll head to Maddie's car which is a Ford Mustang. She lives a few blocks away and I know she won't mind letting me use her car. The Mustang is bright yellow so you can't miss it. That's when you snatch Maggie's backpack and my briefcase and purse, and take off. I'll call the police and report the theft. It all has to seem real."

"I see a problem," Isabelle said. "Even if it is dark, there's still light in the parking lot. Spritzer will recognize us."

Nikki bit down on her lip. "You're right, that is a problem. Alexis doesn't have her Red Bag with her. Wait a minute. Two blocks down, three blocks over, there is a variety store that sells all kinds of junk. One of you has to leave now before they close. Buy a couple of those latex masks kids use at Halloween. Try and get some gloves and maybe something to cover your shoes."

"I'll go. I run five miles every day," Isabelle said. A moment later, she was gone.

Nikki licked her lips and then bit down hard as she picked up the office phone. "I'm using this phone in case she has caller I.D. The minute I hang up, the rest of you leave and wait for Isabelle downstairs. Maggie might smell a set up and get here early. I don't want anything to make her suspicious. It's ringing." Nikki placed her finger over her lip for silence. "Miss Spritzer? This is Nicole Quinn. Jack Emery called and said you would like to speak with me. I'm at the office working late. If you could manage to come by now, I can speak with you. Oh, I'm sorry it's not convenient. Well, my calendar is jammed up till the middle of April. Jack made it sound urgent. Call me the middle of April and I'll try to fit you in. Oh, you can cancel your dinner plans? I'll wait for you. The front door to the building is locked at six so come around to the back entrance. Just press the buzzer and I'll let you in. What? The owner of the building is the one who insists the front doors be locked at six. You know how everything changed after 9/11. This is Washington, D. C. There's ample parking in the back. Fine, fine. I'll be expecting you in forty-five minutes."

Nikki let out her breath in a loud *swoosh*. "She's cagey. Wanted to know why the front door is locked at six. I think she bought it. Get going. She'll be coming in the south entrance so leave by the north entrance and stash the truck. Call for a cab and get out before you come to her street. Good luck. One more thing. When the mugging goes down, whatever you do, don't talk."

"Gotcha," Kathryn said, high-fiving Nikki's outstretched hand. Yoko just giggled. The sound alleviated some of the tension between Nikki's shoulder blades.

When the door closed behind the women, Nikki leaned back in her chair. What was Jack going to say when she told him she had blown his cover? What would Maggie Spritzer do when they were mugged? "Well, I guess I'll find out soon enough," she murmured to herself.

Chapter 7

Nikki applied fresh lipstick and spritzed some of her favorite perfume in the hollow of her throat as she waited for Maggie. While she waited, she allowed her thoughts to wander to Myra and Charles's trip to Spain. Knowing both of them as well as she did, she knew the trip had a dual purpose. Her stomach muscles started to crunch up when she thought about the second reason for their visit. Charles never did two things if one thing would accomplish his end goal. In this instance, Plan B, in case the authorities ever closed in on them. Plan A was to enlist Anna Ryland de Silva's help with Alexis's revenge. Spain was so far away.

Nikki's thoughts were interrupted by the sound of the back door buzzer. She walked out to the hallway and the top of the back stairs to push the buzzer that would unlock the door. She was glad to see that it was already dark outside. She watched as Maggie took her time climbing the stairs.

At the top, Maggie held out her hand, "Maggie Spritzer. You must be Nicole Quinn. This might be a stupid question but why didn't you take the Rutledge name when Mrs. Rutledge adopted you?"

Nikki led the way down the hall to her office. "Because I was born with the name Quinn. Myra left it up to me. Legally, I'm Quinn Rutledge. Why do you ask?"

"I'm a reporter. We're a curious lot."

Inside her office, Nikki motioned to a nubby oatmeal colored chair. "Would you like some coffee, a soft drink, or some wine?"

"No, thank you."

Nikki sat down and crossed her legs. She waited for the reporter's first question. She knew how to play the waiting game. At best, she hoped she just looked curious and perplexed at this meeting. When the reporter started to rummage in her backpack, she knew what was coming.

"I'd like you to listen to this," Maggie said, setting the mini recorder on the desk, clearly out of Nikki's reach, and pressing the play button. Nikki listened intently, hoping the curious look stayed on her face. Maggie turned off the recorder and said, "Would you care to comment?"

"About what? Do you want to sue that person? What is this all about? Do you know the person speaking on the tape?"

Maggie grimaced. "I know him but not as well as you do. Are you saying you don't recognize the voice?"

Nikki just looked puzzled. "Yes, that's what I'm saying. What makes you think I know that person?"

Maggie looked smug. "It's Jack Emery!"

Nikki reared back in her chair. "No! That's not Jack. I'd recognize his voice. You're mistaken. I don't understand."

"Oh, please, let's not play games here. A voice analysis will prove it's Jack Emery. He hooked up with you gals out there at Pinewood. I want to join up."

Nikki hoped she looked as stupid as she felt. "Let me make sure I understand all this," she said, waving her hand toward the mini recorder. "You're telling me Jack Emery has joined our bridge club and now you want to know if you can join. Am I getting this right?"

Maggie snorted. "I'm not stupid, Miss Quinn. That is Jack Emery's voice. I recorded him at the cemetery the night that architect was found in an open grave. He helped those women get away. Those women, your friends. The ones you play . . . ah . . . bridge with."

Nikki leaned forward. "Are you trying to blackmail me?"

Maggie also leaned forward. The two women were eyeball to eyeball. She laughed but it wasn't a pleasant sound. "Blackmail is against the law. I taped District Attorney Emery in court on Monday. The voices match. I asked you if you wanted to comment. I asked if I could join your . . . your bridge club. How can that be blackmail?"

"We prefer to keep our bridge club to six members. I don't agree with you that the voice on the tape sounds like Jack Emery. I don't go to cemeteries and neither do the members of our bridge club. That's what you were implying, isn't it?"

"No, I'm not implying it. I'm stating it as a fact."

"I think you might have a hard time proving an accusation like that. I feel duty bound to warn you that you're treading very close to libel. I think this meeting is over, Miss Spritzer." Her insides shaking at the expression on the reporter's face, Nikki continued, "I would like to give you a piece of free advice. If copies of that tape find themselves in other hands, Mr. Emery will go after you like a dog on the trail of a bitch in heat."

"Don't you worry about this tape. I am going to make copies when I leave here but they won't be given to anyone until I have all my ducks in a row. You're right, this meeting is over."

Nikki watched in horror when Maggie picked up the recorder and stuffed it into the pocket of her jacket. Damn, she was supposed to put it in the backpack. She had to call Kathryn and she had to do it now before Maggie hit the parking lot. Nikki snatched the cell phone off her desk and held it in her lap when Spritzer stood up and turned around. She hit the speed dial and raised her voice several decibels to alert Kathryn. "I'll walk out with you, Miss Spritzer. Just give me a moment to turn off all the lights and lock up. Wait for me in the hallway, please."

"Can't wait to get rid of me, is that it?"

"I do feel you wasted your time coming here. That tape in your pocket is the silliest thing I ever heard. I want to warn you again, blackmail and libel are a serious business and it can turn into an expensive proposition."

Nikki palmed the small cell phone and locked the door to the office. "Damn, I forgot my briefcase. Wait just a minute." She made a production of unlocking the door and going back inside. She turned on lights as she went along. She gasped into the phone. "She put it in her pocket, Kathryn. Can you hear me?"

"Yep. We have it covered."

At the top of the stairs, Maggie turned around and said. "I always try to play fair, Miss Quinn. I gave you a heads-up. My sense of fair play is appeased."

"I'd hate to be you if Jack Emery ever decides to go after you. That's my sense of fair play kicking in."

Nikki opened the door and waited to make sure it closed properly before she headed off to Maddie's yellow Mustang.

"Did you hear something?" Maggie called out.

Nikki stopped, pretended to listen. She looked around. "No. Where's your car? Do you want me to walk you to your car?"

"I don't think that will be necessary. I'm a big girl!"

They came out of nowhere. Nikki screamed

at the top of her lungs and tried to run but one of the masked figures tackled her and she was on the ground. "Get off me! Give me that! Damn you, give me my purse!" Her voice was so shrill it carried all over the parking lot. She risked a glance at where Maggie Spritzer was being shoved up against her Honda.

The action was quick, fast, and frightening.

"Keep screaming," Kathryn hissed in Nikki's ear. "Hold still now, I'm going to fix your face. Thanks for the heads-up." Nikki started to scream and then cut it off when Kathryn clapped her hand over her mouth. "Play dead now. We're outa here."

Maggie Spritzer fought back, screeching as loud as Nikki. Yoko whacked her hand across Maggie's throat, silencing her for the moment. Kathryn ripped the backpack from the reporter's shoulders as she tried to figure a way to get the tape recorder without causing suspicion on Spritzer's part. She started to pat her down, fished the car keys out of her jacket pocket. There was a wad of crumpled dollar bills in her jeans pocket. She took those and then the recorder.

Maggie fought like a tiger. Yoko yanked at a chunk of the reporter's hair and then used her index finger to press a section of her neck. Maggie went limp and sank to the pavement.

"Move, move!" Kathryn whispered. She looked over at where Nikki was struggling to her feet. "You okay? Get back down till she comes around. Let her find you. Do a lot of groaning. See ya."

Nikki assumed her previous position, rolling

around a little to dirty herself. She groaned and moaned wondering how long it would take Maggie to come around. When she finally heard the reporter shuffling toward her, she tried to get to her feet. She pretended to be woozy as she reached for the fender of Maddie's car to pull herself erect. "What happened? Are you all right?"

"I'm going to have a headache for a week. What about you?"

"My ribs hurt. So does my head. He hit me in the neck, too. Son of a bitch, they took my briefcase and my purse. They didn't get the car keys, though. At least we can get back in the building to call the police."

"They took my stuff, too. Not that you care, but they took my recorder as well as my backpack."

Nikki clapped her hands over her head. "You're right, I don't care. Do I look as bad as you do? Did they get your cell phone? They took mine. We have to go inside to call the police."

"I don't think calling the police is a good idea. Those guys are gone. They'll never find them. I'm never going to get my backpack back and you aren't going to get your stuff back. What's the point?"

"Are you crazy? They took my purse. My house keys are in there. I had two hundred dollars and about sixty credit cards, not to mention my driver's license. I'm calling the police. We should probably go to the hospital to get checked out."

"Look, you do what you want, I'm going

home. Don't involve me. If you do, I'll deny it. Once you get into the system, you're there to stay. I keep a spare car key in a magnetic box under the left fender. You of all people should be careful about police scrutiny and no, I don't buy into that sorry story about your little bridge club. Can you make it home or do you want me to drop you off somewhere?"

Nikki stared at the reporter in the bluish light from the lamp post. "I'm going back up to the office. You're welcome to come with me. I still think we should call the police. All right, I won't involve you. I didn't put your visit on the schedule so if I do decide to call them, they can't find their way to you."

Nikki knew the reporter's eyes were on her as she tottered toward the back entrance to her building. She waved half heartedly before she opened the door. Inside, with the door locked behind her, Nikki sprinted up the stairs, opened her office door, then locked it. She collapsed on one of the leather chairs in her lobby. The cell phone was in her hands in less than a second. "Isabelle, she's on her way home. She had a spare key under the fender. Get out of there as quickly as you can. Did you find anything?"

"So far nothing. She's a neat, tidy lady and the apartment is small. Found a stash of condoms and some jewelry in an empty detergent box under the kitchen sink. If she was going to hide something as small as a cassette, I'm thinking it would be with the condoms."

"Kind of takes the romance out of a seduction," Nikki said. "She said she had only one copy but the reporter hasn't been born that I would believe. They're like used car salesmen; all they do is lie. I'll meet you back at the farm."

Nikki headed for the lavatory where she washed her face and hands. She brushed her hair and did her best to clean her jacket with a damp paper towel.

She was at the office door when she stopped and turned around. Maybe Maggie was testing her to see if she really would call the police. Tomorrow she would check the police reports. Nikki flopped down on the same lobby chair and called the police to report her mugging.

Ninety minutes later, Nikki left her law offices for that last time, a copy of the police report in her hands. She hadn't mentioned Maggie Spritzer.

Across the street, sitting in her darkened car, Maggie Spritzer uttered a sigh of relief when the police car exited the parking lot. She waited ten more minutes until Nikki Quinn got into the yellow Mustang. So, it wasn't a setup after all. Just one more crime statistic in the District of Columbia where crime ran rampant. Tomorrow, she'd go to headquarters to look at the police report. It would be interesting to see if Nikki Quinn kept her name off the report.

Maggie headed home, berating herself over and over again about not making copies of the tape. It was the first thing she'd learned in journalism class: back up everything, not once but twice, make copies by the dozen. She'd failed that class if she remembered correctly. Well, hell, you couldn't win them all. If she ever recounted tonight's events to Ted Robinson, he'd laugh his damn head off.

Inside Kathryn's truck, the women congratulated themselves. "We are good, there's no doubt about it," Isabelle cackled gleefully. "I can't wait to see what else that reporter has in her backpack."

"The night's still young. Maybe we should go somewhere to get something to eat," Alexis said.

"I have a better idea," Kathryn said. "I say we go to Georgetown to thank the District Attorney for all he's done on our behalf. What say you?"

"I think that's a smashing idea. But . . . we have to take a gift. Maybe a bottle of wine. Or . . . we could really knock his socks off and give him the tape. Of course, I don't know how humorous Nikki will think that is. We don't have to worry about Myra and Charles finding out since this is all a big secret," Alexis said.

"There might be a problem driving this truck on those narrow streets in Georgetown," Yoko said.

"Well, we'll just have to find a suitable parking space and walk to wherever he lives. Do we have an address?" Kathryn asked.

"It's Nikki's address," Isabelle said. "Isn't it? I'm just guessing here. I can give you directions since I've been there. Are we sure we want to do this? Let's take a vote."

"Two against two. Okay, it was fun thinking

about it. Let's head for the farm. No sense ticking Nikki off," Kathryn said.

Yoko pretended to pout. "I was feeling adventuresome."

Kathryn swung the rig out into the flowing traffic. "Speaking of being adventuresome, did you cancel your class at, what's his name, Harry's *dojo*?"

"Yes. I said it with regret. Harry himself called to find out why I canceled. My answering machine took the message. I called back and rescheduled for tomorrow. I think I can do that two more times."

"Oh, at least that. Sooner or later you're going to have to make a decision. Guys cut you just so much slack before they want you to pony up," Alexis said.

"What are you saying? I cannot buy a small horse. There are zoning laws where I live that do not permit this. Why? Perhaps I should concentrate on the Asian market and forget the *dojo*. Besides, I would just embarrass him in a competition."

"And she's cocky, too. Pony up means to pay up. Like in sex," Alexis said, trying to keep a straight face.

"Oh, I see. Yes, yes, I would consider that. At some point," Yoko added hastily at the horrified looks on her friends' faces.

Isabelle didn't know why or how she had become protective of Yoko. She felt motherly when it came to the shy little woman. "Oh, honey, we are going to need to put a leash on you. Before you make any . . . adventuresome moves, you check with us first. I think we should check out Mr. Harry Wong. We want to make sure he's good enough for you."

"And that he has enough money so you don't have to work," Alexis said. "Unless you want to."

"We need to know how he reacts to children and how he treats his parents. That's very important," Kathryn said.

"Don't you worry, honey, we're going to supervise your love life," Isabelle said.

"I don't want you to supervise my love life. I want to . . . to do it all. I will tell you the details. Afterward."

Kathryn pulled the chain to blow the horn on the rig. "Okay, kiddo, it's a deal."

Chapter 8

Ted Robinson stretched out on his sofa, his two cats crawling all over him. He liked this togetherness. Still, if he had his druthers, he'd pick Maggie to canoodle with. But Maggie hated his guts. She'd betrayed him for her chance to get the big story. He knew without a smidgen of doubt that she'd stolen his cassette that night at the cemetery. The reason he was so certain was because he would have done the same thing had he known she had a recorder.

Minnie curled herself into the nape of Ted's neck. He stroked her small head. He decided right then that he hated women and was forever swearing off the female gender. He knew it was his pride and his ego at stake that was making him think like this. *Now what do I do?*

Well, hell's bells, call that skunk Jack Emery

and ask for advice, of course. Never in a million years. Not in two million years. Jack's rule: Never let them see you sweat.

Mickey leaped from his perch on the top of the sofa and landed half on Ted's head, and half on the pillow. Minnie purred her pleasure in her coveted spot. Mickey hissed and jumped onto the coffee table where he helped himself to a cat treat. "What's wrong with this picture?" Ted muttered.

His phone chose that moment to ring. Ted's arm reached out and then snapped back as though a snake were coiled on the phone. He peered down at the number on the mini cell phone window. Maggie's number. He bolted upright sending Minnie flying to the end of the sofa. He couldn't answer it since he was supposed to be in New York. Well, shit. Screwed again. The phone stopped ringing. He waited a minute before he clicked the message button.

"I know you're home, Ted. I'm outside and can see the lights are on in your apartment. I need to talk to you. I'm going to wait five minutes and call you again. Answer the damn phone because I have something to tell you."

"Oh, no. Oh, no. I leave the lights on for the cats. They're on timers, and you know that, Miz Spritzer," Ted mumbled, his eyes on the digital numbers on his watch. Five minutes passed, then five more minutes with no phone call. He flopped back down on the sofa. Fifteen minutes later, his doorbell rang.

Ted almost jumped out of his skin. The cats beelined for the door. He remained motionless.

Since Maggie had given him back his key, how the hell did she get into the building? Simple, she just waited for someone else to open the door and waltzed right through. Well, let her stand out there until her feet took root.

"I know you're in there, Ted! Either you open the door or I'm going to start bellowing your secrets all over this floor," Maggie shouted to be heard through the door.

What secrets? Oh, shit! Ted swung his legs over the side of the sofa and sprinted to the front door. It took him a minute to undo all four locks. He opened the door and yanked at Maggie's arm. Her feet left the floor as she sailed into the room.

"I knew you were in here, you louse. You didn't go to New York either. I checked; you sent Espinosa in your place. For your information, I was mugged tonight. Not that you care," Maggie sniffed.

Ted leaned back on the sofa. It was probably a lie. She looked fine to him.

"They stole my backpack, my recorder with the Jack Emery cassette, and my keys. It happened in the parking lot at Nikki Quinn's law firm. She got the worse end of it. There were two of them. They stole her briefcase and her purse and knocked her around a little. She filed a police report but I didn't stick around. She promised not to involve me."

Ted hooted with laughter. "Boy, did those women set you up! You fell for it like a rookie reporter. You can't outwit them. You should have figured that out by now. You should be ashamed of yourself for even admitting you got snookered."

Maggie's voice was a tad lame sounding. "I wasn't set up," she insisted. "I've got the bruises and so does Quinn. She could hardly walk. The first words out of her mouth were we had to call the police. If it was a setup, why would she do that?"

"To make a fool out of you. You tipped your hand. What'd you do, play them that stupid tape? Yeah, you did, don't deny it. You called ahead for an appointment and that gave them enough time to set you up. Rookie!" Ted went off into another peal of laughter.

Maggie threw a cushion at him, a murderous expression on her face. Ted continued to laugh.

"So what are you doing here? What do you want? Whatever it is, the answer is no."

Maggie knew when to backpedal. This was one of those times. "Okay, I'm sorry. I did take the cassette. You broke into my apartment and took mine, don't deny it. Okay, we're even. C'mon, Ted, let's get back on track here. I'm sorry. I should have known better than to try to put something over on you. You're way too smart for me."

Ted got up, stepped over the sleeping cats and made his way to the refrigerator. He uncapped one bottle of beer and carried it back to the sofa. "Cut the crap, Maggie. I wouldn't believe you if you swore on your own life. Like I said, you aren't who I thought you were."

"And you are?" Maggie sniped. "You lied about going to New York. And the job offer. If you want to get away from me, just say so. You didn't have to lie to me. I damn well hate liars."

"I hate thieves," Ted retorted.

"I guess if you had given me a ring this is where I'd throw it at you," Maggie sniped again.

"You gave me back my key; same difference," Ted said, hating how terminal the conversation was. He wondered what Jack would do in a situation like this. For starters, Jack would have chopped her off at the knees at the first sign of a problem. Then again, maybe he was giving Lothario Emery entirely too much credit.

"I guess there's nothing else to say then. I'll leave you to your . . . cats. I really am sorry, Ted. I wish both of us weren't so competitive. I do have one question, though. Since you brought me into this in the first place, do you want me to back off now and leave you to whatever you plan to do? It's your baby so I don't have a problem with folding my tent."

"And pigs fly."

Maggie whirled around, her eyes shooting sparks. "You know what, Ted, you sound just like your buddy Jack. I think you turned into his clone. That's not a good thing. I'm taking that as a 'no' on your part which means we are now in competition. Is that how you see it?"

Ted didn't bother to respond. He hated the way his stomach was churning. He didn't like the way his eyes were burning either. He wondered if he was coming down with a cold. He squeezed his eyes shut and didn't open them till he heard the door close. Both cats leaped back onto the sofa and then onto his chest.

Sometimes life was such a bitch.

Ted sat up and reached for the phone on the coffee table. He could call good old Jack and ask what his next step should be. Or he could call the Absolute Total Bottom Line Authority on Women who would give him the straight skinny. Ted hit the number 1 on his speed dial and waited for the phone to be picked up on the other end. The moment he heard her voice, a smile worked itself around his lips. "Hi Mom."

"Teddy! Are you all right? Is anything wrong? You aren't sick, are you? Why are you calling at this time in the evening? Please, tell me you're all right. Did you call to talk to me or Dad?"

"Mom, I'm fine. No, I'm not sick. I called because I need some advice. I called to talk to both you and Dad. How's Dad's knee? Did he decide on replacement surgery or is he still trying to be brave and endure the pain?"

"No, he's tired of being brave. He scheduled his surgery for the middle of May." Now the voice on the phone turned brisk. "What kind of advice can I offer?"

"I met this woman. She's a colleague and we've been seeing each other. We more or less partnered up on a story we're covering but she stepped out of bounds and then I stepped out of bounds and we're at a standstill. No, that's not quite true. I think she dumped me. Maybe I gave her the idea I was dumping her. Whatever, we split up. My stomach is acting up, my eyes are burning. Mom, I feel like crap."

"Teddy, you're in love. Sometimes love hurts.

It's not always bells and whistles. Both parties have to work at it. Sorry is a wonderful word, provided you mean it when you say it. It's not all that hard to say either."

"Mom, she tried to ace me out of my own story. After she agreed to a byline. How can I trust someone like that? She came over here a little while ago and said she was sorry but I sent her packing because I didn't believe her."

"What's she like, Teddy?"

"Her name is Maggie. She has a dog named Daisy. She's nice when she isn't trying to one-up me. We talked about maybe getting married. She covers the Beltway gossip and she's real good at it. I think people read her column before they read the front page. This is a gossip town, as you well know. She brings doughnuts and coffee to everyone in the office every morning. Everyone likes her. Even the guys respect her. She has a lot of freckles and she laughs a lot. When she isn't stabbing me in the back, that is. Well, maybe she's laughing even then but I'm not sure. She's a good cook. Doesn't wear a lot of makeup and doesn't dress up real fancy. You and Dad would like her. I was thinking about asking her if she wanted to go to Indiana with me over Memorial Day so you could meet her. But, Mom, what good is it if I can't trust her?"

"Tell me the truth, Teddy. Can Maggie trust you?"

Ted scrunched his face into a grimace. He'd never lied to his mother. "Well . . . more or less . . . about as much as I trust her. That's a no, Mom."

"I'm going to call your father now, Teddy. You can talk to him for a while. I'm sure you'll do the right thing."

Ted suffered through a long monologue on his father's knee condition, the crooked politicians in Washington, and the spring rains that were plaguing Indiana. When his father finally stopped to take a deep breath, Ted said, "Okay, Dad, I'll call again in a few days. Keep taking your medication. 'Night."

Damn. I knew I should have called Jack. Maybe tomorrow.

With nothing else to do except watch television, Ted opted to head out to an all-night grocery store to stock his pantry. He tried to shift into neutral and make a grocery list but his thoughts were on Maggie and his own bad-ass attitude.

His list in hand, his portable shopping cart in the other, Ted locked his door and headed for the stairs and the all-night market around the corner. He hated the creaky, old elevator that didn't work half the time.

He almost didn't see her. Actually, he heard her before he saw her. Maggie. Sitting on the top step crying her eyes out, her shoulders shaking.

"Maggie, what are you doing here? I thought you left."

Maggie sniffed. "Yeah, well, that's where I was headed but I . . . twisted my ankle and it hurts like hell. That's why I'm crying. Where are you going at this hour?"

"Liar. You didn't hurt your ankle. I was going

grocery shopping." Ted sat down on the steps next to her and said, "Maggie, why don't we call a truce and go back to where we were before we decided to partner up? It was more interesting when we didn't trust each other and kept trying to put one over on one another. Since it was my story to begin with, I'm not giving you back the tape. You okay with that?"

"Do I have a choice? Okay. What about the personal . . . you know . . ."

"That's up to you, Maggie."

"Okay, I'm all for it. Want me to go shopping with you?"

"Well, sure."

Maggie reached for Ted's hand. She squeezed. It took Ted a moment before he squeezed back. He was glad now he hadn't called Jack. He was doing okay on his own. Maybe someday he'd write a book on what men didn't know, would never know, about women. He knew in his gut that Jack Emery was already working on such a book and the damn thing would probably be a bestseller.

Chapter 9

Nikki Quinn paced her bedroom at Pinewood. She felt jittery at having told the others about Jack. Even more nervous about not confiding in Myra and Charles. Wasn't there some kind of saying about chickens coming home to roost? Whatever it was, she couldn't remember it. She jammed her hands into the pockets of her khaki slacks.

She eyed the rocking chair by the window. How still it was, as though it waited for an occupant. Barbara's rocker sat under the high casement window whose sheer curtains were billowing gently in the warm spring breeze. "I could use a friend right now," Nikki said quietly.

The rocker started to move slowly. Nikki automatically reached for Willie and tossed him toward the rocker. Willie seemed to float and then settled in a nebulous grasp. *"I'm here, Nik. Got your panties in a wad, huh?"*

Nikki stopped her frantic pacing and sat down on the edge of the bed so she could face the rocker. "Yeah, pretty much. I told the girls about Jack being my source. I had to. I was kind of surprised that they were okay with it. I haven't told Jack yet and that's bothering me. Not to mention this is all a big secret from Myra and Charles."

"Is it because you think too many people now know about the Sisterhood?"

"Of course."

"You don't have to worry about Jack. Those two reporters are becoming a nuisance. That stunt you pulled in the parking lot was pretty clever. Don't get cocky now because you snookered that reporter. Once she spills her guts to Ted Robinson it will turn on you. They know, Nik."

"Yes, I know they do, but they don't have solid proof. It's hell trying to stay one step ahead of them. Short of kidnapping and muzzling them, I don't know what to do. I should have some kind of plan but I don't. I'm afraid to tell Charles for fear he'll sic those gold shields on them again and it will all end up in Jack's lap. Jack can't do anything. As it is, he's stuck his neck out as far as it will go. He needs to be kept safe and out of this little problem. Barb, he could be disbarred, jailed, God knows what else, if he's found out. Ted and Maggie know about him. There's no such thing as friendship coming first when there's a scoop of this nature in the offing. I have to do something where those two reporters are concerned but I don't know what."

"Why don't you and the others take the bull by the horns and scare the daylights out of them?"

Nikki laughed, a gruesome sound. "If those special guys of Charles' didn't scare them, what makes you think a bunch of women can work that particular miracle?"

"You just answered your own question, Nik. You're women. Run it by the others, see what they come up with. Mom has clout. Tap into it."

Nikki looked down at her watch. "I have to go, Barb. Charles called a meeting for ten. Hey, before I forget, how'd it go in Spain? Myra told me she spoke with you."

"It's as lovely as when we were there as teenagers. I was sad to see how Aunt Annie has changed. Grief can make you old before your time. I think, if the time ever comes, you would be quite content to live there. I know I would."

Nikki whirled around. "What are you saying? Is that a warning?"

"Nikki, it's ten o'clock. You know how cranky Charles gets when you girls are late. You better run."

"All right, but we aren't finished with this conversation."

Nikki galloped down the stairs just in time to fall into line behind the others on the way to the command center.

Isabelle reached behind her to grasp Nikki's hand. A show of comfort. How astute she was. Nikki squeezed back, her thoughts going in a hundred different directions.

Myra wasted no time once she called the

meeting to order. Charles towered above them, busy at his bank of computers. Lady Justice appeared on the three television monitors. For some reason, Nikki always sat up straighter when she looked at the blindfolded Justice.

"I'm happy to report that my old friend Anna Ryland de Silva has agreed to help us. Because nothing about the Sisterhood is secret among us, I want to tell all of you that I had to tell Annie about the Sisterhood. I realize I probably should have consulted with all of you but I took matters into my own hands. I allowed myself that privilege since I'm the one who started the Sisterhood."

Nikki felt her stomach muscles start to crunch up. Was Myra's confession some kind of veiled threat? Was it possible she knew about Jack? She looked up at Lady Justice and suddenly wanted to cry. She bit down on her lower lip as she continued to listen to Myra.

"Annie gave me the keys to the house in Manassas. Actually, it's more than just a house. It's quite a large estate, similar to Pinewood, even larger. There is security and a part-time staff that sees to the maintenance. Annie is in the process of pensioning off all of the staff. We will be taking it over. Temporarily, of course. At some point, Annie will return to the States. What that means is we will be relocating the first day of next week. Charles will stay here but he'll be in communication with us at all times.

"Now, let's get down to business. Charles and I have some ideas but we want to hear from all of you, especially you, Alexis, as this is your mission. Before we do that, do any of you have any questions?"

"I have a question," Alexis said. "Are we all going to Manassas? What about Isabelle and the Barrington farm? Can she take the time off? Sorry, that was three questions."

"Isabelle will come and go. Alexis, you will be with us but out of sight. Kathryn and Yoko will be front and center. We have to be careful because Isabelle's pictures have been in the paper quite a bit. Gillespie and Sullivan know you, Alexis, so you have to stay out of sight until the right moment when you confront the couple. Nikki has a choice to make. Charles wants her to sort through Spanish law but she can do that in Manassas or here where the computers are at her disposal. Now, let's start talking this to death. Alexis, what do you really want us to do?"

Alexis cleared her throat. "I want both of them stripped of everything. I want them to go to prison and not for just one year. When they get out, whenever that may be, I want them to have nothing. I don't want anything to happen to Mr. Sullivan's wife or children. It's not their fault Mr. Sullivan is such a sleaze."

Myra looked around the table. "I think it's all doable. Do you all agree?" The women nodded.

"All right then, this is the plan. I am going to pretend to be Anna Ryland de Silva. Alexis will alter my appearance just enough so that I don't resemble myself. We're going to pretend to be looking for a new brokerage firm because the old one is just too stuffy and conservative. We'll start out with a simple phone call, followed up by a fax. We'll be unavailable for a while after they get back to us. Kathryn and Yoko will be my assistants.

"Charles has outdone himself, as usual, in preparing a dossier on Annie. It is so impressive it made my eyes water just reading it. Those two . . . ah . . . smarmy people will be drooling and salivating when they read it. Just the thought of possibly taking over Annie's account will make them delirious. Their greed will be their undoing."

"Then what?" Kathryn asked bluntly.

"Before we get to the 'then what' part Charles thinks we should monitor their telephones, offices, and their cars so we can be one step ahead of them. That means we will have to have someone plant some listening devices that we can monitor. The 'then what' part is where we allow them to bamboozle us. That's when Annie will arrive and take up residence once we depart. She will accuse them of attempting to defraud her and, of course, press charges. Of course it will make the front page of every financial paper in the world. At which point . . . they're . . . toast. Just for the record, I look nothing like Annie. Charles has scoured every publication, every media outlook, and there are no pictures of Annie anywhere. The aging process this time is in our favor. I think, Alexis, I can arrange it so you're at the prison when the bars clang shut for the first time. What do you think, girls?"

"I'm okay with it if it's what Alexis wants," Kathryn said. The others nodded in agreement. "I think we were starting to get used to the more . . . ah . . . physical punishments. You know, action." The others nodded again as they looked at Alexis.

"It works for me as long as their lives are ruined. I can live with this."

"Then it's settled. We have a few days to work out the finer details of this mission. The house is being readied for us as we speak. To quote Charles, we are pulling out all the stops to make this a success."

Myra handed out folders that contained Anna de Silva's dossier. Included also was a map and directions to the Manassas estate.

"I think, girls, we should each go separately to Manassas and keep a sharp eye out for anyone who might be following. If there's no other business, we're adjourned for the day. Nikki, Charles wants you to stay behind so he can explain what he wants you to do. Can you clear time from the office?"

"It's not a problem, Myra. I'm down to working fifteen hours a week at the office. Things are running smoothly so I'm good to go here."

Leaving Nikki and Charles behind in the war room, Myra followed the others to the kitchen. She smiled, loving the feeling of being part of the girls' social life. She enjoyed listening to them ribbing Yoko about her plan to snare one Harry Wong into, as Kathryn put it, her web.

"So, let me get this straight?" Kathryn said. "You are actually going to show up at the *dojo* for your first lesson but before you get dressed to participate in the drill, one of us is to call you saying there is an emergency and you have to leave. Leaving Harry Wong with his tongue hanging out."

"Yes, yes, you have it right. It will make me look important and that I am not interested even though I am much interested. It is a good plan, isn't it?"

Alexis thumped Yoko on the back. "What would be an even better plan is for you to waltz in there, strut your stuff, and wipe up the floor with all of them. Do some of those high-air *whirly-twirly* things you do, and then do some of that jabbing and kicking. They'll lick your feet in surrender."

Yoko looked puzzled but only for a moment. "Are you yanking my foot?"

The girls, even Myra, burst out laughing.

"That's yanking your chain or pulling your leg," Isabelle said.

"Let's take a vote," Alexis said. "All in favor of Yoko strutting her stuff instead of canceling out at the last second, raise your hand."

"Four in favor of strutting your stuff. You go, girl! Call us and let us know how it goes," Kathryn laughed as she made her way out to her truck. She turned around and called over her shoulder. "Wear something skimpy."

"Oh, yeah," Alexis drawled.

"A leotard will do nicely," Isabelle said in a motherly tone. The motherly tone turned prim. "With a loose flowing jacket." She wagged her finger for emphasis. To her dismay, Yoko laughed but she nodded.

The kitchen seemed incredibly empty and quiet when Myra poured herself a glass of apple juice and sat down at the table. Her thoughts took her back to a time when Nikki and Barbara were eleven. The house had rocked with sound, young people, dogs and cats and even a canary who could sing several bars of the "Star Spangled Banner." The good times. The wonderful times. The happiest times of her life. Tears welled in her eyes at her memories.

"C'mon, Mom, lighten up. Make it a fun day the way you used to."

Myra whirled around so fast she almost spilled her apple juice. "Darling girl, is it really you?"

"It's me, Mom. Don't be sad. Smile for me. I always loved it when you smiled for me and Nikki even when we did something bad. After the punishment we knew you'd give out popsicles and smile at us. Why are you sad, Mom?"

"I'm not sad now that you're here. That might not be quite true. I do tend to get a little nervous before we . . . we exact a particular revenge. So many things can go wrong. I guess once a worrier, always a worrier."

"I know, Mom. It's okay. Relax. Spain was nice, wasn't it? I knew if anyone could get Aunt Annie to bounce back, it was you. I was so proud of you, Mom. I had no idea you could be so feisty."

"Oh, dear, I didn't overdo it, did I? I need to know something, dear. If . . . if . . . it ever comes to us having to go there, will you . . . will you be there? I don't think I'd be able to go if you say no."

"Wherever you are, Mom, I'm right next to you. I have to go now. I hear Nikki. I love you, Mom."

"And God alone knows how much I love you, darling girl." Myra wiped at the tears in her eyes.

"Myra, what's wrong? Did something happen?" Nikki asked, concern ringing in her voice.

"There's nothing wrong, dear." She probably should have mentioned her conversation with her spirit daughter but she wanted to hold the moment close to her heart and not share it. Perhaps later. "You missed the funniest thing, Nikki."

"Oh, what's that?"

Myra told her about Yoko, a smile on her face. When Nikki didn't respond, Myra felt a tinge of alarm. "Don't you find it amusing, Nikki?"

Nikki picked up a bright red apple from the bowl on the table. She shined it on the sleeve of her shirt the way she used to when she was a little girl. "Actually, Myra, it scares the hell out of me. There's no way you could know this, but Harry Wong is one of Jack Emery's best friends. He's got a black belt. He teaches the police officers martial arts three days a week. It's mandatory. He even schools the cadets at the FBI Academy. The man is a legend in his own time."

"Oh dear," was all Myra could think of to say.

"Yes, oh dear. We have to stay on top of that little situation." Nikki bit into the apple with a loud crunching sound. Juice dribbled down her chin. Myra, always a mother, automatically held out a napkin.

"It seems like there's one more new thing to worry about every day. I hope we can keep it all straight."

"I hope so, too, Myra."

Nikki finished the apple. "If you don't need me for anything, I'm going to go for a run."

"Run along, dear. I'm just going to sit here and . . . and drink my juice."

"And think about Barbara's visit?"

Myra just nodded.

Chapter 10

Jack Emery held the phone away from his ear at the mixture of Chinese and Japanese invading his ear. "Harry! Harry! I only understand English and a smattering of Spanish. What the hell is wrong with you? God dammit, Harry, English or I'm hanging up. That's better. What do you mean *she's* there? You want me to come to your *dojo NOW*? Yeah, I know I owe you. All right, all right, I'll be there in twenty minutes."

Jack mumbled and muttered to himself as he changed out of his suit and into jeans and a tee shirt that said "Wong's Martial Arts" on the sleeve. He thought it was a nice touch to show support for Harry whom he respected immensely. As he tied his Nikes, he wondered if Harry was in some kind of trouble with a woman. To his knowledge, Harry had never been involved in a serious relationship. His excuse: no time for frivolity. Obviously, things had changed.

A light drizzle was falling when Jack left the house and headed for his car. He looked around but didn't see anyone of interest except an elderly couple walking their three golden retrievers. Still, just because things *looked* normal didn't mean conditions *were* normal. Only a fool would believe something like that and Mrs. Emery hadn't raised any fools.

Fifteen minutes later, having sailed through every green light, Jack parked his car in the *dojo* lot. He wasn't the least bit surprised to see how crowded it was. Harry had a brisk business and often had to turn people away or put them on a waiting list.

Jack let himself into the small kitchen area where a huge pot of tea was always on simmer. He helped himself to a cup before he headed out to the reception area to meet Harry and try to figure out what the S.O.S. was all about.

Harry spotted him the minute he walked into the reception area. He was dressed for class in his white *gi*, his black belt around his waist. He looked so frazzled, Jack had a hard time believing it was Harry. "She's getting dressed. She's here. What should I do?"

Jack did his best to appear patient. "What the hell are you talking about, Harry? Who is *she*? Are you in some kind of trouble? If you want my help, you have to give me a clue here."

"The girl from the market where I shop. I'm in love with her. She can't see me for dust, Jack. I want to impress her. She's really here now but she always canceled previously. She doesn't return my phone calls. It has to mean something that she's here, right, Jack?"

Jack gulped at the hot tea. Green tea, he thought. "What makes you think I'm some kind of authority on women?"

Harry looked nonplused for a moment. "You said you were."

"Oh." He really needed to stop bragging. "Well, where is she?"

Harry danced from one bare foot to the other. "All the students are in the locker room getting dressed. They don't come out till I ring the bell."

Jack looked around the large room. All the walls were mirrored. Blue mats covered the floor. Other than the mats, nothing else was in the classroom. The reception area, however, was different. Two bamboo benches lined the small area. A teakwood desk held a vase of white flowers. White for purity and serenity, Harry had told him once. Sweet incense wafted about. Takes away the smell of sweat, Harry had said the first time he'd visited. A real bamboo tree stood in the corner. It was lush and full.

"You know how tough I am with my students. Should I go easy on her? If I do that, the others will know I'm interested in her. She's very tiny, fragile. She looks like a beautiful porcelain doll."

"You are smitten, Harry. Look, ring the damn bell and let's get this show on the road. I can't give you an opinion till I see how it's going. For now, do what you always do. Ignore her. Women hate to be ignored. That's a given. If you're thinking about showing off, don't. She knows you're good or she wouldn't be here. Just pretend she's another student. I'd comb my hair if I were you."

Harry smoothed down his shiny black hair, straightened his *gi*, gave his black belt a twist and moved off, his dark eyes miserable. He rang the bell and stepped aside as his students filed into the room and formed four lines. Sixty students. Harry walked to the middle of the room and bowed low. The students bowed low.

Harry straightened up and pointed to a chubby lady in the second row. She moved out of the line to stand in front of Harry. They both bowed. She then stepped to the side and dropped to her knees, her toes and feet flat on the floor for the meditation ritual that had nothing to do with religion. Meditation helped to get a student in the right frame of mind. At the end of the lesson, the meditation ritual would be done again.

Eight minutes later, the ritual over, the warm-up exercises began with the chubby lady conducting them.

Jack stretched his neck to see which of the students Harry was interested in. He waited for Harry to make his way back to the reception area while the warm-up exercises got under way. "Which one is she?" he whispered.

"Second row, third from the left. You can hardly see her. After the warm-up, I'll . . . I'll introduce her as a new student. I do that from time to time so it won't be unusual."

"You better calm down first. Get going, buddy, meditation is over and so are the warm ups."

Harry pranced to the middle of the room and motioned to the chubby lady to get back into line. He pointed to his new student and motioned her forward. "We have a new student this evening. I want you all to offer as much help as you can if she requests it. This, class, is Miss Yoko Akia."

"Oh shit," Jack muttered under his breath. He tried to make himself invisible by slouching lower on the slatted bench. He yanked his Redskins cap lower over his eyes.

He watched Nikki's cohort bow low before the master before she took a step backward and then turned to the class to acknowledge their greeting. She was about to return to her line when Harry called her back. She bowed again and stepped aside. Ah, shit, Harry was going to show off. He could smell his testosterone. *Big mistake, buddy.*

"I'm going to show you some classic moves. Pay attention, Miss Akia. When I finish, we'll engage. Do you understand?" Yoko smiled, nodded, and bowed.

Jack watched the wiry Wong go through his paces. His students kept nodding and smiling as they hoped that one day they, too, would come somewhere near their master's expertise.

Jack remembered his own days under Harry's tutelage. He, like the others in the D. A.'s office, had plotted his death a hundred different ways. It took a full month for the bruises, the aches, the pains and the minute fractures to disappear. He dreaded and hated the two-hour mandatory classes because Harry showed no mercy to any of his students. There was nothing worse than having the master single you out, see him sneer and hear him call you a pussy cat. The times he'd wilted in shame were too numerous to recall, but he'd persevered and prevailed. Harry's training had saved his skin on more than one occasion. For that, he would be forever grateful. His fellow ADA's felt the same way.

Jack tuned back into Harry and his performance. Even at this distance he could see the wicked glint in Yoko's eyes. Suddenly, Jack wanted to run out to the floor and drag the master back to the kitchen. Instead, he leaned back and concentrated on the scene being played out in front of him.

"Do what I do," Harry said. Yoko bowed and followed his instructions. "Don't be timid because you're a girl. I won't hurt you."

Yoko lowered her head. "What if I make a mistake and hurt you?" she asked quietly.

Jack got a whiff of testosterone again. *Harry, you dumb schmuck, she's setting you up. Backpedal. Now.*

Harry Wong, grand master, smiled confidently. "That won't happen, Miss Akia. Now just follow my moves. When we're finished we will engage. Do you understand?"

Yoko smiled. "Yes, I understand."

Jack watched as Harry went through the paces he remembered all too well. As an observer, he could only marvel at the man's agility, his grace, his lightning-like moves. Behind him, Yoko looked clumsy and inept.

Twenty long minutes later, Harry turned back to his new pupil and said, "Now, we will engage."

Big mistake, Harry, Jack thought as he saw the master's feet leave the floor. A nanosecond later, Harry was flat on his back staring at the ceiling.

The class gasped as Yoko pretended horror. "Did I hurt you, Master Wong?"

"Of course not. I'm indestructible. Sometimes a student gets lucky the first time out of the gate." Yoko nodded shyly.

Master and student bowed to each other. Jack groaned. He'd always thought of Harry Wong as his own personal secret weapon. He wondered if that was going to change now.

It happened so quickly, Jack almost missed Harry's second landing. His jaw dropped as Yoko leaped high in the air when Harry's foot and arm shot out. She landed so quickly that the stunned Harry, his eyes wild, took the chop to his neck, a finger jab to his throat, and a violent kick to his side before he landed on his back to stare up at the ceiling a second time.

Ooooh, I feel your pain, Harry. Ooooh, ooooh, that had to hurt. I can't believe that little bit of a thing whupped your ass. It was obvious to Jack that Harry was thinking the same thing. Now, the master was getting angry. *Ooooh, look out little Yoko.*

Harry stood up as he tried to ignore the collective gasp of his class. "Obviously, you have a smattering of knowledge in martial arts, Miss Akia."

"Smattering?" Yoko said as she rocked back and forth on her bare feet.

Shut *UP*, Harry, Jack pleaded silently. He watched in horror as the two bowed and squared off. Harry was outright mad. The porcelain doll was *pissed*. He knew what the outcome would be and he wanted to cry for his secret weapon.

It started out like Miss Pringle's third grade dance class. Wary now, Harry made the mistake of trying to anticipate Yoko's moves. She whirled, twirled, leaped and pranced as she jabbed, kicked and chopped. Harry couldn't keep up with her. He'd whirl, she'd catch him in mid twirl and then she'd chop, her arms like pistons until she had him on the mat and was sitting on his chest. Her tiny hands were like steel claws as she pinned him to the mat. "What does that mean, smattering?"

"That you know a little bit about martial arts. How long are you going to sit on my chest?"

"A little bit? I will accept your apology if it is sincere. I will get off when I am ready."

"All right, you know more than a little. Probably pretty much. You came here under false pretenses," Harry squawked as he tried to shake her loose.

"You tricked the girl at the Asian market to get my phone number. Why?"

"Why? I wanted a date."

"Okay. Pick me up tomorrow night at seven." Yoko leaped to her feet, turned, bowed to the master and then to the class before she strode off.

Harry stood up and winced. "Class dismissed. Two free classes next week."

Jack watched his friend limp over to where he was sitting. "What a pussy cat you are, Master Wong," Jack guffawed. "What's she weigh, ninety pounds? Man, she had you on the ropes. I can't believe you did all this to get a date."

"I never said I was a ladies' man like you. I'm shy. Hey, it worked."

"Yeah, but she beat the shit out of you in front of your class. She humiliated you, hot shot!"

"Nah, nah, I let her win. I'm not *that* stupid."

"Yeah, yeah, you are. Guess it's your turn to hit the hot tub and rub that smelly liniment all over your skinny body. Don't even think about asking me to do it," Jack guffawed again as he made his way back to the kitchen, Harry limping along behind him.

In the kitchen, Harry poured himself a cup of tea. "Where do you suppose she learned the art? She's not that old."

Jack shrugged his shoulders. "This is just a guess but it would be my opinion that she learned this early on, probably as soon as she started to walk. I watched her, Harry. She was in that place you always told us to go to before an event. I could never do that. She tuned everything out. She was in that place, physically and mentally, and she made it work for her. No matter what you say, you were thinking with your dick. Just as a matter of curiosity, when was the last time someone pinned you?"

Harry grimaced as he gulped at the hot tea. "Believe it or not, Jack, no one has ever pinned me. She did it fair and square, too. That, I have to respect. I pretty much feel like a fool. How do I cover that tomorrow if I get the guts to pick her up?"

"Ignore it. Pretend it never happened. It's a wise man who knows when to be humble."

"That's your advice! It sucks, Jack!"

"Yeah, I know. See ya, Harry."

Chapter 11

The cell phone was in Jack's hand even before he fit the key in the ignition. He could hardly wait to tell Nikki about seeing her secret weapon take down his secret weapon. If he lived to be a hundred, he would never forget the stunned look on Harry Wong's face when the ninety pound dynamo pinned him to the mat. Harry would probably never forget it either.

A smile settled on Jack's face when he pulled out of Harry's parking lot. He always smiled when he heard Nikki say, "Jack!" in that breathless voice of hers that he so loved.

"It's me. Boy, do I have a story to tell you!"

"I have one to tell you, too. Where are you?"

"On my way home. Where are you?"

"I'm at the house. Waiting for you. We can swap stories when you get here."

Well, all RIGHT. "Do you want me to pick up anything?"

"A pizza with pepperoni, green peppers and garlic would be nice. I just got here or I would have cooked something. I'm starving. Better buy two. I'll call Bella's now to order them. Go through the drive-through. Wine or beer?"

"Beer! You aren't going to believe where I've been and you sure as hell aren't going to believe what went down. Don't even try to coax it out of me."

"I bet I can top whatever it is you're going to tell me," Nikki teased.

"We'll see about that," Jack said. "See you in a few minutes. Hey, this is really a nice surprise. I didn't expect to see you this week." He broke the connection, the smile still on his face.

Jack looked into the rear view mirror. He knew he had a tail two cars back. So, what else was new? He was so used to it now, it no longer bothered him. What did bother him was the waste of money someone was paying those goons. He wished he knew if it came out of the president's pocket or if Charles Martin subsidized that payroll in some way. He accepted the fact that he might never know the answer to that particular question.

Jack waited till the last minute before he turned on his signal light to turn into Bella's parking lot and then on to the drive-through window. He swiped his credit card through the machine that came through the window on an electronic arm. Within seconds he had two hot pizza boxes in his hand. He whizzed through the parking lot and out to the main road that would lead him to Nikki's house.

Tonight, he was lucky. He found a parking spot two doors down from Nikki's house. Pizzas in hand, he climbed out of the car, locked it and started down the walk. A dark sedan was double parked directly in front of the house. He pretended not to see it.

"Good evening, Mr. Emery."

Jack's response was to flip the bird to the special agent. Well, now they knew about Harry Wong. It wouldn't take a rocket scientist to figure out Harry and his merry band of ninjas were responsible for some of the serious injuries the agents suffered. Jack made a mental note to call Harry and warn him. He worried about Harry. Men in love did stupid things and they tended to get sloppy at their workplace. He should know since he was the perfect example. Still, if he had to make a bet, he'd put his money down on Harry as long as guns didn't enter into the equation.

Jack slammed the door extra loud for the agent's benefit.

Nikki reached for the pizza boxes as she leaned forward to kiss Jack soundly. They ended up laughing before Jack headed off for the upstairs bathroom where he called Harry's cell phone. He wasn't surprised to hear "please leave a message at the sound of the tone." Jack left a detailed message, ending with, "This is your fault, Harry. You wanted me to come to the *dojo*. Stay alert, buddy. These guys play with guns and they have a few scores to settle. Let me know how the big date goes. This is Jack Emery, and I approve this message." Jack laughed to himself all the way back to the living room where Nikki had everything ready and waiting.

Ah, the perfect end to a long day.

A long time later, the pizza boxes and napkins burning in the fireplace along with a fire log, the couple retired to the deep comfortable couch. They cuddled and snuggled. "Who goes first?" Nikki asked.

Jack sighed. "Ladies first. I know you can't top my news, so go ahead, shoot your load."

"Okay, here goes. We're talking pure dumb luck here but guess which one of my sisters has a date with a good friend of yours? Yoko, that's who! She met this guy in the Asian market where she shops and he came on to her, but she's shy. This guy, your good friend Harry Wong, bribed the sales clerk for her phone number and he called her. Go ahead, Mr. District Attorney, try and top that!"

"Oh, I can top that," Jack drawled. "Guess who watched a competition between my secret weapon and your secret weapon? Me, that's who! Your secret weapon wiped up the floor with my secret weapon but Harry was off his feed; he's in love. That little gal pinned him. I couldn't believe someone so small could be so powerful. Harry isn't a big guy but he's all muscle. When you watch him you think he's made of rubber the way he can bend and do all that stuff. Yoko was the same way."

"Damn," Nikki said, propping herself up on one elbow to stare down at Jack, who was resting against a stack of pillows. "I thought I had you that time because they met by accident. This is too weird."

"Weird covers it. They have a date tomorrow. I hate to admit this but your little gal has Harry wrapped. How come you never told me about her?"

"Jack, I didn't know. None of us knew. From time to time she'd do some quirky little thing but I had no idea she was as proficient as she is. Until just recently, Yoko has been a bit of a mystery. She split with her husband. It was one of those arranged marriages. Isabelle kind of mothers her. I think it all started when Julia had one of her assistants give her breast implants. After that, Yoko started to blossom. I have to tell you, she was pretty excited about Harry. God, Jack, what kind of union will that be if it works out between the two of them?"

"An interesting one, that's for sure."

Nikki gave him a good swat. "Listen, Jack, we're all leaving over the weekend for Manassas so I won't be stopping by. We're starting Alexis's mission. It's not like Manassas is a continent away, it's literally just down the road but I won't be able to leave until it's over."

Jack groaned. "I miss you already."

Nikki kissed him lightly as she murmured,

"Then maybe we should make some memories to carry us through the next few weeks."

Jack was off the sofa in a flash. He reached down to grab Nikki and slung her over his shoulder, caveman style. She squealed, to his delight as he bounded up the steps, stumbling only once.

The next morning, Jack thought he and Nikki had created a hell of a memory to carry him through the coming days.

Nikki hunkered down in the war room with Charles, a dozen books spread out in front of her as she tried to make sense out of Spanish law. Charles was so busy at his bank of computers that he hardly noticed her presence.

It was late afternoon and Myra was headed for the District to have an early dinner with Judge Easter. Isabelle was at the Barrington farm and Kathryn had accepted a short overnight run to Pennsylvania to deliver bales of peat moss and pine straw.

Thirty miles away, Alexis Thorne stared at the last entries she'd made in her computer before she typed up a bill to send to her client. Personal shopping didn't pay much but it did pay the rent. She would drop the bill off at the post office on her way to Yoko's nursery where she had agreed to dress the little woman for her date with Harry Wong.

She adored Yoko and liked that she was becoming less inhibited. These days she would even start an argument and usually win. Of all of them, Yoko had made the most personal progress. Isabelle was slowly coming out of her self-imposed exile and was learning to laugh all over again. Myra was more upbeat and Nikki, now that she was back into her relationship with Jack Emery, was proving to be a true sister. Kathryn was combative as ever, just as outspoken, but was struggling to find her lighter side. A man might help but she wasn't sure. Kathryn's emotions were simply locked up too tight. Time, Alexis told herself, was what Kathryn needed.

That left herself, Alexis Thorne. When, she wondered, would she ever again call herself by her given name, Sara Whittier, or was Sara Whittier dead, never to be resurrected?

Alexis swerved into the parking lot and gave a light tap to her horn. Yoko ran out of the flower shop and over to the car. "I am so happy you were not too busy to come, Alexis. This is so important to me. Come, come, I have to tell you about last night. I was . . . I was . . . superb! I was!"

"Well, good for you! Let me get my Red Bag. Are we having tea?"

"Yes. Tea. It is steeping. I bought honey because I know you like honey. Oh, hurry, Alexis. I am closing the shop early. No one comes at this time of day."

"Whoa, whoa. Slow down. This is all going to work. You need to be serene, in control. If you go off half cocked, you're going to blow it. Bet you're glad you got those new boobs, huh?"

Yoko giggled. "You bet," she said smartly.

"Before I forget, Alexis, Mr. Emery was at the *dojo* last night. He tried to make himself invisible, and I pretended not to see him. Since Nikki told us he is more or less one of us, I wasn't worried. What does worry me is, do you think he will tell Harry about me? Now, let me tell you how I came out on top."

Alexis listened, her eyes popping from time to time. "Wow! I would have paid to see that. Congratulations! Mr. Emery won't tell," she said confidently as she pulled out the huge red bag and threw it over her shoulder. "We have four hours, Yoko, till your date."

"And we will need every minute of that time. The bubble bath takes a long time. I must meditate beforehand. I wish to serve you dinner. I hope you like sushi."

Inside the flower shop, Yoko locked the door, pulled the shade down over the window and turned the sign that said open, to the side that said the shop was closed. "Come," she said. Alexis followed her to a beaded doorway.

Alexis looked at the colorful beads and knew somehow that Yoko had made them herself. She'd been here once before, but only in the shop area.

"I have never invited anyone here before," Yoko said, suddenly shy.

"Then I feel honored to be the first person to cross your threshold."

The colored beads parted to show a large room sectioned off with more colored beads. Alexis felt stunned at what she was seeing. For some reason she'd expected either a Japanese or Chinese decor but that wasn't what she saw. The tiny kitchen area was old, the appliances sparkling clean but antiquated. A small table with two chairs sat in the corner. The small living room held two chairs that looked deep and comfortable. A television sat on a small table in the corner. It had the old fashioned rabbit ears. A dark green fiber carpet covered the middle of the floor. There was one picture on the wall of a beautiful woman. She assumed it was Yoko's mother but she didn't ask. The bedroom area had a sleeping mat and a dresser. A fiber carpet matching the one in the living room was on the floor but it held a huge gray-white cat who was sound asleep. A pot of white lilies sat in the corner. Stark, simple, but so clean, Alexis knew she could have eaten off the floor.

"His name is Riff Raff," Yoko said. "He found me, I did not find him. He never leaves the shop. I think he is afraid of the world. I moved in here after my husband left to save money and because I did not like the house we lived in. I know it is . . . not much but it is all I need. I can save for that wet day."

Alexis laughed. "You should see the dump I live in. I tell myself it isn't worth fixing up because I don't plan on staying there. This is nice, Yoko, it suits you."

"I have a dog, too. He is outside during the day but he comes in at night to be with me. His name is Hawthorn. That is what his collar says. He, too, found me. I tried to find his owner but

I could not locate anyone. Hawthorn and Riff Raff are my family. Come, come, I will make sushi for you and we will have girl talk. Do you know how to do girl talk?"

"Oh, yeah. What would you like to talk about?"

"You. I do not want to know about prison. I want to know who you are."

Alexis sat down on one of the two chairs. "My grandmother raised me. She never actually came out and said my mother was no good or that my father was worse, but I knew. I don't know where they are or if they are alive or dead. My grandmother was a wonderful woman. She was heavy on the Bible and she was real handy with the paddle. She made sure I did my homework, wore clean clothes, brushed my teeth. She could peel an apple and not break the skin. I always marveled at that. She loved me with all her heart and I loved her. When I graduated from college, she cried her eyes out. When I started making serious money, I tried to help her but she wouldn't take a penny. I tried buying her a big TV but she said it made her dizzy to look at such a big screen. I would try to take her out to dinner but she said she didn't belong in such places. The only time she would accept presents from me was on her birthday and Christmas. When she . . . when she died and I had to go through her things, I found all those presents in her chest. It broke my heart. I think I would have died if she'd been alive when I was sent to prison."

"I am so sorry, Alexis. We will fix all that for

you. Are you ever going to tell us your real name?"

"My real name is Sara Whittier. On the drive out here I was wondering if Sara was dead, never to be resurrected. It's hard to believe that I will be avenged. Those two smarmy people are so slick, so smart. Because they are con artists themselves, they'll be able to smell a con a mile away. I can only hope Charles knows who he is dealing with.

"Now that I spilled my guts, how is it none of us knew about your martial arts expertise?"

"You never asked," Yoko smiled. "I did not think it was important. We are taught the art of self defense as soon as we learn to walk and talk. It is normal for us, not something out of the ordinary. I do not like talking about myself. When it is my turn, I will tell you anything you wish to know. Tell me about the smarmy people."

Alexis drew a deep breath. "Arden Gillespie is probably one of the most beautiful women I've ever seen. She has incredible blue eyes and they are not enhanced with contact lenses either. She's a natural blonde and her hair has a wave to it. Spectacular is the only word I can think of. Every day she would have a new hair style. She looks like a well-fed supermodel, which means she is not skinny. She has a perpetual tan and always looks like she just came back from some sunny beach. She's smart as a whip, graduated from the Wharton School of Business. And, she's evil.

"Roland Sullivan, I believe, started out being

a respectable broker. All my research bore that out. When Arden came on the scene, he changed. When she became a partner, he changed even more. They both worship money. Once, during the trial, I saw Roland looking at me. I could be wrong but I think he had tears in his eyes at what was happening to me. Tears or not, I went to prison. I think he's just as evil as Arden is. I hate them both. My grandmother is probably spinning in her grave for me saying such things. She taught me not to hate, to turn the other cheek. Sometimes you just can't do that."

"I hate them, too. Your honor will be restored. Would you like a big cup of tea or a little cup?"

"Big cup. Oh, this is good. I haven't had sushi in a long time. So, where are you and Harry going this evening?"

"I do not know. Perhaps a movie. Dinner. Maybe the Asian market," Yoko giggled.

"Well, that poses a bit of a problem. How can we dress you if we don't know where you're going?"

Yoko shrugged. "I guess we'll have to fly with it."

"Wing it."

"Yes, wing it. No kimono, though. I want to look like a slick chicken."

Alexis laughed. "Slick chick, and I think I can arrange that. I see you aren't eating so why don't you go take that bubble bath and I'll clean up here."

"You don't mind?"

"Not at all."

Alexis sat in the little kitchen, her eyes on the

beads that separated the kitchen area from the living room. It must have taken Yoko forever to string the beads and then make a knot between each bead. Maybe Yoko was one of those people who had to keep busy all the time, kind of like herself. If you kept busy, you didn't think or worry.

Chapter 12

Arden Gillespie fished around in her Prada bag for her compact. She tilted her head this way and that to see if her makeup was as flawless as it was when she applied it hours ago. She added a dab of lip gloss, smacked her lips together, and smiled, revealing a fortune in porcelain caps. One manicured nail touched the three-carat diamond stud in her ear. She wondered if there was such a thing as a five-carat earring. Even if she had a five-carat, people would probably think it was Diamonique from the shopper's channel.

The blue eyes her colleagues said were the color of bluebells dropped to the letter on her desk. She sucked in her breath. She'd been sitting here, going over her personal finances, when her secretary walked into the office and handed her a crisp white envelope saying it was marked "personal" and had been delivered by a messenger. That in itself was nothing new or strange since mail arrived hourly by various means. It was the return address that made Arden sit up straighter. Anna Ryland de Silva. Everyone in the world knew who Anna Ryland de Silva was.

Arden licked at the gloss on her lips. Why would someone like de Silva be writing to the firm? Unless . . . For the first time since becoming a full partner, she wished she was the sole owner. Whatever was in the envelope would have to be shared with Roland Sullivan, her partner and her lover.

The word "share" was not in Arden Gillespie's vocabulary. Other people shared. She wasn't one of those other people.

If the word "share" was in her vocabulary, she wouldn't be sitting in this palatial office surrounded by priceless antiques, thanks to one of Washington, D. C.'s top decorators.

With that thought in mind, Arden slit the envelope with an ornate letter opener.

The paper crackled. That meant it was expensive, Arden's favorite word. At first she thought it read like an invitation which in a sense it was. It was short and concise.

Anna Ryland de Silva cordially invites you to her home in Manassas to show, if interested, how your firm would handle her holdings.

The favor of your reply is requested within forty-

eight hours and no later than nine o'clock, Wednesday morning.

The letter was signed by Ellen Markham, personal secretary to Anna Ryland de Silva.

Arden's index finger traced the colorful crest at the top of the paper. She wondered how much it would cost to get such a crest. As she'd learned, anything and everything was available if one had the money to pay for it. Her finger continued to trace the crest as her mind soared. If she could work up a presentation and somehow manage to snare the de Silva account, she would be set for life. Even sharing with Roland Sullivan she would be set for life. And if the wimpy little weasel would divorce his wife and marry her, she'd have the whole ball of wax, at which point she'd make his life so miserable he'd be willing to allow her to buy him out and ride off into the sunset.

So much to do, so little time.

Arden pressed a button and spoke softly. "Bring me coffee, Opal. Has Mr. Sullivan returned yet? Ask him to come to my office the minute he arrives."

Three minutes later, a bespeckled, rosy cheeked Opal brought coffee in a fragile bone china cup on a silver tray. The Kona coffee was flown in weekly from Hawaii for Arden's private consumption. Roland and clients were served Maxwell House coffee in Crate and Barrel mugs.

Arden lit a cigarette, her first of the day. She used a smokeless ashtray that didn't really work and turned on a specially designed exhaust fan that guaranteed a smoke free room. Roland favored cigars and refused to give them up. His exhaust fan was larger and actually worked.

Arden rang for her secretary again. "Opal, stop whatever you're doing and get me everything that has ever been printed on Anna Ryland de Silva. Get as many people as you need to help you. I want *everything.* Call all the papers, the television stations, anyone you can think of. Find out who her friends are. Get addresses and phone numbers. I can't be sure of this but I think I read once that her husband was a count which means she's a countess. ASAP, Opal. Where the hell is Roland? Did he at least call in?"

"He went to his son's school this morning, Miss Gillespie. The boy is getting an award for some class project. Mr. Sullivan said he wouldn't be in till eleven-thirty. I thought you knew, Miss Gillespie. He said no matter what, we were not to call him because the school frowns on cell phones."

"Oh," was all Arden could think of to say. She did vaguely remember Roland saying something about the boy's award but since she didn't like children, his or anyone else's, she'd ignored the comment.

Arden continued to puff on her cigarette knowing she'd have to replace her lip gloss but she didn't care. It was all about her and if other people forgot that, even for a moment, she had no trouble reminding them. Now, if she could just get rid of that ugly picture on the wall by the door, things would be even better.

The picture. That's how she thought of it. *The*

picture was the reason she was sitting in this scrumptious office with her priceless antiques. A duplicate hung in Roland's office. A reminder that they were both responsible for sending Sara Whittier to prison. *The picture* was of Sara Whittier being taken off to prison after her trial. Arden had argued, cried, threatened, and finally had to give up when Roland remained adamant about the picture. To remind them of how low they'd sunk. The picture remained, a daily reminder of her greed. Proof of her guilt in framing Sara. But only Roland knew that because he'd been her willing partner and shared in the money. That part didn't bother her but she knew it bothered Roland. He'd actually said he lost sleep over what they'd done and gone on to say that his wife, who liked Sara, had said there was more to the whole thing than met the eye. Arden had just laughed at him and his Martha Stewart wife.

Arden finished her coffee and crushed out her cigarette. She rang again for Opal who trotted in, knowing the drill: take the cup and saucer, wash the crystal ashtray, spray the room with a deodorizer guaranteed to get rid of the cigarette smell. She did it seven times a day, on the hour.

The minute the door closed behind her secretary, Arden turned on her computer and set to work. By the time Roland waltzed into the office, she'd have something concrete to show him. Forty-eight hours was just that, forty-eight hours. She eyed the picture of Sara Whittier on the wall for a full minute before she deliberately thumbed her nose at it.

The black SUV approached the guard house that led to the Ryland homestead in Manassas. The guard house had its own bath, sitting room, and kitchen along with well-stocked book shelves and a large screen TV. The fieldstone building looked like something out of a Thomas Kincaid painting except for the bars on the windows. Myra pulled up, stopped, rolled her window down and said, "I'm Anna de Silva. I understand from the agency that you are Arthur. Thank you for coming to work for me." She rolled down the window in the back. "These are my assistants, Ellen Markham, Sumi Takamuro, and Carol Sterling.

"Did the agency explain your duties? No one is to come through these gates unless I tell you beforehand. The agency said you were authorized to carry a weapon. I'd like to see it, please."

The guard opened his jacket to show Myra his shoulder holster. Then he pointed to the inside of the guard house where a high-powered rifle could be seen on a rack on the wall. "My replacement is Gerald, ma'am. We're twelve on and twelve off."

"Thank you. If you need anything, call the house number and one of my assistants will fetch it for you. I don't want you to leave your post unless I authorize it."

"Yes, ma'am."

Myra closed the window, shifted gears and

roared through the open gate. She could see in her rearview mirror that the gate closed immediately.

"Wow! This is some place! And no one lives here! How big is the house?" Kathryn asked as the others gaped at the lush landscaping, the vastness of the estate, the mile long driveway lined with tall poplar trees.

"It's huge. I haven't been here in years. Annie doesn't come back here anymore but she makes sure the place is maintained. Her grandparents made their money in cotton and tobacco. It's a typical southern home with wrap-around verandas, floor to ceiling windows. Ten chimneys or so, and of course the tin roof. Nothing on the inside has been changed except the bathrooms and kitchen. The floors are heart of pine, the wainscoting is intact as is the crown molding. Growing up, we weren't neighbors but our parents knew one another. I suppose in today's time you would say our parents arranged play dates for us. We did go to the same schools. Friendships made when very young tend to last a lifetime."

Myra stopped the SUV in front of what was once a carriage house but was now a three-car garage. Overhead there was a fully furnished apartment for the chauffeur.

The buildings were pristine white with ivy climbing the chimneys; and the lawn, the shrubs, and flower beds were manicured to perfection.

Myra pointed to the half-fan windows that were of stained glass. "Annie's grandmother made all those windows, even though it wasn't fashionable for ladies to do such things back in those days. Annie said her grandmother refused to do needlework of any kind. That's what ladies did back then to pass the time. The windows are treasures, to be sure. Come along, girls, I can't wait to show you the inside. It's quite beautiful."

It took the girls three trips to carry all their bags and gear into the house. The last trip was for the computer, printer, and fax, which Alexis set up in less than an hour. She smacked her hands together. "We're open for business, ladies."

Kathryn's face was gleeful. "Let the games begin."

"Now what?" Alexis asked.

"Now we wait for our quarry to call. In the meantime we can explore the house and grounds, think about dinner, or we can have Yoko tell us how her date went last night," Myra said.

Yoko flopped down on a satin sofa, kicked off her shoes and settled herself. The others sat down in a circle and waited expectantly, unsure what they were going to hear.

"The evening was . . . interesting. As you know, Harry is half Chinese and half Japanese like myself. He was raised in Japan, whereas I was raised here in America. He told me all about Japan. We went to a noodle house in Little China. I enjoyed it. It was in someone's house. Harry said he goes there all the time. At first it was awkward. He wanted to know about my background. I did not tell him everything. I remembered what all of you said, do not tell all. So, I did not. He said I was a mystery woman. I liked that. We had no physical contact. He does a lot of bowing so I had to bow. He is more traditional than I am. He has kissable lips."

Kathryn hooted with laughter.

"That's it?" Alexis said, surprise ringing in her voice.

"Yes, that's it. I was disappointed. I think he feels foolish that I pinned him to the mat. Saving face is very important to people of our culture. He says he is modern but he is not. I would not apologize."

"Good for you," Kathryn said.

"Yeah," Alexis said.

"My dear, sometimes you can collect more flies with honey than vinegar," Myra said.

Yoko looked puzzled as she tried to figure out Myra's meaning.

Kathryn reared back as a lively discussion followed.

Yoko just looked more perplexed. In the end, she threw her hands in the air. "I have no wish to live by the old rules. I will probably never go to Japan or China so why should I care about the old ways. America is my home. I want to be like all American women. I do not wish to be subservient to any man. If that is what Mr. Harry Wong expects, then he is going to have to find someone else to do his bidding. I asked him if he watched *Sex and the City* and he didn't know what I was talking about."

Kathryn burst out laughing. "Kiddo, I'm thinking that might be a good thing. You can bet your boots he's going to check it out now, though. I'll take that one step further and wager the next date with Mr. Harry Wong will be an . . .

event. Remember what we said about having to pony up."

Yoko just giggled. And giggled.

Roland Sullivan sat in his customized Porsche in the parking lot staring at the building that housed his suite of offices. He was late but he didn't care. He felt sick all over. Sick and guilty.

He'd felt so proud when his youngest son got his little award at school. Especially when the child looked at him, smiled and waved and mouthed the words, "Hi Dad." Not Hi Mom but Hi Dad. He cringed when he remembered the surprised look on his wife's face when he slipped into the seat next to her. He'd tried to take her hand but she'd moved away, almost falling off her chair in her eagerness to separate herself from him.

Who could blame her? He was a lousy husband, a terrible father. He was, however, rich, an astute businessman, a sneaky adulterer, and the lowest of the low for having framed Sara Whittier for a crime she hadn't committed.

For the past year he'd been trying to figure out a way to break off his relationship with Arden Gillespie but he couldn't come up with anything that wouldn't strip him bare. When you strayed, you paid, one way or another. He wasn't stupid; he knew he was a hair away from losing his family. He'd been spending more time at home but his wife barely seemed to notice. Somehow during the past few years she had made a life for herself and the children that didn't include him, even though he was home in his casual clothes and his slippers. His wife slept in the guest room these days. It was the only room in the house that had a lock on the door. A new lock.

He thought about Arden Gillespie, the woman who had turned his head away from his family. He'd fallen for her so hard he couldn't see straight. She was like the worst kind of addiction. And he was a man with no willpower. If Arden had said, "strip down and dance in the middle of Constitution Avenue," he would have done it. So, it was no surprise that when she came up with what she called a foolproof scheme to defraud Sara Whittier's wealthy elderly clients that he'd gone along with it.

When that was all over, he knew he'd never dance naked in the middle of Constitution Avenue. His addiction had gone south about the same time. He still saw Arden after hours but it wasn't the same. It wasn't even lust. It was a bodily release, nothing else. The whole thing just made him hate himself more.

He might have been able to handle the whole adultery thing if it wasn't for what he'd done to Sara Whittier. Once, he'd tried to find her after his wife in a casual conversation had said she didn't believe for one minute that Sara would steal from her elderly clients. It was like Sara had dropped off the face of the earth. His wife's words rang in his ears to this day. "Sara would never do such a thing but I can see Arden Gillespie doing it." His whole body had turned to jelly at that moment. He still didn't know if it was the look on his wife's face or her words that had put the fear of God into him.

Roland Sullivan wondered if he would ever know.

Chapter 13

Nikki rubbed at her aching eyes. She was beyond tired. All she wanted to do was go upstairs and go to bed but Charles insisted she continue with what she was doing. "I think I probably need new reading glasses," she muttered. "I also need to take a break!"

A moment later, Charles was kneading her shoulders. "We both need to take a break. Let's go up to the kitchen for coffee and something to eat. Have you made any headway?"

Nikki succumbed to the kneading pressure and all but swooned. "Some. Why is it so important to do all this *now*? Maybe if I understood . . ." she let the rest of what she was going to say trail off into nothing.

"From the day we formed the Sisterhood, at Myra's insistence, I've been searching and trying to find a way to . . . for want of a better word, secure our future should the authorities descend on us. Everything eluded me. There just didn't seem to be any way for all of us to get away intact. Myra urged me to redouble my efforts, which I did. You know how she is when she gets a bee in her bonnet.

"Myra has never deviated from her original plan of taking the blame if the authorities closed in on us, but we can't allow that. I'm sure you agree with that. Either we all get away or we all stay and take the blame—which means prison. Part of my plan is airtight. I have things set in motion, but until now I haven't been able to finalize any of the major points. Mainly a location that will be safe if the unthinkable happens.

"Our last mission for Isabelle made Myra even more jittery. She was up at all hours, worrying and fretting. It is starting to take a toll on her. She isn't worried about herself, she is worried about all of you and, of course, me. She's convinced that those reporters are going to be our undoing. As much as I hate to agree with her, I think she's right. I don't think I'm wrong when I say it is becoming more and more dangerous for all of us. It was you, Nikki, who insisted the special agents be called off. Things were in place but at your insistence we had to call them off."

Nikki jerked around. *Call them off. Then why are they still stalking Jack? Is Charles lying to me?* "Charles, those agents were brutal. Scaring someone is one thing, beating them half to death is something else. I'm sorry but I can't and won't go along with something like that."

"You knew the risks going into this. You all did. You agreed that we would do whatever was necessary to survive and not get caught. You knew, Nikki. I don't think you would have been quite as upset if it had been someone other than Jack Emery. In activities such as ours you cannot change horses in midstream. I'm sorry about the cliché."

Charles was right and she knew it. Talk about being between a rock and a hard place. Clichés were running rampant. Still, she had to try. "We all drew the line at murder, Charles. Now, that's a fact. Ted Robinson had to have his spleen removed. Jack got beaten to within an inch of his life."

"In my business, Nikki, it's called collateral damage. At the risk of repeating myself, you all agreed when you turned security over to me. It's my job to keep you all safe. There is no way on this earth that I will allow Myra to go to prison. Or the rest of you, for that matter. I will do everything in my power to make sure you're all kept safe. That's something you have to live with.

"Now let's go upstairs and relax with a nice cup of hazelnut coffee and a thick ham sandwich."

Nikki wasn't about to leave it alone. "Why Barcelona?" she demanded.

"Because of the law of sanctuary. I plan to discuss all of it at our next meeting. We have Myra to thank for coming up with the idea. Anna de

Silva is going to deed the monastery to Myra. Spanish law forbids an outright sale. It's the only way, Nikki. It may never happen but a plan has to be in place. None of us would be safe here in our own country. In short, Nikki, there are no other options."

Nikki knew he was right about that, too. No options meant no options. End of discussion.

"What else is bothering you, my dear?" Charles asked as he waited for the bookshelf to slide back into place.

"I don't know how I or any of the others will like living in a foreign land. Foreign lands are places to visit, not to live. I'll make the sandwiches and you do the coffee."

"That sounds like a plan," Charles said cheerfully. "I suggest we eat on the terrace. The fresh air will clear away the cobwebs in our heads. Look at it this way, Nikki. You'll all be together. You know what Myra always says: home is where your stuff is. I tend to agree."

Nikki sliced ham, her thoughts jumbled. "That sounds like a plan, too," she said. She watched as Charles settled things on a silver platter. Place mats, silverware, sugar, cream, linen napkins and plates. As she spread mustard, Charles walked outdoors to clean off the table and wipe down the chairs. Tears burned behind her lids. What would any of them do without Charles? More than likely, they'd all fall apart.

Nikki cut the sandwiches in two and placed them on the bone china plates. She wondered why they weren't eating off paper plates. Then she remembered Charles saying paper and plastic plates were for picnics. As long as she didn't have to do the dishes, she didn't really care what kind of dishes she used.

Nikki followed Charles out to the terrace. "How pretty the terrace looks with all the flowers. They all seem to be blooming at the same time. Spring is wonderful, isn't it, Charles?" Nikki settled herself and then burst out laughing. "I feel like I'm sitting right in the middle of a box of Crayolas. I think every color in the box is right here on the terrace."

Charles smiled as he bit into his sandwich. He chewed thoughtfully. "Are you feeling better, Nikki?"

Nikki pondered the question. "Maybe it's the lawyer in me but I don't like uncertainty. The first thing we learned in law school was never ask a question you don't know the answer to. It's that kind of feeling. I understand where you're coming from, Charles. Because of the uncertainty, you have to make plans for our safety whether we like it or not. Of late, there seems to be more tension, more fear, less confidence. Mistakes are bound to happen. We aren't perfect."

Nikki pushed her plate away. "Charles, how did you walk away from your old life? How did you leave that life behind? Maybe if I understand that part of it, I can come to terms with what *might* happen."

Charles dabbed at his lips with the linen napkin before he reached for the silver coffeepot and poured. "In my case, it was death versus life. I didn't see that I had any choice. I was fortunate that other people helped me escape to your fine shores. I didn't allow myself to look back. I had many black days in my life but those early days were the blackest. I was glad to be alive. Myra helped. There were days when I thought I couldn't handle it without her help. In my case, I had no warning, no time to prepare. In short, my dear, in the beginning, it was a crippling experience. That's why I'm doing my best now in case something goes awry so that we will all be able to handle it. Think of it as a safeguard, my dear."

Nikki stared across the terrace at a beautiful crimson petunia plant that was as big as a bushel basket. She wished life was as beautiful as the plant she was looking at. She closed her eyes and minutes later was sound asleep in the warm spring sunshine.

Charles quietly gathered up the remains of their lunch. Before he left the terrace, he opened the large striped umbrella so that Nikki wasn't in the direct sun. Only then did he allow his shoulders to droop.

Myra Rutledge, a.k.a., Anna de Silva, sat at the huge oak table finishing the breakfast Alexis had prepared. Toast, coffee and grapefruit.

Kathryn, with the appetite of her profession, grumbled. "Tomorrow I hope we have home fries, scrambled eggs, bacon and a ton of toast. I hate grapefruit. I don't just hate it, I *really* hate it."

Alexis clapped her hands. "That's great,

Kathryn, because tomorrow it's your turn to cook. I, for one, am going to look forward to a hearty breakfast. In my defense, we didn't bring much food with us if you recall. Isabelle is bringing the grocery order later this morning. I ordered tons of food."

The women bantered back and forth, their eyes on the kitchen clock. Would the firm of Sullivan and Gillespie respond to Myra's invitation promptly at nine o'clock or not?

Myra looked at Kathryn. "You know exactly what to say, don't you, dear?"

"I do, Myra. As little as possible. I will be clipped, cold, professional. I've got it covered. I rehearsed all night in my dreams. What are we having for lunch?"

"The same thing we had for breakfast unless Isabelle gets here early. If your next question is what's for dinner, I don't know yet. Everything depends on Isabelle," Alexis said.

It was two minutes to nine when Yoko got up from the table to clear it. "Would anyone care for more coffee?" All the women held out their cups. Yoko emptied the pot and handed it to Alexis to make fresh coffee while she stacked the dishwasher.

With only three seconds to go till nine o'clock, the women removed their gaze from the clock and transferred it to the portable phone next to Kathryn's coffee cup.

Even though they were expecting it, the ringing phone startled them all. Kathryn held up three fingers and didn't click on the phone until the end of the third ring.

Kathryn's voice verged on frosty when she said, "De Silva residence. This is Ellen Markham."

"This is Roland Sullivan, Miss Markham. I'm responding to Mrs. de Silva's inquiry. We will be faxing our proposal in a few moments unless you tell me otherwise. We will of course follow up with a hard copy."

"That will be satisfactory. Mrs. de Silva can see you tomorrow at two o'clock. Mrs. de Silva has been conducting interviews for the past ten days. Your firm, because you are the smallest, will be Mrs. de Silva's last interview in her quest for new representation. Mrs. de Silva will announce her decision in twenty-four hours. Shall I pencil you in for two o'clock, Mr. Sullivan?"

"Yes. Two o'clock will be fine."

"Will Miss Gillespie be with you?"

"Yes, Miss Gillespie will be with me. She is my partner, Miss Markham."

"Two o'clock, Mr. Sullivan. Do not be late. Mrs. de Silva takes points off for tardiness." Kathryn wiggled her eyebrows as she ended the call.

"Perfect," Myra said.

"Yeah, perfect," Alexis said. "Don't get cocky; those two are snakes."

"Yeah, but this time, we're in control. We're holding the cards, Alexis. This is going to work. Don't go jinxing us now. How about some more coffee while we talk about what we're going to have for dinner?"

Alexis grinned but not before she wadded up the dish towel and threw it at Kathryn.

* * *

Back in the District at the firm of Sullivan and Gillespie, Roland Sullivan wiped at the perspiration on his brow. "The woman sounds like a holy terror. I don't think I ever heard such a cold voice in my life. If that woman is one of the layers we have to penetrate to get to de Silva, we might as well forget it right now. She had no trouble telling me we were last on the list to be interviewed because we are the smallest firm. She said they've been interviewing for the past ten days. Our appointment is tomorrow at two o'clock. She also cautioned me not to be late because de Silva takes points off for tardiness."

Arden Gillespie eyed her lover and partner with a calculating eye. "Darling, don't underestimate our combined power. You can be incredibly charming when you want to be. You did charm me. And I know how to treat women. I can sweet-talk anyone and that includes women."

Roland fed papers into the fax machine, one by one, a devilish light in his eyes that Arden couldn't see. Maybe, just maybe, this was a way for him to sever his connection with Arden. Give her enough rope and she'd hang herself. Finally, he'd be rid of her and some way, somehow, he might be able to appease his guilt over Sara Whittier. He might even be able to get back into the good graces of his family.

"I know just what I'm going to wear," Arden trilled. "I bought this beautiful Armani suit. I even had shoes dyed to match. We'll go in my Mercedes. Or do you think we should hire a chauffeur? Just because we're a small firm doesn't mean we should look tacky. Everyone knows good things come in small packages. In other words, Roland, big doesn't mean better. Wear your Brioni suit. You look so . . . so dashing and cosmopolitan."

Like he was really going to show up wearing a Brioni suit after reading Anna de Silva's profile that said she was a simple woman with simple tastes. Anything ostentatious was an automatic turnoff to one of the richest ladies in the world. He couldn't help but wonder how Arden had missed that part of de Silva's profile.

Roland ignored his partner as he kept feeding papers into the fax machine.

Life, Roland decided, was about to get mired in muck. He felt so depressed, he wanted to go home to hear his wife tell him everything would be okay, like in the old days when he was just starting out. Back then she'd been so supportive. That was then and he hadn't screwed up yet. It wasn't going to happen and he knew it. Things would never be okay again and he knew that, too.

Chapter 14

The newsroom hummed with activity but Maggie Spritzer paid little attention. It was always like this around midmorning for some reason. She typed the last few words of her column, ran spell-check, and printed it out. Her extension would ring off the hook tomorrow when the ladies of Washington turned to her column. My oh my, what would they say when they found out Senator Myers's wife charged 900 dollars' worth of spring flowers to the taxpayers? They'd probably fall off their breakfast chairs or spill their morning coffee when they went on to read how the Secretary of State's wife didn't use her pooper-scooper. On Massachusetts Avenue no less. The big question was, would she be fined or would she trade on her husband's political position? Did the world care? Probably not, but the social ladies of Washington would have something to buzz about over their luncheons and teas for at least three days.

Maggie dropped off her column in her boss's in-box and prepared to leave the newsroom.

Today, Maggie was wearing a flowered spring dress with matching jacket. She carried a tote, hating it because she missed her old L.L.Bean backpack. The colorful tote matched her outfit. Ted Robinson whistled approvingly as she approached his desk. "What's up, Slick?" he asked, using the new nickname he'd given her.

Maggie perched on the corner of Ted's desk, showing a generous portion of leg and thigh. "Wanna go for coffee? I just turned in my column and have tomorrow's done in draft form. I'm free as that breeze outside. How about you? I have something I want to show you," she whispered.

"Then I'm your man." Ted shouted across the room, "Hey, Espinosa, cover my phone, okay?"

Ted adjusted his baseball cap, slipped on his backpack, and followed Maggie from the room. She led him out of the building and around the corner to a greasy spoon that had scarred formica tables, six stools, two bar tables and the worst coffee and food in the entire District. Free refills were the joint's claim to fame. The place was jamming.

Maggie got in line while Ted moved to one of the bar tables where a sportswriter from the paper was sitting with one of the financial guys. "Yo, Garrity, can I have this table when you're done?"

"Sure, Robinson, if you don't mind getting your ass kicked by one of the other twenty people waiting for it."

"But did they ask as politely as I did? C'mon, I've been up since forever and I need some of this swill to get me going."

"It's all yours, buddy," the sportswriter said, sliding off his chair. Ted immediately plopped down, ignoring the boos and hisses. A couple of minutes later, Maggie joined him to more boos and hisses. Both reporters ignored the disgruntled customers.

"Well, whatcha got? May I say you look particularly springy this morning. Is something going on that I'm not aware of?"

"Spring is in the air. Flowers are blooming. The sun is shining. The trees are almost in full leaf. Do I need a better reason? As to what's up, take a look at this," Maggie said, sliding a thick stapled sheaf of papers across the small table. "Tell me what you think."

Ted looked at an aerial photo of a large estate. "It looks like a scaled down castle of some kind. I've seen this before but can't quite place it. Ah," he said, as he scanned the text. "Anna de Silva. She's a countess or something. You got some dirt on her? What?"

Maggie grinned like a Cheshire cat. "I followed some of the ladies from Pinewood out there yesterday. Actually, I was tailing the Asian gal. I followed her from her nursery to Pinewood and then I followed a dark SUV to Manassas. That's where they are. I don't know if all of them are there or not. There's more security out there than there is at Pinewood. Doesn't that make you wonder? And, Anna de Silva lives in Spain. She is not in residence in Manassas."

Ted's eyes narrowed. "And this all means . . . what?"

"They're on the move, Ted. They're going to do something. They relocated so they could do whatever it is they're going to do. I spent all night on the computer and called in every favor owed me to get the goods on the de Silva woman. I think she's aiding and abetting, Ted."

Ted snorted. "All the way from Spain? Don't you think that's a bit of a stretch?"

"Did I mention I spent all night on this stuff? It's my female gut instinct, Ted."

No way in hell was he going to touch *that.* "Okay, spit it out."

"I think . . . and you and I agreed more or less, that Myra Rutledge is behind this little group of vigilantes. She's got the money and the power. Stretch that mind of yours and digest this. Myra Rutledge, Judge Cornelia Easter and Anna Ryland de Silva are best friends going back to the age of five. Easter doesn't have the money the other two have. De Silva is one of the richest women in the world. Myra can hold her own in that regard but she is not quite as rich as de Silva. Are you following me, Ted?"

"I'm with you."

A strange voice said, "Are you *ever* going to give up this table?"

"Not any time soon. Beat it," Maggie said, menace ringing in her voice.

"Okay. Why would the ladies of Pinewood relocate to Manassas if something isn't going on or about to go on? Didn't you say Myra Rutledge and Charles Martin took a vacation? Five bucks says they went to Spain. By the way, how do you know that?"

"I have a source at the airport who is a mechanic," Ted said. "He calls me anytime that Gulfstream takes off. He did some checking and the flight plan was to Barcelona, Spain."

"Aha! And why do you suppose they went there? For reinforcements. More money. De Silva's clout. Her house in Manassas. A bunch of reasons, Ted. De Silva is going to become a player in this mess. I am ninety-nine and nine-tenths percent sure of that."

Ted slurped on his coffee. He looked up as a waitress held her pot aloft. He nodded. So did Maggie. The waitress poured liberally. "They should condemn this place," Ted said.

"What could they be up to, Ted? How does de Silva figure in this? Is it just her money and her house that they need? If that's the case, wouldn't a phone call have sufficed? Why go all the way to Spain?"

"Maybe they wanted a short vacation? You did say they were best friends."

"Keep reading, sweet cheeks. The woman hasn't been back here in close to twenty years. What's that say for her tie to her old homestead, where, by the way, she has maintained a skeleton staff to oversee things? They call her a woman of simple tastes. They say she suffered a terrible tragedy and that's why she's reclusive. They were on their yacht with an inexperienced crew when a terrible storm came up. The husband and both children were swept overboard but somehow she survived. Details are sketchy and she doesn't give interviews. That's why she's never left her mountaintop. Take a gander at her digs in Spain. Any bells going off in your head?"

Ted stared at the pictures for a long time. "This picture," he said, tapping a photo of Anna de Silva's Spanish home, "says it used to be a monastery that Count Armand de Silva inherited, which then passed on to Anna at his death." He looked up and across at Maggie. "Isn't that the order of things? A spouse dies and the surviving spouse inherits."

"C'mon, Ted, think. Put it all together and tell me what you see."

"What's to see, Maggie? Obviously, Myra Rutledge is taking advantage of an old friendship to enlist de Silva's aid. De Silva must have agreed if the ladies have relocated to the old homestead. If de Silva is really a recluse, she won't be coming here. That tells me she offered financial aid and the use of her home but she is not going to be an active player in . . . whatever they're up to. I assume you think I'm missing something. Enlighten me. Can we leave? I can't drink any more of this coffee."

Maggie gathered up the de Silva file and

slipped it into her tote. She slid off the high-backed chair, smoothed down her dress and jacket. "I'm ready."

As the two reporters exited the greasy spoon, they were followed by snide comments and more boos and hisses.

Outside in the bright sunshine, Maggie looked up at her tall companion. "I've got things to do but I want to leave you with a thought. Go back to the paper and bone up on the law of sanctuary."

Ted removed his baseball cap and smacked it against his leg. "I'll be dipped in shit! So that's where all this is going. Talk about clever. Good work, Maggie! Really good work!"

Ted never paid compliments. Maggie beamed. "Am I back in your good graces?"

"Yes, you are."

"All right then. I shared all this research. Where's the tape you stole from my house?"

Ted didn't hesitate. "I gave it to the boss. It's in the safe at the paper. It's going to stay there until we need it. Am I in *your* good graces?"

"You are." Maggie stood on her toes and kissed Ted lightly on the tip of his nose. "Come by around seven," she said. "I threw some stuff in the Crock Pot this morning. You can bring some French bread and a good bottle of wine if you're interested."

"Okay. Where are you going now?"

"Home to try and figure some things out. I have a lot of loose ends I need to tie up or at least try to make sense of. I might have more to tell you tonight."

The two reporters separated, Ted going one way, Maggie the other way.

Instead of heading for the *Post*, Ted continued down the street. A walk around the block in the warm sunshine was just what he needed. His thoughts were thousands of miles away on a mountain in Spain. What did it all mean? He was so engrossed in his thoughts as he loped along that Jack Emery had to grab his arm to spin him around.

"Hey, earth to Ted! What's with you? You must be getting ready to crucify someone in that paper of yours. Either that or you're in love again. Which is it?"

"Well, if it isn't Mister Crime Fighter himself out and about on this lovely spring morning. It isn't even lunchtime so that makes me wonder where the defender of the people is going. Is your destination worthy of a mention in the *Post*?" Ted guffawed at his own wit.

Jack grimaced. "Nothing that exciting. I've been sitting in court since eight this morning. After cooling our heels for ninety minutes we were told the judge, his clerk, his secretary and the bailiff ate some bad sausage in the cafeteria earlier. No court. I couldn't resist taking the long way back to the office. What's up with you?"

"Not a damn thing, Jack."

"Now that's a lie if I ever heard one. Wanna stop for coffee?"

"Guess you want to pick my brain, huh? Guess what, Jack, my brain is empty. I'm up for a good cup of coffee and maybe a fried egg sandwich. You buying?"

"Don't I always? You look rather smug this morning, Ted. Want to share?"

Ted snorted. "That will be the damn day. How's things going with Nikki?"

"Not a clue. Like I said, I just live in her house."

"Yeah, I always say that, too. By the way, where are we going for that coffee and egg sandwich?"

"Sadie Green's Café. Shouldn't be a crowd now; breakfast is over, too early for lunch."

"You seeing anyone besides Nikki?"

"Marcey Williams. She's an ADA in the office. You on or off with Maggie?"

"It's a day-to-day thing. One day we're on, one day we're off."

Jack opened the white painted door of Sadie's café. The café smelled of fresh coffee, cinnamon and bacon. His mouth started to water. They took their seats at a window table with a green checked tablecloth. A waitress appeared the moment they were seated. She had two matching napkins wrapped around the silver. "Coffee?" Both men nodded and then gave their order.

Wariness shone in both men's eyes as they looked at each other across the table. "What do you want to talk about, Ted?"

"The weather? Looks like spring has finally sprung. It was a hell of a winter, wasn't it?"

"Yeah, it was a hell of a winter. Supposed to be a hot summer," Jack said.

"Are we having a titillating conversation?"

"I'd call it boring. We're both working too hard not to say anything. Saved by our food,"

Jack said as he looked up at the waitress. "This is why I like coming here. You don't have to wait an hour for your food and it's hot when you get it." He watched as Ted poured ketchup all over his sandwich and then cut it with a knife and fork.

A worm of unease settled itself between Jack's shoulder blades. He didn't know why but he felt Ted knew something he didn't know. What was it Nikki said? When you were in control, you were in the catbird seat. Then she laughed and asked, and what does the cat in the catbird seat do? When he shrugged his shoulders, she laughed again. Why, darling Jack, you purr. Ted was purring.

Ted wiped up the mess on his plate with a stray piece of toast, then he said, "How come the Pinewood ladies relocated?"

Jack didn't have to pretend to be surprised. He was. "Huh?"

"The ladies of Pinewood. Your significant other. How come they relocated?" Ted said, enunciating each word carefully as though Jack was an idiot.

"Now, how the hell would I know something like that? For starters, I didn't know the ladies of Pinewood had relocated. You seem to know more than I do. Why don't you explain it to me?" *Oh, Nik, you are definitely not going to like this.*

Ted gulped the last of his coffee. "Ha!"

Jack fished around his pocket for the money to pay the check. He stood up and said, "Don't you think you're a little old to play these stupid games? Who the hell cares if the Pinewood ladies moved or went on vacation, or decided to go camping? Certainly not me. Keep up with this silliness and you're going to get your dick in a sling and then what will Miz Spritzer do? You think about that, Mr. Hotshot Reporter."

"Let me worry about my dick. I'm just trying to apprise you of the latest developments so that when the hammer falls you can't say I didn't drop all these little hints."

"Guess you don't think much about your missing spleen these days, eh? Well, guess what, I do think about it and that's why I'm keeping my nose out of anything that doesn't concern me. You do what you want, Ted. Be careful, okay?"

"Yeah, Jack, I'll be careful. Thanks for breakfast," Ted said as he headed for the men's room.

"Any time."

Outside, Jack let his breath out in a long agonized sigh. Washington, D. C., the nation's capital where it was impossible to keep a secret. Nikki was going to pitch a fit when he told her about his breakfast meeting with Ted.

Chapter 15

At five-thirty Maggie Spritzer decided to take a break so she could check the contents of her Crock Pot. As she peered down into the bubbling food she wondered what she should call the mess bubbling away. She hoped it would taste as good as it smelled. Ted loved comfort foods cooked in one pot, but then so did she.

Daisy nipped at her toes, a signal that she wanted to go for a walk. Maggie slipped into a pair of clogs she kept by the front door. Inside, she liked to go barefoot. "Okay, get your leash and we'll go for a walk." The little brown and white dog beelined to the bedroom, dragged the leash and dropped it at Maggie's feet.

Forty minutes later, owner and dog were back in the apartment. Daisy went off with her dog biscuit and Maggie returned to her computer. She perched her reading glasses on her nose and rummaged through her files for the fiftieth time. She wished she knew what she was looking for. Whatever it was, it wasn't smacking her in the nose. It was here, she knew it. Why wasn't she homing in on it? Damn, maybe she was just too tired to see the obvious. "Okay," she muttered, "let's start over."

The ladies of Pinewood. She had a file on all of them, thanks to Ted who said he got the files from Jack Emery. Maybe her problem was that someone else had made the files and the folders, and that was what was throwing her off. In the blink of an eye, Maggie had new file folders in her hand. She labeled all of them before she created a new file on her computer. Just hit the highlights. You can fill in the details later, she told herself.

By six-thirty she felt she was making progress.

Myra Rutledge. Rich. Money out the wazoo. Mother of Barbara Rutledge who was killed by a diplomat's son or nephew. That part wasn't clear but didn't really make a difference. Guy has diplomatic immunity, but was never punished for his crime, left the country. Flash forward several years to ladies of Pinewood taking a trip to China. Maggie drew a big fat zero with a red magic marker. Then she wrote, "no further details."

Nikki Quinn. Myra's adopted daughter. Once engaged to Jack Emery, who was now a District Attorney. On again, off again romance. Has own law firm. Top-notch defense lawyer. Myra's right hand in more ways than one. Her legal eye would be on everything. A huge red question mark followed Nikki's name.

Charles Martin. Powerful man. Scary man. Maggie added a long line of red question marks after his name. British. Brains. Who exactly was Charles Martin? Jack Emery managed to get beaten within an inch of his life when he started poking around into the Brit's background. Ted was minus a spleen when he followed in Jack's footsteps. She herself had been paid a visit by some pretty scary dudes. All of the above due to Charles Martin. Maggie noticed her hands were shaking as she added another line of red question marks.

Move on, girl, move on. The only problem was, she couldn't move on because she had the shakes. Just remembering the intimidating men who had paid her a visit made her so jittery she couldn't think straight. Yet, here she was, defying them by poking her nose into things that obviously concerned those same men.

Maggie was like a disgruntled squirrel as she rummaged in the drawers of her desk for a cigarette. She'd given up the foul habit long ago just the way Ted had, but she kept a pack of cigarettes in a plastic bag for emergencies. She finally found the package and fired up a cigarette. Daisy barked as a plume of smoke circled upright.

Maggie continued to puff, choke and sputter but she didn't put the cigarette out. Instead, she shooed Daisy out of the room, closed the door and turned on the overhead fan. When the cigarette was down to the filter, she put it out and lit a second one. "Oh, God, why am I doing this?"

When Maggie finished her second cigarette, she sealed up the plastic bag and shoved it in the drawer. Then she shoved in Charles Martin's file and slammed the drawer. She wished there was a key to lock the drawer but there wasn't.

The doorbell rang. Ted! Maggie ran to the door and pulled it open. She literally fell into Ted's arms.

"Smoking, huh? What happened?" She told him. "Yeah, that guy and his buddies are enough to make you drink *and* smoke. Look, I'm starved. Let's have dinner and then we can hash this all out. Maybe I can help you." Ted held out the loaf of French bread and the bottle of wine.

They ate with gusto until there was nothing left but a few stray vegetables in the bottom of the pot. An inch of bread remained on the cutting board and the wine bottle was empty.

"What *was* that?" Ted asked, pointing to the pot.

"*That* was everything in the refrigerator plus a can of beans. I even threw in some left over Chinese from the other day. I thought it gave the whole thing a little extra zip."

They made small talk as they washed the dishes and tidied up the kitchen. When they were finished, they retired to Maggie's spare bedroom that she used as a home office.

"Wow! This looks like my place! You better

not ever call me sloppy again," Ted said as he stepped past piles of files and stacks of paper. "Did you at least make some headway?"

"I thought so until I made a file on Charles Martin. I thought if I created my own files on all of those people, I might get a better grasp on them. Following someone else's notes doesn't work for me.

"The women are such a diverse group. As far as I can tell, they have nothing in common. And one of them, the doctor, is still missing. Think about it, Ted. A doctor, a truck driver, a woman with a menial job, an architect, a lawyer, and an Asian woman who owns a nursery. There's no common ground here."

"Of course there is, you just aren't seeing it." Daisy took that moment to leap onto Ted's lap. She sniffed him from head to toe before she leaped off and onto Maggie's lap. "Don't feel bad, it took me a while to figure it out."

Maggie stared across the room at a picture of a colorful sailboat skimming over whitecaps. Someday, she was going to have her own sailboat. She sighed as she wondered if she would get seasick. "Just tell me, Ted."

"Nikki Quinn. Think about it. Those women probably engaged or tried to engage her legal services at some point. She brought them all together, somehow, some way."

"That does make sense."

"I tried sifting through court records to find out if any cases went to trial for those women but I came up with zip except for Isabelle Flanders, but Nikki Quinn didn't handle her case until recently. This is purely a guess on my part but I think all those women fell through the legal cracks and were denied justice. The Rutledge woman, too. So, she gets all these women that Quinn screens and we have the ladies of Pinewood. When Senator Webster disappeared, so did Doctor Webster, whose name is Julia. Now, they're down to six. The Thorne woman has no background. It's like she was born the day she started to work as a personal shopper. By the way, when I checked her out, I found Nikki Quinn was her sole reference. Quinn said Thorne shopped for her because she was too busy. Most of Thorne's clients are elderly. She does a good job, her clients love her.

"We know about Isabelle Flanders because we were part of it. We know the Hershey woman set her up. She wants revenge, so she goes to Nikki Quinn.

"I wasn't able to come up with anything at all for the truck driver other than that her husband died way too young. She's an engineer, so was her husband. They bought an eighteen-wheeler and took to the open road when they found out he was ill. Neither Jack nor I can figure out how she fits into the group. Ditto for the Asian cutie."

"We're assuming here, Ted," Maggie said. "So, let's assume a little more. The ladies go to China. That must mean they were after the man who killed Myra Rutledge's daughter. That's one down. The Websters disappear. That's two down. The Flanders woman makes three. What's your best guess as to who they're working on now?"

"Whatever they're doing in Manassas has to be either for the Thorne woman or the Asian cutie. I'm thinking we should do a little B&E. If the ladies are in Manassas, the Quinn law firm will be unattended. You know how to get in since you were mugged in the parking lot. You said the front is locked at six o'clock. Want to take a crack at it?"

"Now? You want to do it *now*? You really do run with an idea, don't you?"

"Why not? We need to work off that heavy dinner," Ted said, his eyes alight with excitement.

"What about the alarm system? There's quite a bit of light in the parking lot. Even though it's getting late, there might be other people working in the building. For all we know, the police might be keeping an eye on the building after the mugging. I think it's risky, maybe even dangerous. Convince me, sweet cheeks."

Ted's chest puffed out. "There's an element of risk in everything we do. You can slip and fall in the shower. You can get hit by a car crossing the road. Your microwave oven can blow up in your face. I say we do it. I'm real good with a slingshot."

"You're no David, Ted. Cops play with guns. G-u-n-s!"

Ted shook his head. "No, no, I'll shoot out the lights in the parking lot. Jack showed me how to disarm an alarm system a couple of years ago. I think I remember how to do it. Parking lot lights go out all the time."

Maggie looked horrified. "You *think*?"

"Okay, I'm sure. We'll need a few things to take with us. You game?"

Maggie looked around at her safe little apartment that she'd furnished one piece at a time. Then she looked at her dog who was sleeping on the sofa. If she was arrested, she might not be able to come back here. Who would take care of her dog? She'd get one phone call if she was hauled off to jail. Instead of calling a lawyer, she would have to call her mother to drive down from Delaware to take Daisy. Then again, if she went along with Ted's plans they might find out for certain that Nikki Quinn was the adhesive that glued the Pinewood ladies together. *Think Pulitzer*, she told herself. "Okay, I'm game. What do we need to take with us?"

"A heavy duty magnet, not one of those little ones on your fridge. Screwdrivers, big and small. Small flashlight. I want you to change your clothes. Dress like a lawyer. You'll need a briefcase and if you have a hat, wear it. You'll be the lawyer, I'll be the client in case anyone is in the building. Go on, get dressed."

Maggie shouted from the bedroom. "What about *those guys*?"

Yeah, what about those guys. Ted walked back to the bedroom. He whistled approvingly, to Maggie's delight. She was wearing a dark pinstripe pantsuit, high heels and a soft white fedora. "I modeled this outfit for the paper's fashion show last year. I liked it so much, I bought it and never got another chance to wear it. Damn, where's my briefcase? I haven't used that in ten years." She rummaged in the closet for the Gucci case. It looked flatter than a pancake. She stuffed two folded towels into it to plump up the brown leather.

"We have to sneak out of here," Ted told her. "How about if we go down the stairs and out through the basement? We'll go out one at a time, walk over to the Avenue and catch a cab. I'm hoping those goons think we're in for the night. Look, we'll deal with it if they catch on."

Maggie adjusted her fedora. "I hope those aren't famous last words."

"Yeah, me too."

Forty minutes later, Maggie knew there was no point pretending she wasn't nervous. Ted had appointed her the "lookout" after he shot out the parking lot lights with the homemade slingshot he'd fashioned on the fly. Her voice jittery, she asked, "How long is it going to take you to pick the lock?"

"Hey, I'm almost a pro. I did it. These latex gloves make for slow work. Be sure to put yours on. Now, where's the alarm?"

"At the top of the stairs and around the corner. There's a dentist on the floor; his offices are at the end of the hall. When Quinn's business went south after that horse trial, she rented out office space to a dentist. I read that in the paper in an ad the dentist took out. Dentists close at five o'clock so that means no one should be on this floor at this hour."

"I wasn't planning on getting my teeth cleaned, Maggie, but thanks for sharing that information. Hand me that magnet. I think we have ninety seconds, maybe a full two minutes since whoever comes in this entrance has to climb the stairs. If we're lucky it's a three minute delay. You'd think there would be an elevator," Ted grumbled.

Maggie didn't realize she was holding her breath until she saw the tiny red light turn to green. She slumped against the wall. Ted joined her, his face wet with sweat. "Did you lock the door after we entered?"

"Yes."

Maggie headed down the hall on wobbly legs, Ted trailing behind her. She pointed to the plate glass doors that led to the firm's offices. Ted set to work. Maggie leaned against the wall again as she forced herself to take deep gulping breaths to steady her nerves.

"Told you, a piece of cake. No lights. We have to work in the dark. Point the beam of that little flashlight downward at all times. I don't suppose you know where the file room is, do you?" Maggie shook her head. "Then let's split up. Keep your eye out for a safe. It's probably a built-in and probably in Quinn's office. Whistle if you find anything."

"Did you lock the office door?" Maggie asked,

her voice still quaking as she teetered along in her high heels.

"Of course."

Twenty minutes later, Maggie was on her knees, off in the corner, her penlight pointed at the floor as she pawed through the T's for Alexis Thorne. She whistled. "Hey, Ted, I found one of the files. Are we taking it or are we making copies?"

Ted pondered the question. "Take it," he said boldly. "The copy machines are rented and they have a digital counter. If the office manager is on the ball, she'll know what the number was at the close of business today. I don't think anyone will be looking in the files tomorrow morning. Unless we screw up."

"The rest are here, too, all five of them," Maggie announced.

"Good. Take them all. Hurry up, we have to get out of here."

Maggie rocked back on her heels. "How come this was so easy? Shouldn't these files be hidden? Why are they even here?"

"How many people do you know who break into a legal firm? A law office is considered as safe as a church. We did the unexpected. There was an alarm if you recall. That's the good news. The bad news is Jack didn't tell me how to rearm the alarm."

"What?"

"C'mon, c'mon, put those files in your briefcase. Whoever was the last one out tonight will think they forgot to set the alarm. If there's a night watchman he'll get blamed. Be sure you put everything back exactly like it was."

Maggie stuffed the five files between the two towels in her briefcase. She took a long minute to look around. Satisfied that everything looked the same as it did when she entered, she stood up. "Okay, let's go. Are you sure you can't arm the system? It's going to be a dead giveaway. Won't it be the reverse of whatever you did to disarm it?"

"I don't think so. I'd need one of those digital counters to reset it. Maybe if I can find the fuse box I can turn off the power. They *might* think there was a power surge. It's a risk no matter what. Are you sure those files weren't under lock and key?"

"Hell, yes, they were under lock and key. I picked the lock with my hatpin. See!" Maggie said, pointing to the hatpin on the side of her fedora.

"Oh."

"Are you ready?"

"As soon as we find the fuse box. I didn't see one when I went through the rooms. I wonder if there's a supply room or a storage unit. Give me a minute."

Maggie waited, tapping her foot. When she saw the hall light go out, she panicked, but followed Ted's voice. He snapped the lock and the two of them sprinted down the dark hall and down the two flights of dark stairs. At the outside door, Ted looked at the door and grinned. "Self-locking. Take off those shoes and run like hell."

Run they did, across the dark parking lot and out to the street before they slowed down to allow Maggie to put her shoes back on.

Hand in hand, they walked along, trying to decide where to go.

"The paper," Ted said.

"Good choice," Maggie said.

Chapter 16

Nikki had no idea why she was drinking coffee at four o'clock in the morning with her eyes closed. Then again, two hours of sleep in forty-eight hours might account for her droopy eyelids. She was so tired she was cranky and out of sorts. Walking over to the sink took every last ounce of her energy. She turned when she heard her name called.

"Go to bed, Nikki. Thank you for all your hard work." Charles pointed to his briefcase that contained all the work she'd done in the past two days.

Nikki looked down at the travel bag. "Are you going somewhere, Charles?" Did the man ever sleep?

"I'll sleep on the plane. But, to answer your question, I'm going to Barcelona. I expect to be gone at least five days. Possibly less if I accomplish everything on my agenda. I will be returning with a guest. Get some sleep, my dear. Go along now, I'll lock up. The information you gathered was just what I need."

Nikki struggled to summon up enough energy to respond. "It's old Spanish law, Charles. While you're there, check on things. I'm sure a lot of the old laws have changed over the years. Fly safe."

By the time Nikki's feet touched the bottom step, Charles was gone.

In her room, Nikki looked around. How could everything look the same? She fell across the bed and was instantly asleep.

Nikki rolled over, her arms grappling for a blanket that wasn't there. A phone was ringing somewhere and a voice was urging her to do something.

"No, no, don't roll over. You have to get up, Nik. Hurry, it's important. The phone is ringing. Nikki, get up. Now. Time is of the essence."

Nikki ground her face into the bedspread. "I can't, I'm too tired. Go away, I'm going to sleep all day," she mumbled.

"Get up, Nikki. You have to get up. You can sleep later."

"Go away, Barb. Come back when I wake up." Nikki rolled over onto her back. "Now you woke me up. What's so damn important? Listen, the phone stopped ringing. That means the person gave up."

"Now, Nikki. Please, you have to get up."

"All right, all right, I'm getting up. Can I take a shower?"

"No, you cannot take a shower. Check the phone."

Nikki reached for the phone on the nightstand, clicked a button and listened to her office manager's frantic voice. "Nikki, call me as soon as you get this message."

If there was one thing she didn't need right now, it was bad news. Well, whatever it was, it was going to have to wait till she showered and had a cup of coffee in front of her.

Twenty minutes later, dressed in khaki slacks and a bright yellow sweater, Nikki made her way downstairs to make fresh coffee. She was stunned to see Isabelle sitting at the kitchen table.

"Wow, you look . . . tired," Isabelle said. "I just got here a few minutes ago and made coffee. Where's Charles?"

Nikki looked at the kitchen clock. It read 9:20. "He left for Spain around four this morning. He had me working on Spanish law for forty-eight hours. I had only two hours' sleep and it wasn't restful. How are things at the farm?"

"We're ahead of schedule. That means we're doing well. I try to get over here every morning around this time to just sit without someone hassling me over something. Thirty minutes of R&R. Any news from Manassas?"

Nikki shrugged as she held out her coffee cup. Isabelle poured. "I've been out of the loop these past two days. You probably know more than I do."

"Today is the first face-to-face meeting with Gillespie and Sullivan. I think it's scheduled for two o'clock this afternoon. Kathryn just said to stand by. Can I make you something to eat?"

"Toast with jam if you don't mind. I have to call the office. Maddie called and she sounded frantic."

"Go ahead. Do you want me to leave the room?"

"No, no. The District probably turned the water off again. They do that early in the morning for some reason. Maddie always gets upset when it happens. By the way, Isabelle, you're lookin' good these days."

Isabelle smiled. "My world's right side up thanks to all of you. Go ahead, make your call. I'll be quiet."

"Maddie, it's Nikki. What's wrong? What?" She listened, the color draining from her face. "Oh my God! Did you call the police? Thank God you didn't. Okay, I'll be there in an hour."

"What's wrong?"

"Someone broke into our offices last night. Maddie was the last to leave the building and she set the alarm. It was off this morning. Sometimes we have power surges so she didn't think too much about it till she checked the surveillance tape and saw that someone broke in. Guess who?" Nikki didn't bother waiting for the architect to guess. "Ted Robinson and Maggie Spritzer, that's who. They took the files from my office. Before you can ask, they were locked up but not in the safe."

Isabelle dropped the slice of toast in her hand. "What . . . what's going to happen? What exactly does that mean, Nikki?"

Nikki seethed with fury. "Plenty. You know when we had the surveillance cameras installed, I didn't want to pay the extra money to run the wiring to have them built into the wall. Maddie finally wore me down and I caved in. I'm going to have to give that woman a raise. Those reporters had no clue they were on film. We got them red-handed."

"But Nikki . . . was it just the Sisterhood files?"

There was no point in lying. "Yes, just the five files. If they read them and there's no reason to think they didn't, then they know Alexis's real name. They'll figure out we're after Gillespie and Sullivan."

Nikki gathered up her car keys and purse. She snatched a slice of toast from Isabelle's hands and accepted a coffee to go.

"Call me," Isabelle shouted as Nikki raced through the open doorway, coffee sloshing all over her khakis.

All the way into the District, Nikki cursed herself over and over again. How could she have been so stupid as not to have put the files in the safe? The break-in was so over the top she had difficulty comprehending it.

Forty minutes later, Nikki swerved into the parking lot. She moved like greased lightning once she turned off the engine. By the time she hit her office, she was breathless with her gallop up the back stairs. She bellowed at the top of her lungs. "Show me! Make copies."

"I made six copies," Maddie said as she slipped the tape into the tape player.

Horrified at what she was seeing, Nikki watched the two reporters in action. First they picked the lock on the outside door, then Ted disarmed the alarm system. The camera caught the sweat on his forehead and Maggie's panic. She felt sick when she saw Maggie Spritzer pick the lock on her office file cabinet. She continued to watch as Maggie perused the files. Ted appeared and the surveillance camera followed him to the storage room where he cut the power and then turned it back on. They were still on camera as they raced down the stairs and out the door.

"Give me that!" Nikki shrieked. She knew she was losing control but she couldn't seem to help herself.

"Take a copy. I'll put the original in the safe. Don't worry, I marked it. Now you can go. Kick some ass, Nikki."

"Count on it!" Nikki shot back.

Anger, unlike anything she'd ever experienced, flooded through her. Common sense told her she had to calm down, to get her wits about her before she did something that would backfire on her and on the Sisterhood. That was when she realized she was going eighty miles an hour. She eased up on the gas pedal and took a deep breath. Right now she didn't need a cop stopping her for speeding.

Nikki drove around the *Post*'s parking lot three times before she found a parking spot. Now that she was here she realized she needed a plan. She couldn't storm the newsroom like some demented woman. She needed to be rational. Rational meant she should call Jack.

"Emery here."

"Jack, it's me. Listen to what I have to tell you. Tell me what to do before I do something I'll regret." Nikki rattled off the morning's events.

"Jesus. Where are you?"

"I'm in the *Post*'s parking lot. Time is of the essence, Jack. Help me out here."

"I'm thinking. I'm thinking. Give me a minute. Okay, here's what you do right now. Go into the building, give the tape to one of the guards and ask him to deliver it to either Maggie or Ted. Write off a little note. Tell them it's a copy, the original is in a safe deposit box at the bank. That means the next move is up to them. Then meet me back in Georgetown at the Brickyard. I'll buy you lunch."

"Jack, what if they made . . . make copies?"

"We'll deal with that when the time comes. I'll leave now."

"Don't you have to be in court?"

"Just got out. The verdict came in at 9:30 this morning after three days of deliberation. We won."

"Are you absolutely sure this is the way to go? I'm beside myself. Isabelle is the only one who knows. Charles left this morning for Spain. The others are in Manassas. I'm stalling. I'm going, Jack. See you in thirty minutes."

Nikki climbed out of the car, popped the trunk. She rummaged until she found a manila envelope. She slipped the tape into the envelope and closed the clasp. On the front she wrote,

"Ted Robinson or Maggie Spritzer. This is a copy, original in safe deposit box." She signed her name.

Clutching the envelope to her chest, Nikki walked boldly to the entrance and then over to the security guard. She showed her legal ID, handed him the envelope and said, "Can you have someone deliver this immediately? It has to do with a court case I'm trying and I need an immediate response. Thank you."

Nikki left the building and ran to her car. She was shaking badly when she started the engine. Charles would be livid when he found out what had happened. The others would be beyond livid. Right then she wished a hole would open up and swallow her. She felt sick to her stomach. Sick with fear at her stupidity.

"Spritzer! Robinson! Delivery!" a voice shouted from the door to the newsroom.

Ted Robinson loped over to the messenger. "I'll take it!"

Maggie appeared at his elbow. "What is it, Ted?"

"I think it's something neither one of us is going to like. Read the message."

Maggie blinked. "Why would she be sending us a tape?"

"If this is what I think it is, she had a very good reason for sending it."

Maggie followed Ted into the conference room and over to the VCR. He slid the tape into the slot and then stepped back to watch it. At one point, he threw his hands in the air and said, "Goodbye career." He looked over at Maggie who couldn't get her tongue to work. "I didn't see any cameras. I even looked."

Maggie hugged her arms to her chest and rocked back and forth. Instead of a Pulitzer, she was going to get a six by nine cell. She finally found her voice. "Maybe we can cut a deal. We give her the files after we make copies. We let her hear the tape."

"Are you crazy? She's got us, make no mistake about that. I bet they have you on tape during that mugging, too. The one you didn't want her to report. That chick just fried our asses and we didn't even see her light the match. We are not making any copies so get that thought out of your head. If she goes to the cops, guess who will try the case?"

Maggie started to cry. "Oh, God! This was all your idea, Ted."

"Hey, you went along with it. You were right there, baby. You're the one who lifted those files. Your fingerprints are all over them."

Maggie cried harder.

"She's going to tell that Martin guy and he's going to tell those goons of his. We're as good as dead. Maybe I should call Jack."

"I love this job. I love my life. I'm sorry I ever got tangled up with you. I can't believe I was stupid enough to go along with you on that stunt." Maggie sniffed and blew her nose before she started to cry all over again. "I had a chance, we both did, of getting a Pulitzer. Now we're never going to get it."

"Stop acting like a female who got dumped on. Let's put our heads together and try to figure a way out of this. We have the tape from the cemetery to barter with. Talking to Jack is not out of the question. We might have to do some sucking up."

"He's not going to help us. *He's one of them!*"

"Fine, then you come up with a better idea."

Maggie stalked her way out of the conference room. It was up to Ted to remove the security tape and carry it back to his desk where he looked at it like it was a snake about to strike. Past tense; he'd already been bitten. He sat quietly for a long time, his head in his hands.

Ted looked up when he heard a loud thump. Maggie dumping the files on his desk. How could five folders make that kind of noise? "I had the boss open the safe. Since you're the brains of this outfit, you figure out where we go from here."

Ted thought for a moment, staring at the tape. "The fact that she gave us this security tape means Quinn didn't go to the police. Yet. We both know she can do that at any time. Once the ball starts rolling, it's all out of our control. We get fired for starters. We go to trial unless we cop a plea. No competing paper will hire us. The bright spot is we get six months unemployment. She dumped this in our lap so that means she's waiting for us to make a move because she's holding all the cards. The security tape we're holding means squat. A good defense attorney will find a way to keep it out at a trial. I know how those guys work."

Maggie perched on the corner of Ted's desk. "Go ahead, call her and set up an appointment. I don't want this crap hanging over my head."

"Maggie, look at me. Swear to me that you did not make copies of those files."

Maggie met his gaze head-on. "I did not make copies. You were with me the whole time. When we got here, we read the files and then we had them put in the safe. When would I have had time to do that?"

"Did you make notes?"

"No, I did not make notes. I do, however, remember every single thing I read. You read the same files, and I know you remember what you read, too. You want to carve out my brain?"

"Well, they can't take that away from us, now can they?"

Maggie sniffed as she dabbed her eyes again. "Who is going to make the call?"

Ted played with the paperweight on his desk. "I suppose that's your way of telling me you don't want to make this a woman to woman thing. You think she might go easy with me because I'm a friend of Jack Emery. All right, I'll make the call."

Ted pulled out his cell phone. "Well, shit, Maggie, what's the number?"

"How should I know? Call information. You're stalling. I'm going to wash my face." Ted rolled his eyes as he listened to the information operator. He jotted down the number on a pad. Before he made the call, he took five deep breaths. He didn't feel one bit calmer as he dialed the number.

"This is Ted Robinson. I'd like to speak with Nicole Quinn."

"Miss Quinn is out of the office, Mr. Robinson. Would you care to leave a message?"

"Ask Miss Quinn to call me." Ted left his cell phone number and the main number at the *Post.* He broke the connection and hit his speed dial to Jack Emery's private cell phone. He listened to a metallic voice telling him to wait for the sound of the tone before leaving a message for the cellular customer he was trying to reach. Ted ended the call without leaving a message.

Maggie came up behind him. Washing her face hadn't helped her red eyes.

"Well?"

"Miss Quinn is out of the office this morning. I left my cell number and the number at the paper. Jack's not answering his cell. He might be in court."

"Now what?"

Ted jammed the manila envelope into his backpack. "Now, we wait."

Chapter 17

Alexis paced the length and breadth of the second floor terrace of the Manassas estate. Kathryn and Yoko watched her, helpless expressions on their faces.

Alexis stopped, leaned over the table and said, "I don't want to be this uptight. But just the thought of those two coming here is making me sick. I want to snatch that woman baldheaded. Him . . . I just want to turn him into a eunuch. The worst part of the whole thing is I can't confront them." She snapped her fingers in fury. "They're going to be right here, *that* close."

"We're going to do it all for you, baby," Kathryn said. "I can't positively guarantee this but I think you'll get your chance at those two.

For now, you'll be able to listen in. Is there anything else, any little tidbits you want to share with us where the two of them are concerned?"

Alexis shook her head. "I told you everything I could remember. Arden has a black belt in shopping. I know, just know, she has one of those American Express black cards. She got all that by sending me to prison. There's nothing she won't do for money. She corrupted Roland. As good-looking as he is, his eye never wandered until Arden came on the scene. I'm almost certain Roland's wife knew. She stopped coming to the office once Arden established herself. No, no, that's wrong. She did come by one time about three months after Arden signed on. She never came to the summer picnic or the Christmas parties after that. She used to arrange them and everyone always had a lovely time because Mrs. Sullivan cared enough to make it work. It was kind of sad that day she came to the office. She was all dolled up, heavy makeup. She was dressed in something real fancy, kind of slinky, actually. She had her hair done up, jewelry on. That's not who Mrs. Sullivan is. It was really out of character and sad at the same time. She said she came by to take Roland to lunch. Arden cut her down to size in two minutes. In one breath and with one demeaning look, Arden managed to let Mrs. Sullivan know she looked overdone and she, Arden, had a business lunch with Mrs. Sullivan's husband and a client so she might as well just *run along.*

"I followed Mrs. Sullivan out to the elevator

and tried to be nice and told her in so many words that I thought Arden was too full of herself. She didn't cry but there were tears in her eyes. She gave me a big hug. I was so damn mad I let Roland know that his wife had stopped by to take him to lunch and that she was all dressed up. He looked at me like I had sprouted a second head and wanted to know why I hadn't told him earlier. I told him what Arden said to his wife and he was livid. He did not have a luncheon engagement that day with Arden or anyone else. He was very clear about that."

"Does any of this help?" Alexis asked.

Kathryn looked thoughtful. "I don't know. We're winging this part of the way until we get a handle on both of them. Today is get-acquainted day." At Alexis's worried look, she said, "You have to trust us, okay?"

Alexis's head bobbed up and down. "Okay. Anybody else call?"

"No, it is very quiet," Yoko said.

"Sometimes that's a good thing," Alexis said over her shoulder.

"Yeah, sometimes," Kathryn said. She looked over at Yoko. "We still have three hours till show time. Let's kick this around a little. What's up with Myra this morning?"

"She has been on the phone all morning with Charles. I think they have a secret. I think it has something to do with the lady who owns this house. Are you nervous about meeting those awful people?"

Kathryn hooted with laughter. "On the contrary. I can't wait to cut those two down to size. I have to practice my haughty look a little more." Together the two young women made faces at one another, laughing and slapping at each other, either in approval or disapproval.

From her position in the sunroom, Myra watched them, a smile on her face. She tried to remember when she was that young and could laugh the way Kathryn and Yoko were laughing. Barbara and Nikki had laughed together all the time. Girl talk, girl secrets. A veil of sadness slipped over Myra's face.

"Why so sad, Mom?"

"Darling girl! I was thinking about how you and Nikki used to laugh like Kathryn and Yoko are laughing. I was feeling a little sad. Actually, I was feeling a little lonely. I'm not myself when Charles is gone. He's going to fetch Annie back with him. I'm looking forward to her return. Nellie is excited, too."

"I have to go now, Mom. Nikki needs me. I just wanted to say hello and to tell you how much I love you. I'm so proud of you, Mom."

Myra was about to say something when she felt a featherlight touch on her cheek. A lone tear built in the corner of her eye and trickled down her cheek. She squeezed her eyes shut to savor the bittersweet feeling.

The exclusive Brickyard restaurant lived up to its name. The outside eating area for good weather was all brick with little winding paths leading to brick-based tables and benches. Rough hewn beams stretched across the eating area that dripped tendrils of glossy green plants. Ficus trees were lush and full and placed strategically to give privacy to the diners. Somewhere beyond the lush greenery a waterfall could be heard. Scarlet and yellow tulips sat on all the tables in matching colored pots. It was the perfect place to conduct a business meeting, a liaison, or just a small group meeting to play catch-up and enjoy the exquisite food.

Nikki ate at the Brickyard often and the hostess immediately showed her to her favorite table near the waterfall. Known as a good tipper, she was always given preferential treatment. When the waiter appeared at her elbow, she decided not to wait for Jack. Even though she was one of the first customers, and it was early for lunch, she decided it was five o'clock somewhere in the world. She threw caution to the winds and ordered a double scotch on the rocks for herself and a Bud Lite for Jack. When the drinks came, Nikki took a healthy gulp and immediately felt lightheaded. She gulped again and wondered if her eyes were crossed.

Nikki was fiddling with her watch, opening and closing it, just to have something to do with her hands so she wouldn't pick up the tumbler of scotch. She looked up, relief in her expression when Jack sat down across from her.

"Guess the dark stuff hit the fan, eh?"

Nikki leaned across the table. "Jack, they fucking broke into my office during the night! I have to tell Myra and Charles and you know what that means," she hissed.

Jack nodded glumly as he swigged at his beer. "I don't know what other body part Robinson can live without."

"Right now, I don't care. Damn!" Nikki yanked at her cell phone, looked at the number of the incoming call. She hated people who talked on their cell phones in restaurants. She got up, walked behind one of the lush ficus trees and returned the call to her office.

"It's Nikki, Maddie. What's up?" She listened. Her slumped shoulders squared imperceptibly. "I'll call you back in fifteen minutes. In the meantime, call Isabelle, her number is in my Rolodex. Tell her to call the kennel trainer and arrange for the guard dogs to be returned to Pinewood, ASAP. I'll get back to you shortly."

Back at the table, Nikki looked at Jack. "It was Maddie. Ted called the office to speak to me. I told her I'd call her back in fifteen minutes. Time, Jack, is of the essence. I can't wait for them to do something. I have to take control. I'm going to invite the two of them out to Pinewood."

Jack set his beer bottle down with a thump. "And . . ."

"There is no . . . and. They will become our . . . *guests*."

Jack made wet circles on the pristine tablecloth with his beer bottle. "Have you thought this through, Nikki?"

"No. I can't have them running around loose flapping their tongues. Jack, those two can destroy us. You, too. Don't even think you can talk them out of this. I've got them red-handed and

I have to act on it. Charles . . . Charles won't have it any other way. Neither will the others. There are no other options and you know it."

A young waiter with a spiked hairdo appeared. Without looking at the menu, Nikki said, "We'll both have the special, whatever it is."

"How long can you . . . hold them as your . . . ah, guests?"

"Indefinitely," Nikki said coldly. "The guard dogs will be back this afternoon. Only a fool would even think about tangling with them. Forever if necessary."

Jack squinted and looked into his empty beer bottle. He held it aloft and wiggled it to get the waiter's attention. "What about their families, their jobs, their pets?"

"I'll take care of it." Nikki gulped the last of her drink in one long swallow. Her eyes started to water as she excused herself to go behind the ficus tree again. Jack slumped in his chair as he waited for her to return.

Nikki was all lawyer when she sat back down at the table. Her voice was cool, professional and brisk. "My clients will meet me at Pinewood at six o'clock this evening. Ah, here's our lunch. I wonder what it is."

"Is that it?"

"That's it, Jack."

On her way back to Pinewood, Nikki made two phone calls. The first was to Isabelle, the second to Myra. She stated her business the same way she'd made her final comment to Jack, brisk, cool and professional. When she clicked off, she slid a Bruce Springsteen tape into the player. It was her way of shifting her emotions into a neutral zone.

"Not a bad decision since you made it on the fly."

"Barb!"

"Yeah. Hey, slow down and lower the volume. You can't hear yourself think."

"That was the object. I don't know what else to do. I can't let them run around loose. Those two reporters could bring us all down."

"That's true. Mom wouldn't look good in prison garb. You probably should put them in the apartment over the garage. The dogs will be deterrent enough."

"That's what I was thinking. Isabelle and I will get their pets, pack a bag for them. They'll be more than comfortable until Charles gets back and we decide what to do with the two of them. It isn't kidnapping if they agree to stay. I'll make sure we record everything they say. Do you think it will work, Barb?"

"I don't see why not. What did Mom say?"

"I think I rattled her. She was cool, though. She told me to do what I thought was right. Isabelle agreed. I still can't believe they were brazen enough to break into my office. I'll never feel safe until I know there are no other copies out there. They can tell me anything they want. I will have no choice but to believe them. If I were in their position, I'd make sure I covered my ass one way or the other."

"That's you, Nikki. Yes, Maggie and Ted are bold

and brazen, but when it comes to breaking the law, the journalistic privilege does not exist. They're dead in the water if you go public and they know that. No reputable paper would represent them. They'd have to go the tabloid route."

"Going public means we all go down. I can't go down that road. I can threaten but that's it. Or, I can have Charles do what he does best. I don't want to go down that road either. Damn, how the hell did this happen?"

"You underestimated them."

"Yeah, yeah, I did. Shame on me."

"It's going to be okay. My money is on you, Nik. Hey, gotta go."

Nikki shook her head to clear her thoughts. Well, now she had a plan. Sort of. Kind of. She turned the volume back up and felt a little better as Bruce entertained her the rest of the way home.

Isabelle was waiting in the kitchen when she got to Pinewood. She'd made a pot of coffee and changed out of her work clothes. "I'm all yours. Just tell me what you want me to do." She poured coffee the minute Nikki sat down.

"Okay, we have to stock the pantry and the fridge for our guests. That means dog and cat food, too. One of us has to go to Safeway. We also have to clean the apartment over the garage. Take your pick."

"We don't have to go grocery shopping. We can call in the order; they'll deliver and carry it up the steps. We just have to tip *big.* The two of us can clean the apartment. It will be ready for our guests when they arrive. What say you?" Isabelle said.

"Works for me. Call in the grocery order and don't forget the kitty litter and some pee pads in case they can't take the dog out. There's a veranda on the back of the building so the dog can go out there. Order enough for . . . let's say two weeks to be on the safe side. I'm going to change my clothes."

Isabelle's jaw dropped. "You're actually going to help me clean?"

Nikki whirled around. "Of course. Myra made Barbara and me learn how to clean. We had to scrub our bathroom, do our own laundry and make our beds. We had to muck the barn, too. And we raked leaves, mowed grass, and planted flowers. Oh, yeah, Myra made us iron our own clothes. I know how to do it. I cleaned my own house for years until my hours got so long. Then, I had to hire someone. However, I refused to buy an iron. The cleaners worked for me."

Isabelle looked perplexed. "Guess you used a mop, huh?"

"Are you kidding. It was on our knees scrubbing. It was a good thing, Isabelle. We didn't mind. I like cleaning my own house, I just don't have the time."

Isabelle laughed. "Since you're such an expert, you get to do the bathroom."

"You got it. We should have heard something by now, don't you think?"

"It's only three o'clock. Soon, would be my guess."

"Isabelle, do you see any other way?"

"If you're referring to the reporters, no, I don't see any other way."

"I have a real bad feeling about this."

"Yeah, me too," Isabelle said.

Chapter 18

Roland Sullivan sat at his desk, his eyes on the small digital clock on its top, a gift from his wife. The desk set was from his wife, too. The bookcase across the room, under the window, held pictures of his family in the early years. He was sad to note there were no later photographs. Maybe that was because he was never home to be included in family pictures. He regretted his absences more and more these days.

The thick file on Anna Ryland de Silva sat in front of him. He wondered if he should go through it again. What was the point? Either the woman would hire the firm or she wouldn't. Being last to be interviewed didn't do much for his ego.

Arden knew the file inside out. If anyone could clinch the deal, it was his partner. The mere thought of her rubbing it under his nose made his stomach jump. He was waiting for her now, trying to imagine how she would look. Professional, sexy, charming, aloof. All of the above. He, on the other hand, had paid attention to de Silva's likes and dislikes. He'd dressed down, going with creased khakis, tasseled loafers and a button-down Oxford shirt. No power tie today. He'd chosen his jacket with care, finally choosing a light tweed that was one hundred percent cashmere. He hadn't even bothered to get a haircut. Arden had chastised him about that.

Roland looked at a picture of his wife waving into the camera. What a beautiful smile she had. His stomach jumped again when he remembered how he'd tried to get her to talk to him last night. He'd practically groveled, saying he needed her advice. She'd chopped him off at the knees with one look. "You gave up the right to ask me for *anything* a long time ago, Roland." Calling him Roland had been the last straw. She always called him Rolly. A pet name from the early days of their marriage. Calling him Roland meant she was beyond angry.

It wasn't just his wife who was upset. The kids treated him like a guest, a rare visitor whom they treated with courtesy. Courtesy, for God's sake. Well, screw it.

Sensing a presence, Roland looked up and did a double take. "Arden?"

The willowy blonde whirled and twirled. "What do you think? Is it too much? Do I look *real?*"

Roland could only gawk. The lustrous blond

hair was slicked back into a tight bun at the nape of her neck. Her earrings looked like they came from a discount store, as did the strap watch on her wrist. The manicured nails were minus the blood red polish she loved and were cut short with a coat of clear polish. Her outfit was a denim skirt with matching jacket and a white tee. He knew she'd picked it up at a thrift shop because it looked worn and a little wrinkled. Any other time, Arden wouldn't be caught dead dressed as she was now. Her shoes weren't the Chanel or Ferragamo that she usually wore. He made a bet with himself that they came from Wal-Mart.

"Well, you're definitely dressed down."

"We should leave now. I borrowed a car from a neighbor of mine. It's a four-year-old Saab but it still looks good. Maroon in color. You can drive a stick so you're the driver. Ohhh, Roland, I can smell our bank accounts filling up."

Roland thought he'd never seen his lover and partner so giddy. "There's an old saying, my dear, don't count your chickens before they hatch."

"For God's sake, Roland, do you always have to be so negative? If I listened to you and those little ditties of yours where would we be now? Certainly not a contender for the de Silva account. And . . . you wouldn't have that little Hawaiian vacation spot or that ski chalet in Aspen."

Roland's voice dropped an octave. "That's true, but I'd probably sleep a lot better at night."

"Take a sleeping pill," Arden snapped.

Roland moved like lightning. He reached for Arden's arm and pulled her into the room. He moved his big hand till he had his partner's neck in his grasp. He literally dragged her to the wall and shoved her face up against the photo of Sara Whittier. "Don't ever tell me to take a sleeping pill again." He dropped his hand. "We should be leaving. Mrs. de Silva frowns on tardiness. I read that in her file."

Arden's eyes glittered. "Will you stop with that Sara Whittier crap already. It's over and done with. Get over it. How many times did you go to Aspen and Hawaii last year? I rest my case."

The short drive to Manassas was made in silence. From time to time, Roland looked down at the small map he'd taken off the Internet, courtesy of MapQuest. Twenty minutes later, Roland steered the Saab onto the long driveway leading to the house. He slowed and came to a complete stop at the guardhouse. He blanched slightly as did Arden when they saw the beefy guard with a gun at his waist. It was impossible not to see the rifle hanging on the wall inside when Arthur stepped toward the car, his hand on the gun butt.

"Two forms of ID, sir. You, too, ma'am."

Roland opened his wallet, removing his driver's license and a credit card with his picture on it. Arden handed her cards to Roland who handed them to the guard. Before Arthur retreated into the guardhouse, he said, "Roll your window up, sir, and leave it up until I tell you to roll it down."

"What is this, Fort Knox?" Arden demanded angrily. "She's just a rich old lady, why does she need all of this?"

"Because she can afford it and probably because she wants to keep people like us out of here. She's a multibillionaire. If you were in her position, you'd have helicopters hovering over your residence and don't deny it."

"It's so . . . over the top. It's like she's stressing her importance," Arden sniped.

"And yet she's a recluse," Roland sniped back.

The phone inside the guardhouse buzzed to life. The guard picked up the phone and moved out of sight. "Yes, ma'am, they're here now. I'm checking their IDs. You want me to open the gates at precisely 2:27. Yes, ma'am."

Arthur returned to the Saab. Roland lowered the window to accept their identification cards. "The gates will open at 2:27. Raise your window."

Arden sniffed. "He acts like he's Gestapo."

"Stop it, Arden. The man is doing his job. You just don't like it when other people are in control." He handed the cards back to her. He almost laughed at the tacky-looking purse she carried. He wondered where she'd gotten it. Not that it mattered.

Roland crawled up the driveway, parked, got out, went around to open the door for Arden. "Guess we go to the front door."

"Obviously. We aren't servants or tradespeople."

"Ladies first," Roland said as he stepped aside to allow her to lead the way.

The door was opened almost immediately. Yoko stepped back and bowed her head slightly. "I am Sumi Takamuro, Miss Markham's assistant. Follow me, please, Miss Gillespie, Mr. Sullivan. Miss Markham is waiting."

Arden was so busy eyeing all the antiques and priceless objects of art, she kept tripping over her own feet. Roland had to steady her twice by reaching for her elbow. He knew his partner was impressed beyond words. He wasn't. He liked modern houses with clean lines, lots of glass and raw wood. He could never live in a mausoleum like this one.

Sumi knocked once on an ornate mahogany door and opened it at the same time. She stepped aside and said, "This is Miss Gillespie and Mr. Sullivan, Ellen."

Kathryn Lucas got up and walked around her desk. The cut of her business suit was so severe, the material so exquisite, it shrieked dollar signs. The white linen blouse under the jacket was unwrinkled and so beautiful, Arden had to suck in her breath. "Ellen Markham," she said, extending her hand. Her grip was bone crushing and Arden winced. Roland matched the pressure.

"Please, be seated. I'm Mrs. de Silva's personal assistant. I can give you exactly twenty-seven minutes today." She looked over at Sumi and said, "Set the clock."

Arden was stunned to see the Asian woman set the time on a three dollar kitchen timer.

"Shall we get right to it," Kathryn said. She opened a folder and pretended to read the contents. "I've studied this at great length. I have to wonder how you can guarantee half of what's in here."

"When it comes to investments, Miss Markham, we never use the word 'guarantee'. You have to give your broker credit to know when to buy, when to sell and when to hold tight. Our record, as you can see, is impeccable," Roland said. "We're not in business to lose money. Our object, our goal is to make everyone as rich as possible. I have no intention of blowing smoke in your direction. At times, things go awry. We can't predict what's going to happen so we hedge our investments and are on top of them twenty-four-seven. We're only a phone call away, again, twenty-four-seven."

Arden decided it was time to jump in. "We might be a small house but we deliver quality. That, we *can* guarantee." *How much did she pay for that suit?*

"Admirable," Kathryn said coldly. "Have you studied our bottom line on the P&L report?" Both brokers nodded. "Well?"

"We're prepared to pay three percent if the balance drops below your present bottom line."

"Five!" Kathryn said. "That five percent would have to be in an escrow fund. Five percent of our bottom line."

"That would be impossible, Miss Markham. We'd have to mortgage our business, liquidate our personal holdings and it still wouldn't be enough."

Kathryn leaned back in her chair and steepled her fingers just under her nose. "Banks love to lend money. If Mrs. de Silva were to decide to go with Sullivan and Gillespie, banks will stand in line to loan you money. Five percent."

Arden looked at Roland. Roland looked at Arden. Kathryn watched them both and fought not to laugh. Yoko turned away so she wouldn't burst into giggles. In the end, greed won out.

Arden's voice was shaky. "Are we to understand you are considering our firm, or was that a hypothetical?"

Kathryn let them squirm for a full two minutes before she replied. "The decision is mine to make. I will be honest with you, the larger firms had a problem with the percentage. I would need confirmation from the bank. Meetings will be required. Mrs. de Silva's name will be on the escrow account. Do you have a problem with that?"

Hell yes, she had a problem with that. "No, not at all," Arden said quickly.

Kathryn thought Roland Sullivan looked sick. She looked straight at him waiting for his response. He couldn't seem to make his tongue work so he nodded.

Kathryn looked over at Yoko, her eyes a question.

"Seven minutes remain, Ellen," Yoko said.

"There is one other thing." Kathryn opened a folder and withdrew a stack of newspaper clippings. She pushed them across her desk. "I need an explanation for this lawsuit and the young woman who worked for you. It stands in your way."

Arden bit down on her bottom lip. "The firm managed to weather the . . . incident."

"Incident? A woman going to prison is not an *incident.* I have a transcript of the trial right here," Kathryn said, pointing to a mountain of bound folders. "I found Miss Whittier's version quite credible, as did Mrs. de Silva. Where is this young woman today?"

"We don't know," Arden said quickly. "After she got out of prison, Miss Whittier dropped off the face of the earth. Roland tried to find her. We aren't heartless. We wanted to give her a little stake to start over but we couldn't locate her."

"Well, Mrs. de Silva's people will be able to find her. I should talk to her before I make my final decision. But, since time is of the essence, I can wait a little while longer."

Arden's insides quaking, she decided she had nothing to lose. "It will be you, Miss Markham, who makes the final decision?" she asked.

"Yes. Do either of you have a problem with that?"

"Not at all," Arden said. "What happens if your people can't find Miss Whittier?"

Kathryn stood up to indicate that the meeting was over. "I'll make a decision at that time if they are unsuccessful. Thank you for coming out here today. I'll be in touch. Be sure to let me know when and if you can secure a loan. Sumi, show our guests to the door."

Kathryn turned her back and walked out of the room, closing the door softly behind her. She fell into Alexis's arms. "How'd I do?"

"Great! You were great."

"Dear girl, you really had them transfixed," Myra said.

Yoko bounded into the room, giggling. "You should have been an actress, Kathryn. I could see the greed in their eyes."

"Trust me when I tell you they'll stop at a bank on the way back to the office," Alexis said.

"In that outfit?" Kathryn said.

The women went off into another peal of laughter.

"Alexis, how do you feel, dear?" Myra asked.

Alexis shrugged. "I peeped out the door at them. I thought I wouldn't be able to contain myself, that I would rush out and strangle both of them. It didn't happen. I did want to cry, though, when they called me by my real name. I think it went well. In other words, I'm satisfied."

Kathryn hugged her. "We aim to please. Can I now please get out of these clothes?"

"Absolutely, Miss Markham," Myra said.

Chapter 19

Roland Sullivan did his best to talk between his clenched teeth. He was furious.

Arden lowered the window on the passenger side and lit a cigarette. "Will you relax, Roland. We can do this. Stop at the first restaurant you see and we'll talk." She blew a perfect smoke ring as she leaned her head back against the leather headrest.

"Are you out of your mind? We cannot do this. Let me be more specific, I will not agree to this. I am not going to mortgage my holdings so you can get rich. I started my business on a shoestring and I'm not going to mortgage it, nor any of my properties. My house is paid for. I hope you're listening, Arden."

"You only have what you have because of . . . let's be blunt here, Roland. You have what you have because we framed Sara Whittier and raped her accounts. Let's not be shy about it. We're both wealthy thanks to our dastardly deeds."

"I know. It's my cross to bear. The answer is no, Arden."

Arden blew another perfect smoke ring. "It would be more money than either of us ever dreamed of. When Wall Street hears de Silva signed on with us, the big boys will want to play with us. Millions and millions, Roland. Look, there's a small café, let's stop there."

Roland dutifully slowed and turned into the parking lot of the Sweet Grass Café. Normally, he would have walked around to open the door for Arden. Today he got out of the car and walked toward the entrance. Arden had to run to catch up to him.

The café was a cozy little place with small round tables covered by colorful tablecloths. Sawdust littered the floor. Sweetgrass baskets hung on all the walls and could be purchased by the patrons. It was well past the lunch hour and too early for the down-home dinner the café was known for. Two signs over the counter said beer and wine were available and smoking was not an option. The only occupants were two elderly white-haired ladies and two waitresses.

Roland headed for a table well away from the two old ladies. He didn't bother holding a chair for Arden. She grumbled as she pulled out her own chair and sat down.

Roland flipped open the menu. He had three choices—pot roast, crab cakes, or fried chicken. He opted for the pot roast with mashed potatoes and two sides. Arden ordered the crab cakes with a garden salad. Both ordered coffee. The minute the waitress was out of earshot, Arden fixed her gaze on Roland who met it defiantly.

"They're going to try and find Sara. Doesn't that bother you, Arden?"

"If we couldn't find her, they aren't going to find her either. She's gone. Forget about Sara Whittier. It's because of Sara that we're sitting here with the brass ring within our grasp. Open your eyes, Roland. This is the big time."

Roland stirred cream into his coffee. What he really wanted was a triple shot of Old Granddad. "Big time, my ass. Did you hear the same things I did? What bank would be crazy enough to grant us a loan of that size to go into escrow without our names on the account? If you believe that, you are really stupid. The answer is *NO!*"

"Look, Roland, this is the chance of a lifetime. I know a bank that I am almost certain would grant a loan. The escrow account will be in their bank drawing interest. We can agree the bank holds the interest. Between the two of us we can make some robust profits for de Silva. We talked about it in detail. Your ideas are as good as mine are. We *can* do this. We really can. If we mortgage everything we have, drain the offshore accounts, we can come up with fifty, maybe seventy-five million easy. If you're worried about your primary residence, *the one you share with your wife*, we can exclude it.

"I did listen to the Markham woman. It's true

she didn't confirm that she would give us the account. What she wants is to see if we're willing to put everything on the line. She said two of the big houses outright refused. I grant you five percent is a lot but not enough to make us say no."

Roland leaned back so the waitress could put his plate in front of him. Suddenly, he was ravenous and couldn't wait to dig into the mashed potatoes and gravy. His wife Patsy used to make meals like this. She called them comfort food. He wondered if he would find comfort after he finished the food on his plate. He looked across at Arden's plate. She was mashing the crab cakes with her fork. He wasn't at all surprised when he saw her make a dollar sign as she carved and sliced at the food on her plate.

"It is enough to say no. I have no intention of ending up selling shoes in a department store. I don't think you'd do well working as a domestic somewhere."

"You are so negative. You need to think ahead. We did so many projections we were dizzy. You agreed that we could do it."

"That was before Markham came up with that five percent. That is an ugly percentage. If it was three, I might consider it. *Might* is the operative word."

Arden's eyes were desperate. "What if I agreed, between us, to personally suck up the other two percent? There will be more than enough money to last us ten lifetimes if we play our cards right. Would you agree to that?"

Roland pondered the question as he sopped

up the last of the gravy on his plate with a chunk of homemade bread that melted in his mouth. Maybe he'd ask the waitress if he could buy a loaf to take home with him. "I might."

Arden sighed loudly. "I'll call the banker tonight at home and talk to him. You can listen if you like." She gave herself a mental shake and switched into her seductive mode. "Think about it," she whispered, "we're naked in bed talking to a stuffy banker on the speakerphone who only has sex twice a month with his overweight wife in the missionary position."

Roland fell into the trap and totally forgot about asking for a loaf of bread to go.

Maggie Spritzer moaned and groaned as the car ate up the miles. "I don't mind telling you I'm scared, Ted. How did we miss those security cameras?"

"Because we're stupid. Okay, okay, I'm stupid. The goddamn things looked like recessed lighting. I'm not a high-tech person. You missed them, too. You said you didn't want to fight it."

Maggie watched the countryside flash by. "A reporter without credibility . . ."

"There's no point in beating this to death. We're going to apologize. We are going to promise to lay off. We are going to return the files and swear on our parents and everyone on earth that there are no notes and no copies because it will be the truth. Then we are going to hope those women take pity on us and take us at our word. Then and only then, I am going to kill Jack Emery for involving me in this shit in the first place."

"It would have been a Pulitzer, Ted," Maggie muttered.

"Well, that is not going to happen now so get that thought out of your head and don't ever think about it again."

Maggie worked at her seat belt so she could turn to face Ted. "We do have one other option."

"We're out of options. I don't want to talk about this anymore. What?"

"We could join them. We know Emery is one of them. If we were on the inside, we'd really get the straight skinny on all of them. That would fly when we did our exposé. The journalistic world would forgive us for that little breaking and entering we did."

Ted took his eyes off the road long enough to glare at his companion. "Don't go down that road, Maggie. We're here. Let me do the talking, okay? Just agree with everything I say. I want to give you something to think about so listen up. No one, I repeat, no one knows we're here unless you blabbed to someone. The ladies of Pinewood are a law unto themselves. They have the kind of backup you and I can only dream about. That's another way of saying we're at their mercy and we have to be properly contrite and believable. Tell me you understand everything I just said."

Maggie mumbled something that sounded like she agreed. "Do you ever wonder what it's like to have so much money you can afford all this?" she asked, waving her arms about.

"No! The gates are opening. Oh, shit, look at those dogs!"

Maggie took one look at the snapping, snarling dogs and squeezed her eyes shut. The huge iron gates closed silently. A moment later the dogs turned docile and headed back to wherever they came from. The reporters stayed in their car until Nikki appeared to escort them into the house.

The fine hairs on the back of Ted's neck moved in the early evening breeze. The look on Nikki Quinn's face and the set of her shoulders told him whatever was about to happen was going to be downright ugly. He was wary of looking at Maggie. He hoped she wouldn't start to cry. He felt his skin prickle when he heard the door close behind him. Maggie must have had the same reaction. He could see her shoulders start to tremble.

Nikki nodded toward the round oak table as she fiddled with the whistle around her neck. "Coffee? Soft drink?"

Both reporters shook their heads. Ted tossed the manila folder onto the table.

Nikki picked it up and carried it over to the kitchen counter where she opened it and withdrew the files. She spent a good twenty minutes going through each page in an effort to convince herself that nothing was missing. She picked up the larger envelope and a smaller envelope fell out. "Is this an extra . . . *something* for me?"

"Oh shit," Ted mumbled under his breath. Both he and Maggie slumped in their chairs.

Nikki opened the clasp on the smaller envelope. A small cassette tape dropped to the counter. "I think I know what this is. Do either one of you want to confirm it?"

"It's the tape we made that night at the cemetery when Jack Emery helped you women," Ted said coldly.

"I take it I wasn't supposed to get this."

"That's right, you weren't supposed to get it."

"How do you explain this then?"

Ted didn't see any advantage to lying. "The files and the tape were in the safe at the office. When we asked for our package I guess the boss thought we meant both envelopes. There are no copies of anything, if that's your next question."

Nikki's face was grim. "For your sake, I hope that's true," she said.

Ted's stomach crunched into a knot. "Now what?"

Maggie squared her shoulders. She struggled for bravado. "Okay, we're guilty of breaking into your offices. However, let's not lose sight of the fact that what you and your friends are doing is far worse. You could go to prison for a very long time if you turn us in because we'll sing like the proverbial canaries. We'll cop a plea and probably get off with probation. Our paper will go to bat for us. We both know that. Yeah, yeah, we might lose our jobs in the end and maybe even our credibility, but are you willing to take that chance, Miss Quinn? While we're at it, you set me up in the parking lot, didn't you?"

Nikki was about to respond when Isabelle knocked at the kitchen door before she walked in. "Oh, company! Am I interrupting anything?"

Maggie and Ted both noticed the whistle hanging around Isabelle's neck. It matched the one Nikki wore.

"No. Coffee?" Nikki asked.

"Don't mind if I do." Isabelle poured herself a cup and lounged against the kitchen counter. "What should we talk about?" she asked cheerily.

Maggie was still feeling brave. "How about that night at the cemetery when you guys dumped Rosemary Hershey into an open grave?"

"Oh, that! A simple case of mistaken identity."

"Like hell! You damn women are out there breaking the law left and right and we caught you fair and square. You win this round. We turned over all our proof. That puts you in control. For the time being. I'd like to leave now."

Isabelle brought the cup to her lips. "I bet you would."

Nikki looked genuinely regretful. "I'm afraid we can't allow you to leave," she said. "We'd like you to be our guests for a little while."

"What does that mean exactly?" Ted asked.

"You're a smart man, Ted. What do you think it means?"

"You're kidnapping us is what it means to me."

"The word 'kidnapping' has such an awful connotation. You called my office for an appointment. My office manager can verify that. I invited you out here to Pinewood. She will verify that, too. Actually, you're free to leave. Your other option is to follow us out to the apartment over the garage where we'd like you to stay while you're visiting. Of course if you really don't want to accept our hospitality, we understand. It's your choice. Isabelle, open the door."

Isabelle opened the door. The snapping, snarling dogs circled the steps leading to the back door. "Just wade through the dogs. When you get to the gate, we'll open it."

Maggie and Ted looked at one another. In a resigned voice, Ted said, "We accept your hospitality."

"Your cell phones, please. Just put them on the table. Empty out your pockets. Isabelle, pat them down. While I take our guests to our guest house, remove the distributor cap from the car and let the air out of all four tires."

"You're a bitch!" Maggie snarled.

"Takes one to know one," Nikki snapped in return. "Follow me and don't make any sudden moves or the dogs *will* attack you. I would like to share with you that these dogs patrol twenty-four hours a day."

"This is kidnapping," Maggie blustered as she followed Nikki, Ted on her heels.

"Let's not do that dance again. You are our guests. We've gone out of our way to make sure your stay with us is as enjoyable as possible. Come along now, don't dawdle. The dogs get nervous when one is out and about too long. To prove how considerate and caring we are, we're going into town to fetch your pets." Nikki opened the garage door and ushered her guests up the stairs to the second floor. "I think you will be quite comfortable here. Everything you could possibly want is here: the latest bestsellers, the latest videos, a wide screen TV, a Jacuzzi and a plentiful supply of beer and wine. Wonderful food, ample room, a veranda in the back where the animals will be able to run and play. There is an intercom between this apartment and the main house. You can call us anytime if you need something. Think of this as a vacation you promised yourself but didn't have the time to take. Enjoy the evening."

Nikki joined Isabelle in the kitchen. "If you're ready to go, let's do it."

"How did they accept it all?"

Nikki laughed. "All things considered, rather well. They'll adjust, they have no other choice."

"Just to be on the safe side, let's leave our cars *outside* the gate while we're hosting our guests. Reporters are very . . . ingenious."

"Good thinking," Nikki said as she gathered up her purse and car keys. She locked the kitchen door behind her.

"When are you going to . . ."

"Tell everyone? Soon."

Chapter 20

The words exploded out of Jack Emery's mouth like bullets. "You did *WHAT*?"

Nikki played with the wristband on her watch. She refused to be cowed by Jack's outburst. Her gaze was rock steady and right on. "You heard me the first time. We had no other choice, Jack. Those two can ruin all of us and that includes you, too. Stop looking at me like that. I'd do it all over again if I had to."

Jack raked his fingers through his new haircut. "Of all the harebrained stunts, this one tops the list. How long do you plan on housing your . . . guests?"

Nikki's tone turned defensive. "As long as it takes. For all intents and purposes, the two of them ran off to get married. I have it covered.

We sent letters to their boss. Resignation letters. We paid up the rental leases on their apartments for six months plus all their utility bills. Both of them used automated checking. Like I said, we have it covered. They goddamn well broke into my law offices. They had the tape of you at the cemetery. Let me be the first to tell you your voice is loud and it is recognizable. Ted said he played it for you. I was protecting you, too."

Jack continued to finger-comb his hair. "Son of a fucking bitch! This one is really going to come back to bite you, Nikki."

"Yeah, well, I guess I'll have to bite back, won't I? I can't unring the bell. It's done. We even took their pets out to the farm. They are *guests*, Jack."

"Bull*SHIT*! You fucking kidnapped them! You stepped way over the line this time."

Nikki's voice turned colder than ice. "Have it your way."

"Now what?"

Nikki's gaze didn't waver. "Now it's business as usual. I'd really like to stay but I have to get back to the farm. Isabelle is holding the fort."

Jack wasn't about to give it up. "Well, hell, yes, you better get back there to see to the welfare of those two reporters. You don't know Ted Robinson very well. Or Maggie."

Nikki turned on her heel to leave. "Is that a warning? Duly noted. I'd like to add that Ted and Maggie *don't know me very well.*"

Jack sat down on the brick steps. "I don't give

a hoot about those two. Well, I do and I don't. Dammit, Nikki, you know what I mean. I'm worried about you and the others."

Nikki stood on the sidewalk under a maple tree that was almost in full leaf. Morning sunshine filtered down through the leaves, warming her. "Assuming you were a betting man, Jack, who would you be betting on right now?"

Jack shook his head from side to side, refusing to answer the question. Nikki's shoulders drooped before she took off on a jog to her car that was parked in the next block. She was crying when she unlocked the door and slid behind the wheel. She lowered the window and craned her neck to see Jack who was still sitting on the steps, his head cradled in his hands.

Nikki did her best to shift her thoughts away from the current situation by thinking about the other Sisters in Manassas. When she got to the farm she was going to call Myra and talk it out. Then again, maybe she wouldn't do that. She hated to infringe on Alexis's revenge with a problem she couldn't do anything about at the present.

Jack had been disturbed. No, more than disturbed; he'd been pissed to the teeth. Out of concern for her, of that she was sure. Still, she would have preferred a little more of a show of support on his part.

On any other day, Nikki would have enjoyed the ride to Pinewood with the trees dressed in their spring finery. She was tempted to stop at several roadside stands that were alive with rows and rows of spring flowers but today she had tunnel vision and tunnel thoughts, if there was such a thing. Instead of worrying about Ted and Maggie, she should be worried about how things were going with Alexis. "I need to talk, Barb!"

"Whatcha want to talk about, Nik?"

"Did I screw up? Barb, I didn't have a choice. I'm worried about what Charles will say because it *is* kidnapping. Damn it, what was I supposed to do? Let them blow the whistle on us?"

"Nik, relax. Things will work out. Charles will know how to handle this when he gets back. Stop beating yourself up over this."

"Why does kidnapping those two reporters bother me and yet being a member of the Sisterhood, exacting revenge on cases that fell through the cracks, *doesn't* bother me? Can you explain that to me?"

"It's simple. Maggie and Ted can bring it all down around your ears. If you hadn't done what you did, they would have turned you all, and that includes Mom, Charles, and Jack, over to the authorities and you'd be sitting in prison. You reacted like anyone would react in order to protect everyone. I would have done the same thing, Nik."

"Honest Injun?" Nikki said, using the phrase she and Barbara had used when they were kids and questioning each other's honesty.

"Honest Injun, Nik."

"That makes me feel a little better. I'm still worried about Charles, though."

"Don't be. Things will work out. See ya, Nik. I'm going to check on Mom."

Nikki smiled all the way to Pinewood. She always felt better after a talk with her dearest friend who was no longer of this earth.

Arden Gillespie was dressed to the nines and could have passed for a high fashion model. She had the twelve bankers eating out of her hand, something Roland Sullivan knew he never could have done even on his best day.

It was the end of the second day of banking meetings and a hair wasn't out of place on her beautiful head. The gloss on her lips was just as shiny as it had been at eight this morning when they'd entered this elegant boardroom. He wondered if her face hurt from all the smiling she'd been doing.

Roland knew Arden was sweating but the bankers didn't know that. The key, she'd said last night over a late supper and rousing sex, was to be cool and unruffled and to let them know there were hundreds of banks who would love to partner with Sullivan and Gillespie if they chose to pass on the loan. She was pulling it off, too, to his amazement.

Sullivan looked down at the Rolex on his wrist. It was ten minutes to five. Bankers liked to wind up the day at five sharp. Ten more minutes and they'd have their answer. At least he hoped they would. With stone-faced bankers, one never knew what was going on in their heads.

One of the bankers, the oldest, the most distinguished of the twelve, leaned forward and said, "I understand Mrs. de Silva has become a bit of a recluse since the tragic death of her family some years ago. We have no wish to intrude on her privacy. All we'll need is a letter of intent signed by Mrs. de Silva and her main brokerage house. If that can be arranged, then Virginia State and Trust will grant the loan. It will be the largest in the bank's history. In case you didn't know this," the man droned on, "Mrs. de Silva's great-grandfather was one of the bank's founding fathers. I used to give Anna all-day suckers when her daddy brought her into the bank as a little girl. I wonder if she remembers," he said vaguely.

"I'll certainly mention it when I see her, Mr. Peacher," Arden said smoothly. They had it. She'd pulled it off. She wanted to look over at Roland and shout it to the heavens. Instead, she kept her cool and with one exquisite manicured nail, opened a pale yellow folder. "Since Mrs. de Silva is in residence, I don't think she'll mind a late afternoon fax of confirmation. She's most anxious to wrap up this business. Believe it or not," she trilled, "unlike the rest of us working people, the Countess detests dealing with money issues. She's anxious to return to Spain to wind up her affairs there so she can take up permanent residency in Manassas."

Peacher stood up, reached for the paper Arden handed him and said, "Then we shouldn't keep the Countess waiting, should we?"

"I'm sure the Countess will appreciate the courtesy, Mr. Peacher."

Roland felt like he was glued to his chair. It was a deal. It was a fucking deal! Arden had charmed, bullied, cajoled the board and they were a hair away from a done deal. His eyes started to water at the vast sums of money that would be within his and Arden's grasp. He could hardly wait to go home to share the news with his wife. A celebration dinner was certainly called for.

Behind him somewhere, he could hear the fax machine whirring. Everyone was suddenly on their feet, their hands outstretched. Roland unglued himself from his chair and stood up on wobbly legs. His partner was beaming as she smiled and shook hands all around, making small talk. He knew *schmoozing* was part of the game but all he wanted to do was get back to the office to see if Ellen Markham had signed off on the fax. Until he had that piece of paper in his hands, this was just a banking exercise and not a deal.

Finally, the last hand was shaken and they were out in the bank lobby, which was eerily silent. A guard opened the door, smiled and told them to have a nice evening.

"I want to scream and jump up and down, Rolly, but I know those guys are watching from the window. We did it! I honest to God think we did it. If that fax is in the machine when we get back to the office, you and I are going to celebrate like we've never celebrated before! All night long, Rolly, all night long!"

All thoughts of rushing home to his family disappeared. All Roland heard were the words, *all night long.*

Arden slid into the passenger side of Roland's Porsche. She buckled up before she fired up a cigarette. She blew a stream of smoke, then screamed at the top of her lungs. Roland burst out laughing as he, too, let out a roar of pleasure.

"Baby, baby, baby, tonight is our night!" Arden squealed in pleasure. "In your wildest dreams, did you even *think* this was a possibility, Rolly?"

Roland answered honestly. "No, I didn't. We aren't out of the woods yet. That Markham woman has to say yes to the bank. And then there is that other little matter of Sara Whittier."

"I refuse to allow you to rain on my parade, Roland. Hire a new batch of private detectives to find Sara. Pay her off. Give her a million dollars and get rid of her. We can afford it. The court found her guilty. Sara Whittier is old news, darling. I don't want you wasting your time thinking about her. And, it's time to take down those damn pictures in the office. That's the first thing I'm going to do when we get back."

Twenty minutes later, Roland downshifted as he roared into the parking lot at the offices of Sullivan and Gillespie. "Give some thought to that Markham woman finding her before we do. Sara Whittier can make a good case for herself."

"Oh, pooh. You worry too much. When do you think we're going to meet the Countess? I've never met a Countess. Do we have to bow and curtsy? I'll kiss her ass if I have to. All that money! I'm going to buy houses all over the world. I'm going to allow myself to be waited on hand and foot. I'm going to get a massage and a facial every day. I'll hire a personal trainer. One of us should buy a plane; one of those

Gulfstreams. We'll travel with our laptops making Countess de Silva richer than she already is."

Roland climbed out of the car and walked around to open the door for Arden. "There is something I want to do, Arden. I want to pay back all of Sara's investors. I want to do it so I can sleep at night. If you don't want to do it, then I'll do it on my own."

Arden stood tall and smoothed down her skirt and suit jacket. "Darling, think about the repercussions. If there's a way to do it without it funneling back to us, I'll go along with it. We'll talk about it and work out a way to do it." She stood on her toes and kissed him long and hard to seal the bargain.

Patsy Sullivan stared down at the parking lot from her husband's office. Her eyes filled with tears but her jaw was grimly set. She backed away from the window and looked around the office; the office she'd never step foot in again. Never.

Patsy Sullivan did two things before leaving the offices of Sullivan and Gillespie. First she quickly made a copy of the papers in the fax machine. The second thing she did was to take down the two photographs of Sara Whittier from her husband's office and the one in his partner's office. She slipped both into her carryall and left the firm by the rear entrance.

Patsy walked around the block to a private parking lot and paid her fifteen dollars to retrieve her Volvo station wagon. While she waited for her car to be brought to her, she called home. Her youngest son answered the phone, sounding so grown-up that Patsy felt tears well up in her eyes. "Hi, honey, I just called to say Mommy is on her way home. And, I have a surprise, candy apples, but only if you eat all your dinner. Tell Martha I'll be home in half an hour. Be nice to your sister, honey." Her son's whoop of pleasure allowed the tears to roll down her cheeks.

"I hear the fax machine!" Yoko said.

"Well, don't just stand there! Go get it! Let's see what our pigeons have to say."

Yoko ran out to the hall and down the steps to where the fax machine was. She didn't bother to read the papers, she just yanked them out of the machine and raced back to the kitchen where Myra, Alexis and Kathryn were preparing dinner. She handed over the two sheets of paper to Myra.

The women waited patiently as Myra read the papers in her hand. "Ladies, the Virginia State Trust is prepared to grant an astronomical loan to Sullivan and Gillespie. Do you believe that? They must be fools!"

Alexis couldn't help herself. Both clenched fists shot in the air as she danced a little jig. "That has to mean they mortgaged everything they own. It's *sooooo* much money."

Myra smiled. "Annie told me her grandfather was one of the founding fathers of the bank. Maybe it was her great-grandfather. I don't suppose it matters since they'll grant the loan, which we will help ourselves to as soon as Charles gives us the go-ahead. Tomorrow morning, Miss Markham will inform Miss Gillespie and Mr. Sullivan that Countess de Silva would like a face-to-face meeting. Miss Markham will also let them know that it still is not definite that they have the account. The Countess will make her decision after she meets with them. They also need to be informed that we've hired the best private detectives in the area to find Miss Sara Whittier. We want that to hang over their heads."

The women all hugged Alexis. "You happy?" Kathryn asked boisterously.

"Oh, yeah," Alexis drawled. "Those two are spending their money right this moment."

"I hope they have a good return policy," Myra said quietly.

Chapter 21

If Roland Sullivan had had a tail, it would have been between his legs as he walked into his house two days later at eight o'clock in the morning. His wife ignored him as she ushered the children out the front door to wait for the school bus. She kissed them both and told them to have a good day.

Patsy's eyes burned when the children looked longingly at their father's back. She was glad her older children weren't here to see what was about to transpire between their parents.

Still in her robe, Patsy walked back to the kitchen where she poured herself a cup of coffee. She wasn't a mean person or a vindictive one, but this morning she'd had enough. She poured the remainder of the coffee in the pot down the sink. She leaned against the kitchen counter, eyeing her husband over the rim of her coffee cup with "Mom" written on it. There was a matching cup in the cabinet that said "Dad". Roland always drank his coffee out of it. The kids hadn't given it to him, she had. She reached behind her for the cup, held it in the air and then dropped it on the ceramic tile at her husband's feet.

"What the hell! Why did you do that? What's wrong with you?"

"You're what's wrong with me, Roland. Look at you! You look like what you are, an adulterer. You reek of perfume, marijuana and *sex*. You've been gone for two whole days without even a phone call. You're wearing the same clothes you left here in the day before yesterday. That alone tells me all I need to know about where you've been. I'm filing for divorce and I want you out of this house before the children get home from school. If you aren't out of here, I'll call the police to forcefully remove you. I *will* do it, Roland."

Roland stared at his wife, a look of horror on his face. He looked around at the cozy comfortable kitchen his wife had decorated. The kids liked to do their homework at the old oak table. They sat at the table to eat their after-school snacks, usually sliced apples, a cookie and a glass of milk. He'd personally never seen them at the table but Patsy had told him about it. The kitchen always smelled of cinnamon and vanilla. He liked this kitchen, liked having his morning coffee sitting at the table by the big bow window with the ferns hanging from the hooks Patsy had screwed into the window frame.

"You can't mean that, Patsy. I know I haven't been home much lately but I've been working on this stupendous deal. I think we nailed it down two days ago. I've been working around the clock finalizing the details. Last night I worked through the night on all the last minute details," Roland lied with a straight face. "I told you about Countess de Silva. Don't you remember?"

"You're a liar, Roland. I wouldn't believe anything you said if your hand was on the Bible when you were saying it. I want you out of here before the children come home from school. Now, if you'll excuse me, I have to get dressed."

Roland's hand snaked out to reach for his wife's arm. Patsy shook herself free and froze him in place with a scathing look. "Take your hand off me. God knows where that hand has been."

"Patsy, wait! This deal will make us rich beyond our wildest dreams. We'll be able to travel all over the world. You can quit your job. We can hire private tutors for the kids when we travel. We'll have houses all over the world with servants, chauffeurs, nannies for the little guys. I can work on my laptop. I won't have to go to the office every day. We hit the big time, Patsy. Don't do this. Take a step back and give me a chance. I did all this for *us*. That's why I've been gone so much."

Patsy started to laugh and couldn't stop. Finally she was able to gasp, "And you think I believe all that? None of that means *diddly* to me. I like this house. I like being a Mom and a teacher. I like going to the kids' activities and driving them everywhere. I like having dinner with my kids and I like tucking them into bed at night and listening to their prayers. When was the last time *you* did that? I don't want houses all over the world. I don't want or need all that. Do not, I repeat, do not ever say you did all that for me. You did it for that woman you're screwing around with. I was at your office the other day, Roland. I saw you kissing Arden Gillespie in the parking lot. It looked to me like your tongue was all the way down to her belly button so don't lie to me and say you worked late. When the kids went to sleep that night, I drove to the office and it was locked and dark. Then I drove to her apartment and there was your car right in front of her building. You make me sick. Pack your bags and get out of here. I'm sick and tired of being made a fool of."

"Patsy . . . Look, I'm sorry. Don't do this. Please. I'll find a way to dissolve the partnership. I'll never see her again. I'm begging you, Patsy, don't do this," Roland moaned.

Patsy ignored his pleading and walked away, then turned around and retraced her steps into the kitchen. "Go to the authorities and tell them the truth about Sara Whittier. I know you had something to do with that young woman going to prison. You and that . . . that . . . slut you've been sleeping with. Do you think I'm stupid, Roland? After Sara went to prison you suddenly had bushels of money. You bought vacation homes, you bought that Porsche. The bank accounts quadrupled. I am so glad I never spent a penny of that money but you wouldn't know that, would you? I've been living off my salary, I've been supporting the kids and paying the mortgage on this house. That money you worship is evil money. That's all I have to say."

Roland sat down in the breakfast nook. He had no idea how long he'd been sitting when he looked up to see Betty, Patsy's part-time housekeeper. She put a cup of coffee in front of him. A blank expression on his face, he stared up at the woman. Yesterday, if he'd been asked to describe Betty, he wouldn't have been able to do so. She had a plain, honest face that was now registering disapproval.

Roland gulped at the scalding coffee. He burned his tongue but he barely noticed. He looked over at Betty who was emptying the dishwasher. "This is a nice kitchen, isn't it? I like the brick and the green plants. Patsy has a good eye for decorating."

"Yes, she does, Mr. Sullivan."

Roland looked at the refrigerator where all kinds of magnets, notes and schedules covered just about every inch of the doors. His family was a busy family that he was no longer a part of. He felt like crying.

Carrying his cup of coffee, Roland made his way up the stairs to the second floor. He passed his wife who was on the way down, her purse over her shoulder. "Be sure you're out of here before the children get home. Take everything you need now, because I don't want you coming back here unless you're invited. I plan to change the locks later this afternoon. Take *everything*, Roland."

Everything meant he'd have to make at least a dozen trips unless he rented a U-Haul. Well, that wasn't going to happen. First things first. He showered, shaved and dressed in casual clothes before he hauled out his suitcases. He'd had no idea he had so many clothes. Clothes that Patsy or Betty laundered, suits that Patsy took to the cleaners.

Roland lost track of all the trips he made out to his car. He'd have to get a hotel room until he found a suitable apartment.

When his car was packed to the top, he called the Marriott to engage a suite for an indefinite period of time. He made four trips before he finally settled into the suite decorated in bright orange, yellow and brown. He'd be here only to sleep so he would have to tolerate the decor until a suitable apartment could be found. Roland opened the minibar and popped a bottle of Beck's beer. He gulped at it, finishing it in three long gulps. He opened a second bottle. Now, he had to sit here and think about what had just happened to him and what, if anything, he was going to do about it.

While Roland Sullivan contemplated his future, his wife Patsy was being escorted down the hall by an intern to District Attorney Jack Emery's office.

Jack got up from his desk to walk around and

shake hands with Mrs. Patricia Sullivan. He wondered if he knew this pleasant-looking lady because her name sounded familiar. Right now she looked frazzled.

"What can I do for you, Mrs. Sullivan?"

The woman played with her wedding ring, sliding it up and down over her knuckle. "I'm not sure, Mr. Emery. Maybe I should have gone to an attorney but I thought he might send me here so I . . . I decided to come here on my own. A while back, four years or so, a young lady—this young lady," Patsy said, pulling Sara Whittier's picture out of her bag and handing it over to Jack, "was sent to prison for something I am almost certain she didn't do. I hate that I'm here saying these things but I have my children to think of."

Jack looked down at the picture he was holding. Alexis Thorne stared up at him. His stomach immediately crunched into a hard knot. *Son of a bitch.*

Patsy Sullivan continued. "I think my husband and his partner framed Sara Whittier and I think they're going to do something else that . . . that is . . . sort of like that," she finished lamely.

Jack licked his bottom lip. He hoped his voice didn't give him away. "Do you have any proof? What makes you think . . . ?"

Patsy didn't wait for him to finish. "First of all I want you to understand something, Mr. Emery. My husband and I are having serious marital problems. I insisted he move out of the house this morning. He's been having an affair with his business partner. No, no, my coming here has nothing to do with their affair. I've accepted that and have tried to move on. Now, Roland and his partner are a hair away from securing the account of one of the richest women in the world. My husband was bragging this morning about how much money we would have. I can't prove anything but I suspect the two of them are going to somehow scam this woman. I guess what I want to know is if there is a way your department can conduct some sort of investigation into . . . into whatever it is the two of them are doing. I would like to find Sara Whittier but I don't know how to go about it. I thought you might have some advice for me. I know as sure as I am sitting here that the young lady did not do what she was accused of.

"After Sara went to prison, my husband and his partner had money to burn. No one even questioned it. I did, though, for all the good it did me. Sara was . . . is a lovely person. She truly cared about her elderly clients. She was incredibly diligent. She would never cheat them the way my husband and his partner said she did.

"Isn't this matter something your office would investigate? Or, should I go to the police? I don't know what to do, Mr. Emery."

Well, shit, he didn't know what she should do either. "I can't initiate an investigation unless I have more to go on than what you're telling me. I need proof, Mrs. Sullivan."

Patsy stood up. She looked dejected. "I think I knew you were going to say that. I went to the police the last time and they didn't do anything. None of them would believe me. Sara wouldn't do what she was accused of. You have so many resources, Mr. Emery, can't you find her for me? She might have proof. I suppose that's an empty hope. If she had proof, she wouldn't have gone to prison. I'm sorry I took up your time."

Jack literally leaped off his chair and raced toward the door where Patsy Sullivan was standing. "Look, I can't promise anything. What I might, and I stress the word *might*, be able to do is to make some inquiries on my own. Please, don't get your hopes up. By the way, did you discuss this with your husband?"

Patsy snorted. "I talked till I was breathless. He got extremely angry. Of course he denied every accusation I made. He said I didn't know what I was talking about. This morning, after I told him to leave, I also told him to find Sara Whittier and make things right. Of course he ignored me.

"Roland used to be a decent man. He was a good husband and a doting father. Then Arden Gillespie started to work at his firm. In very short order, Roland made her a partner. I don't know if that was before or after the affair started. I blame her more than I blame him but he didn't have to go down that road if he didn't want to. By the way, do you know a good divorce lawyer?"

"As a matter of fact, I do. Her name is Nicole Quinn. If you like, I can give her a call."

"I would appreciate it, Mr. Emery."

Jack watched as the woman's eyes filled with tears. He patted her shoulder and again promised to do what he could on his own time. He asked for her home phone number. Patsy handed him a business card that said she was a special needs teacher. Her home phone, her cell phone, her email and fax number were listed on the card. Jack stuffed it in his pocket. It wasn't until he got back to his desk that he realized Patsy Sullivan had forgotten to take the picture of Sara Whittier, a.k.a., Alexis Thorne, with her.

Jack looked at the clock on the wall. It was 10:50. He didn't have to be in court till one o'clock. He could take an early lunch even though he wasn't hungry. He needed to call Nikki to report what had just happened and he didn't want to call from the office.

Outside in the bright spring sunshine, Jack whipped out his cell. Nikki picked up on the second ring. They made small talk but it was obvious to Jack that his lady love was still ticked off at him. He did his best to be lighthearted and jovial even though he didn't feel that way. "I called you for a reason, Nik. Tell me what, if anything, you want me to do." He repeated the conversation with Patsy Sullivan in precise detail. "She wants me to find Sara Whittier."

On the other end of the cell phone, Nikki Quinn's mind raced. "What do you think, Jack? Do you think a meeting between Mrs. Sullivan and Alexis might help us?"

"Jesus, Nikki, I don't know. I thought you guys had a lock on this thing. Why risk rocking the boat with a meeting that isn't going to solve anything? At least at the moment. My advice would be to leave it alone. I don't see anything wrong with telling Alexis she has one person on the outside who believes in her. I think she might like to hear that.

"Oh, I almost forgot. Mrs. Sullivan asked me if I knew a good divorce lawyer. I recommended you. When it comes right down to it, she might not go through with it. The man is her children's father. She did seem pretty determined, though."

"Thanks for the endorsement. I'll let you know if she calls. I think you're right and I will tell Alexis. You aren't going to believe this but Kathryn said Virginia State Trust okayed that mega loan. Do you believe that?"

"Hell no! I for one will never use that bank. By the way, how are your guests?"

"My guests are fine. Charles gets home tonight. He'll take over. For all I know, he might give them their walking papers. I did what I had to do, Jack."

"I know. I'll call you later, okay?"

"Love you, Jack. I mean it."

Jack's voice turned flirty. "Bet you say that to all the guys who call you on your cell phone."

"Nah, only the ones whose names are Jack."

Jack laughed as he snapped his cell phone shut. Now, he was in the mood for some Dirty Dogs. He made a bet with himself that he could eat five of the fully loaded dogs and burp only once.

Chapter 22

The limousine glided to a smooth stop outside the guardhouse. Arthur, working the midnight shift, snapped to attention. "Mr. Martin, Mrs. de Silva said I was to open the gates for you no matter what the hour. You're free to go up to the house."

Charles closed the back window. Anna de Silva laughed aloud. "I am so enjoying this cloak and dagger experience. However will we tell the man that I am the real Mrs. de Silva?"

"Just say you had a face-lift," Charles quipped.

"I've been thinking of getting one of those. Face-lifts, I mean."

"Whatever for? You're beautiful as you are. Never tamper with perfection, my dear."

Annie laughed again. "That's something my

husband would have said. Oh, Charles, I can't believe I'm home again. It seems like a hundred years since I've been here. Do you think Myra will be up and waiting for us?"

"I can personally guarantee it, Annie. I'm sure the others will be awake also. They can't wait to meet you."

"But it's three o'clock in the morning."

"So it is. Look, your house is lit from top to bottom. I think that answers your question. I wouldn't be a bit surprised to find a lovely buffet all set up. The prodigal returns. That kind of thing."

Annie rolled down the window. She sighed happily. "It smells like home. It really does. Spring here is so different from Spain." She sighed again. "I should have come back a long time ago."

Charles placed a hand on Annie's arm. "You weren't ready before. You're the living proof that you can go home again. Ah, I just saw the back light go on. I can promise you on the count of five all my ladies will be waiting outside for you."

Before the limousine came to a full stop, Annie was out of the car and running to the back entrance. Myra, also running, met her halfway. They hugged, laughed and cried and then it was Charles's turn. "Oh, my darling, I missed you so," Myra said, kissing him soundly. "Come, come, it's chilly out here." Myra linked her arm with Charles' as she made introductions all around.

In the large kitchen with a fireplace big enough to roast a pig, Annie danced and twirled around, looking at everything, touching this and that, remembering when she lived here as a child. "I'm not going to sleep. I'm going to sit right here and wait for the sun to come up. Then I'm going to explore every inch of this place to test my memory. Oh, food, good! Myra, how can I ever thank you for shaking me loose from that Spartan existence I was living?"

Myra, still holding Charles's hand, smiled. "No thanks are necessary, Annie. That's what friends are for. We should be thanking you for going along with this charade. Because of you, we're actually going to make it work. Our pigeons are in the coop so to speak. Now, let's sit down and eat this wonderful food the girls prepared for your arrival. I'll bring you up to date as we munch along. But first I need to speak with Charles so if you'll excuse me for a moment. I'll be right back."

Charles felt a prickle of alarm as his lady love led him into the dining room and closed the door behind her. "Charles, when I said our pigeons are in the coop, I wasn't exactly truthful. Actually," she said, wringing her hands, "we have two extra pigeons. They . . . ah . . . just more or less flew into the coop. Nikki did what she had to do. She did tell me more or less after the fact, but I agreed. So did the others. I suppose we could have called you but what could you have done from Spain? Nikki had to act quickly."

"Dear girl, will you please just spit it out."

Myra did just that. "Now, we don't know what

to do. How long can we keep those two reporters incommunicado?"

To Myra's relief, Charles smiled. "Nikki did that, eh? Good for her. I'm glad she stepped up to the plate and acted as quickly as she did. If you don't mind, I think I'll grab a sandwich and some coffee and head out to the farm. I slept on the plane so I'm rested." He wiggled his eyebrows and said, "But I'll be back later."

"In that case, you may go," Myra twinkled. "I missed you, Charles."

"Not half as much as I missed you, old girl."

Myra did a little eyebrow wiggling of her own. "Listen to them, Charles. Isn't it wonderful to hear Annie laughing like that. I just know Kathryn is regaling her with all kinds of stories. It's a good thing, isn't it, Charles?"

"Yes, it is a good thing. Annie has a reason to get up in the morning now. She told me on the flight over that she's going to buy a whole bunch of dogs, cats and even a parrot."

In the kitchen, Myra made a sandwich and filled a thermos for Charles. Five minutes later, he was gone.

Myra sat down at the table with a cup of coffee and a sandwich of her own. She looked around at the women who now filled her life. "Did you bring Annie up to date?"

"Oh, Myra, they only got to the tip of the iceberg. They told me they had enough stories to last a week. Kathryn was just telling me about your road trip. She promised to take me on her next job. I can't wait."

"Business first, Annie. Right now, we need

you in the Sisterhood. Afterward, you can ride shotgun with Murphy. Now . . ."

Nikki bolted upright, her eyes frantic. She listened to the quiet that surrounded her. What had woken her? She slipped out of bed and walked over to the window. The sky was clear, the moon almost full. Her gaze went to the garage. It was dark and quiet. That had to mean her guests were asleep. She turned around to see the rocker moving back and forth. "Barb?" she whispered.

"Uh huh."

"Did you wake me? Is something wrong?"

"No. Charles is home. His car just arrived. See the headlights arching on the window. Relax, Nik."

"Easy for you to say. I just know he's going to chew my head off. I have to go downstairs."

"Go ahead. It's four in the morning, you know."

"I know what time it is. Are you going to be here for a while?"

"I'll wait for you. Calm down, okay?"

Nikki slipped into her robe and slippers. She raced down the stairs to the kitchen in time to see Charles rearming the security system. She allowed herself to be hugged and kissed on the cheek.

Her voice was shaky, fearful, when she said, "Charles, I did something . . ."

"I know all about it, dear. Myra told me when I dropped Annie off in Manassas. I would have done exactly the same thing. Thank you for stepping up to the plate the way you did. If you hadn't acted as quickly as you did, we could be facing a disaster."

Nikki was so relieved she grew light-headed. "What are we going to do with them, Charles? We can't keep them over there forever."

"I'll decide before it gets light out. It might be a good idea to invite myself for breakfast." His eyes twinkled as he patted Nikki on the shoulder. "Right now, I'm going to take a shower and get out of this suit. Coffee would be nice when I come back down."

"I can do that, Charles. As Myra says, run along."

The moment Charles disappeared up the back staircase, Nikki took great gulping breaths before she started to make fresh coffee.

"Told you it would be all right."

"You really get around, don't you?"

A tinkling laugh. *"I'm everywhere. You're on the edge, Nik. Relax. It's all going to work out. As far as I know, Charles has never failed to make things come out right. Just trust him."*

"I do but you have to admit, kidnapping two reporters is a bit over the top."

That same tinkling laugh again. *"Not when you compare it to the alternative. I'm going to drop in on Mom and Annie. It will be nice to see her again."*

"Barb, can you . . . ah . . . what I mean is, can you . . . see . . . feel . . . Annie's family? How does all that work? Why don't they speak to Annie?"

"Maybe Annie isn't open to it like you and Mom were. Some people aren't."

"Couldn't you . . . ah, you know, goose them a little in that direction?"

The tinkling laugh circled overhead. *"Not my job, Nik. See ya."*

Nikki whirled around when she felt a hand tap her shoulder. "Oh, Isabelle, you startled me. What are you doing up so early?"

"I heard Charles. What did he say? Is he okay with our guests being in residence?"

Nikki sighed as she watched the coffee dripping into the pot. "Believe it or not, he was great about it. Said I did a good job and he would have done the same thing. He complimented me, Isabelle. God, I feel like someone took ten thousand pounds off my shoulders."

"That's great. It's out of our hands and into Charles's capable hands. We should celebrate. Then again, maybe we shouldn't. Isn't there some kind of saying about chickens coming home to roost or something?"

Nikki laughed. "It is indeed out of our hands. Today is the day Gillespie and Sullivan meet the bogus Anna de Silva. Alexis must be like a cat on a hot griddle. I know I would be if I were in her shoes."

"I wish we could be there! I hate being out of the loop," Isabelle said as she held her cup toward Nikki.

Nikki carried her own cup over to the table and sat down. "Jack called me yesterday. He told me that Mrs. Sullivan showed up at his office yesterday and told him she thought her husband and his partner framed Alexis but that she had no proof. And, she went on to tell him she thinks they're scamming this new client they are trying to woo, but again she has no proof. She asked him if he knew a good divorce lawyer and he recommended me."

"How come you didn't tell me this yesterday? Not that it would have made any difference," Isabelle grumbled.

"Because I went to bed at nine-thirty and you weren't here. I'm telling you now. Oh, here's Charles!"

"Good morning, Isabelle," Charles said, bending over to kiss her on the cheek.

"It's good to see you back home, Charles. It's been kind of lonely with everyone gone."

"Well, I am back now and I will be cracking my whip," he joked. He reached out for the cup of black coffee that Nikki held in her hand. He sat down and relaxed. "Is there anything I need to know?"

"Not really."

"Well then, the sun is creeping over the horizon so I guess it's time for me to pay a visit to our guests. I'll need a whistle, Nikki."

When the kitchen door closed behind Charles, the two women rushed to the kitchen window. They watched him cross the yard to the garage, climb the steps, knock on the door, and then disappear from view. They looked at one another, their eyes full of questions.

Nikki shrugged. "We'll just have to wait and see what happens. More coffee?"

"Well sure, fill 'er up."

* * *

Ted Robinson opened the door, his hair standing on end. He was dressed in boxer shorts and a tee shirt that said he was a Redskins fan. A dog yapped at his feet as two cats hissed at this intrusion. "Whatever you're selling, we don't want it."

"Good morning, Mr. Robinson. Allow me to introduce myself: Charles Martin."

Ted jerked his head backward. "Yo, Maggie, you better come out here. Our host is here." He turned back to face Charles. "We don't do breakfast. Actually, we don't do much of anything these days except read and watch television." His tone changed. "What the hell do you want?"

Charles brushed past Robinson to enter the apartment. Maggie appeared wearing a long white nightgown, her curly hair just as messy as Ted's.

"Please, sit down," Charles said.

"Why should we?" Ted snarled angrily.

"Because I told you to. It wasn't an invitation. It was an order. You are in no position to quibble, Mr. Robinson." Ted and Maggie immediately perched on the edge of the couch.

Charles waited a moment until he was sure he had the reporters' attention. "You have caused my friends and myself considerable angst. That's why you're here. I want you to know I can keep you here forever if I so choose. I can also spirit you away and you'll never be found."

"That sounds like a goddamn threat," Ted blustered.

"It is, Mr. Robinson."

"Or? I sensed an *or* in there somewhere."

"Or I can simply allow both of you to leave. I can, if you are interested, guarantee you both positions at the *New York Post* if you care to relocate."

Both reporters stared at Charles with suspicion and hope in their eyes. "And why would you do that?" Ted demanded.

"To avoid having to kill you," Charles said. To both reporters it sounded like Charles was discussing the weather.

"We'll take it," Maggie said quietly. "Ted?"

Ted nodded. "Are there any other . . . restrictions?"

Charles smiled. "I've killed many people while I was in service to the Queen. I will always be able to find you. There is no place you can run to. No place you can hide that I won't be able to find you. If you ever breathe one word that I don't like, and I will know if you do, I will kill you. It's that simple."

Charles stood up and walked to the door. "You are now free to leave. You have one hour. When you're ready to go to your car, call the house and I'll call off the dogs."

When the door closed behind Charles, Maggie wrapped her arms around Ted. "We're going, aren't we?"

"Damn straight we're going. Hurry up and pack."

"Is this the end of . . . this . . . this crap? I don't want to die, Ted."

Ted's eyes were narrowed to slits. "We'll talk

when we're out of here. It's not the end of the world, Maggie. Think of it as an adventure."

Maggie looked up at the tall man standing next to her. She shivered at what she was seeing in his eyes and face.

Chapter 23

Arden Gillespie walked into Roland Sullivan's office dressed in a long mud-colored sack dress with matching straw sandals. She wore no jewelry and her lustrous blond hair was pulled back into a severe bun. Roland thought she looked awful and said so. He was wearing a charcoal gray suit, white shirt and power tie. His wing tips were polished to a high sheen.

He didn't want to go to Manassas. He didn't want to meet Anna de Silva because then this whole damn thing would be *real.* He wished he could turn the clock back to another time. To before AG. Before Arden Gillespie. Back then he was happy, truly happy making a go of his small brokerage house, happy with Patsy and the kids. Happy planning for holidays, vacations, and just hanging out in his family room in the evenings, holding Patsy's hand while they watched television, talking about their day, sharing a bottle of wine.

Greed and lust were terrible things even though the lust was pleasurable at the time, and spending money as if he printed it himself, just as pleasurable.

"What did you do with the pictures?" he barked.

"I took mine down and trashed it. What did you do with yours?"

Roland looked at the blank space on the wall where Sara Whittier's picture had hung for so long. "I didn't do anything with it. I thought you took it down. Are you telling me you didn't?"

"No, I didn't. What difference does it make as long as it's gone? By the way, what's wrong with you? You look terrible. You could use some concealer under your eyes. Not sleeping?"

"No, I'm not sleeping. You might as well hear it from me. Patsy booted me out of the house. She's filing for divorce. I moved to the Marriott four days ago."

Arden looked honestly surprised. "Why?"

"Because she knows about us. She saw me kissing you in the parking lot last week. She staked out your apartment those two days we celebrated. I know I've told you this before but I'm going to tell you again, She never believed Sara Whittier did what we accused her of. She also thinks we're scamming de Silva. You want to run with that one, Arden, because I sure as hell don't. My gut tells me she's going to . . . I don't know what, but I know she's going to do something."

"That means you'll have to give her half of

everything," Arden said. "Sara is a dead issue. Did you hire a detective to find her like I told you to do? You didn't, did you? Why is it you leave everything up to me, Roland? All right, all right, I'll take care of it when we get back from Manassas. We should leave now or we're going to be late."

Roland turned away to stare out the window. "I just realized something. You don't have a conscience, do you?"

Arden stamped her foot. "It's a little late to be worrying about a conscience. Need I remind you that you were right there when all that business with Sara was going on. You couldn't wait to buy that fancy place in Aspen. So just shut up, Roland. I never want to hear you mention Sara Whittier to me again. Let's just get this over with so I can dump these clothes and fix my hair. I'll drive today," she said coldly.

Roland wished he had the willpower, the guts, to tell Arden to go to hell. He picked up his briefcase because he never went anywhere without it, and followed his partner from the room and out to the borrowed Saab.

They were halfway to Manassas when Arden took her eyes off the road long enough to look over at Roland. "Why didn't you move in with me?"

Roland didn't bother to answer. He stared out the window at the passing countryside, his thoughts jumbled. His mother always used to say money was the root of all evil. He wished she were still alive so he could tell her she was right.

Arden's voice turned cold. "You are going to

make an attempt to be civil and charming when we meet de Silva, aren't you?"

Roland stirred himself long enough to reply. "You don't have to worry about me."

"You screw this up, Roland, and I'll make sure you live to regret it. This is our chance at the brass ring. Listen to me, I don't give a hoot about that plump little wife of yours who thinks she has a brain and can threaten me through you. Nor do I care that she kicked you out of your house. Buy another one, a bigger, better one. If you're hung up on your kids and she won't let you see them, adopt some. Get a cat, for God's sake. Are we clear on all this, Roland?"

Christ Almighty, what did he ever see in this woman? Suddenly, he felt sick to his stomach. He was tempted to ask Arden to stop the car so he could upchuck but then he noticed she was making the turn into the de Silva estate. He took deep breaths to try and calm himself.

Arden waited for the guard to open the gate. This was all so . . . so royal, for want of a better word. She told herself she could now buy herself something just as grand as this lavish estate. She, too, could have a guardhouse to keep unwanted people away from her royal self. The thought so pleased her, she smiled.

And then they were standing at the front door ringing the bell. Yoko opened the door and ushered them inside. "Follow me, please. Miss Markham is waiting for you."

Arden stopped in her tracks. Roland bumped into her. Yoko kept on walking. "But I thought we were to meet with Mrs. de Silva," Arden called out. Yoko ignored her comment. Both brokers hurried to catch up.

Kathryn Lucas didn't bother to get up from her chair behind the highly polished desk. She motioned for Arden and Roland to sit down. Precisely in the middle of the desk was a bright red folder. She opened it, pretended to read. Her expression gave no clue as to what she was reading or thinking. Across the room, Yoko was watching the three with interest so she could report later to Alexis, Myra, and Annie.

Kathryn removed her reading glasses and looked across at the two brokers. "I must admit, I didn't think you would be able to secure a loan of the size we stipulated. Mrs. de Silva was as surprised as I was until I reminded her that Virginia State Trust was the new name of the bank her great-grandfather founded. After your meeting with Mrs. de Silva—if she doesn't change her mind, which she's been known to do at the eleventh hour—she will give the order to begin the transfer of her accounts to your firm.

"Mrs. de Silva likes to ask questions. Sometimes the questions are personal and sometimes they concern business. Honesty is always an excellent policy. Mrs. de Silva can give you ten minutes. Sumi will take you to the sunroom now to meet with Mrs. de Silva." It was an abrupt dismissal.

Yoko stood up and motioned for Arden and Roland to follow her.

Myra Rutledge, a.k.a. Countess Anna de Silva, was sitting on a straight wooden chair dressed in a long flowing white muslin dress. Her back was ramrod stiff and she had a magazine in her hands. She wore ropy sandals and a crown of spring flowers. She smiled as she extended her hand, palm down. There was no other furniture in the sunroom, not even a carpet. The sun coming in the wraparound windows was blinding.

Arden walked forward, uncertain if she was supposed to kiss the extended hand or not. What the hell, she dropped to one knee and did just that. Roland followed suit.

"It's nice to meet you, Countess," Arden said. Since there was no place to sit, she simply stepped backward and waited. Roland did the same thing.

Myra smiled again. "I want to congratulate you on securing the loan I required. Ellen and Sumi tell me you had to mortgage all your holdings. I approve. That proves to me you are dedicated to doing a good job for me. I'm sure you will be rewarded handsomely. I like to be upfront with the people who work for me. I am a demanding client. I do not tolerate excuses. Now, tell me about your families. I understand, Mr. Sullivan, that you have children. I am very fond of little ones. A picture will suffice."

Roland reached for his billfold and withdrew a small family snapshot. The picture was an old one where everyone was smiling into the camera.

"What a lovely family. Absolutely charming. I insist you all come to dinner one evening. I would love to meet your children. Ellen, before Mr. Sullivan leaves, set up a dinner meeting."

Myra turned her attention to Arden as she enjoyed the stricken look on Sullivan's face. "I understand you're a single career woman. Commendable. You don't look the part," she said sharply. "I expected business attire similar to Miss Markham's. I assume there is a lot to be said for . . . comfort."

Arden grappled for something to say in her defense. "I don't think one's ability should be judged on his or her apparel. I work a very long day that doesn't leave much time for shopping. I do like to be comfortable. I apologize if my outfit offends you." She cursed the article she'd read on de Silva that said she liked simple things. Then she cursed herself for believing it.

"Oh, it doesn't offend me," Myra said breezily.

Arden knew when to keep her mouth shut so she clammed up.

"Tell me what you will do if you fail to turn a profit on my holdings. You'll be wiped out financially."

"We won't fail. The word simply is not in our vocabulary," Roland said flatly.

"In that case, I must say good-bye. I will anticipate your first report. I don't ever want to hear one excuse about a stock, a fund, a bond, whatever. You're being paid to anticipate every market trend. Oh, dear, just one minute. Did your firm make good on Miss Whittier's accounts?"

"Of course," Arden lied coolly.

Myra looked over to where Kathryn was standing. "We really must find that young woman."

"We have several serious leads, Mrs. de Silva."

Confidence rang in Kathryn's voice. "We'll locate her, it's just a matter of time."

"You've never failed me yet, Ellen. Good-bye, Miss Gillespie, Mr. Sullivan."

Yoko appeared out of nowhere and escorted the couple from the barren sunroom and out to the front door. She opened it and then said, "Miss Markham will call you to set up an appropriate dinner date." It was all she could do not to push them out the door. She did, however, slam the door harder than was necessary before she scampered back to the sunroom where the others waited for her.

"Oh, Myra, you were wonderful!" Annie said. "Kathryn, you should have been an actress, and you, Yoko, you were exquisite. Darling Alexis, what do you think?"

Alexis liked this lady. She was everything Myra said she was. She smiled at the excited Countess. "I enjoyed watching them lie. I wish you could see Arden when she's dressed up. As I said before, they are both spending money in their minds. That's all either one of them thinks about."

Myra pulled off her gray wig and tossed it aside. "Wouldn't it be exciting if Alexis were to call Miss Gillespie and say, 'I understand you've been trying to reach me.' Then arrange a meeting between the two of them with the rest of us standing by in case of . . . foul play."

Yoko clapped her hands. "A wonderful idea. Should we do it before we clean out the bank account or after?"

Alexis sat down on a wicker chair. "It's not enough! I thought reducing the two of them to paupers would be enough but it isn't."

"Darling girl, they're going to go to prison. You said that's what you wanted," Myra said.

Alexis dropped her head into her hands. She started to cry. "I know that's what I said and I meant it. It just isn't enough."

Kathryn spoke. "I think what Alexis is trying to say is, it isn't personal enough. She wants to get her licks in and I for one understand that."

"I do, too," Yoko said.

"Then let's think of something that will make it personal," Annie said briskly. "I used to get wonderful ideas. Isn't that right, Myra?"

"Absolutely. All right, ladies, let's adjourn to the kitchen for coffee while we kick this around," Myra said.

Two hours later, Alexis was beaming from ear to ear. "It works for me!"

Countess Anna Ryland de Silva positively glowed. "I told you I was an idea person."

"We need to talk, Roland. Look, I'm sorry your wife is divorcing you. I guess I am surprised at your reaction. For some crazy reason, I thought you didn't care and that's why you stepped so willingly into my arms. You did come willingly, Roland. If you have regrets now, there's nothing I can do about it. We're going to be working very closely together so now might be a good time to set some ground rules. I say that because I assume our . . . relationship has come to a screeching halt. Or am I wrong?"

Roland removed his jacket and yanked at his tie. "No, you aren't wrong. I thought you were going to call a detective agency to find Sara Whittier. If those women out there in Manassas get to her before we do, all this," he said, waving his hand about, "is going to come crashing down around us. I'd get on it. Promise a bonus to the detective. Tell him we need to locate her yesterday."

Arden knew he was right. She hurried to her office and closed the door while she made her calls. An hour later she was convinced she had a dedicated detective who promised there would be no charge if he didn't locate the missing subject in thirty-six hours. That was good enough for her. She marched her way down the hall to Roland's office to tell him. She was stunned to see him sitting with his feet propped up on the desk, guzzling scotch. A *big* tumbler of scotch.

"We should have located Sara a long time ago and paid her off. Where are we going to get the money to do it now, Arden?" He sounded like he didn't care one way or the other.

"That is a problem. I guess I'm going to sell my jewelry and my Mercedes. You're going to have to sell your Porsche and your boat. That will be some serious money for starters. We'll pay her the rest once she relocates out of the area. Assuming she's still in these parts. For all we know, she could have gone back to Mississippi."

"I did try to find her once," Roland said, slurring his words. "She just dropped off the face of the earth. I should have tried harder."

Arden could feel anger starting to build. "You know what they say about letting sleeping dogs lie. I wish you'd get over it."

Roland continued drinking. "What do you suppose it's like being in prison? Eating that awful starchy food, being locked in a little space, having to shower with other people watching, working for twelve cents an hour. Going to bed at nine at night, getting up at five. Seeing visitors once a week, assuming anyone cares enough about you to visit. How did Sara survive all that?"

"Will you stop that!" Arden screamed shrilly. "I'm sick and tired of hearing you whining like this. It's over and done with. I have no desire to go to prison so I don't think about what it would be like. Obviously it isn't as bad as you say it is because Sara survived and even got out early for good behavior. Sara is a survivor just like I am. I don't know what the hell you are other than a *wuss*. Right now, you're a drunken *wuss*."

Roland finished his drink and immediately poured another. Arden eyed him with disgust before she left the office.

In her office, her mind raced. She knew in her gut that Roland was somehow, someway, going to screw things up. Maybe it was time to do something about him. Now that his fat little wife was dumping him, who would miss him if he disappeared? Then again, if he died, she'd be five million dollars richer from the Key Man insurance partner policy. She could handle the de Silva account on her own if she hired a few buttoned up financial MBAs. Her mind continued to race as idea after idea flitted through her head.

Chapter 24

Arden Gillespie paced her office in short, jerky steps as she puffed furiously on a cigarette she neither wanted nor needed. Each time she walked around her desk she stopped long enough to look at the screen of her computer monitor. Where were the accounts? They should have been transferred by now. Markham said she would set the transfer in motion the day they went to Manassas to meet with the Countess. A prickle of apprehension rippled up and down her arms as she puffed on her cigarette.

Arden wondered if she should mention her concerns to Roland who seemed oblivious to what was going on. He was more concerned with finding a new apartment and getting used to his secondhand car. She knew he was depressed over the fact that he had to sell his

Porsche and his boat. He was now driving a secondhand Lexus with 70,000 miles on it. All he did was whine about it. Today, he would be a snarling bear when she told him the private detective had had no luck in locating Sara Whittier. The detective had gone on to say he wasn't giving up because now it was a challenge.

The cigarette in Arden's hand had burned down to the filter. She stubbed it out and lit another one. The room was already cloudy with smoke. She wondered if the smoke alarm would go off. It was a nonsmoking building. Well, rules were for other people, not her.

She was in front of the computer again. Where were those goddamn accounts? A call to Ellen Markham would probably answer the question. Would calling that frozen ice queen be a sign of eagerness or insecurity? Or would it come across as professional? She was rattled and she knew it.

Arden opened the door to let the smoke from her office billow out into the hall. She walked back to the kitchen area to get a cup of coffee. She was surprised to see Roland leaning against the sink sipping his own cup of coffee. She tried for a light tone. "How's the apartment hunt going?"

"I found an apartment, fully furnished. I'll be moving in over the weekend."

"Is it nice?" Arden asked, making small talk.

"It's not the Ritz but it's all I need. There's an extra bedroom for the kids if Patsy lets them stay overnight." He shrugged.

Finally, Arden couldn't stand it any longer.

"The detective hasn't found Sara Whittier and the de Silva accounts haven't been transferred. I didn't want to call the Markham woman without your approval."

Roland, who had been staring into space, brought his focus back to Arden. "It's been three days! You're just telling me this now! If you don't want to call the Markham woman, try calling the brokerage houses where the accounts are. The broker's name is at the top of the account. You have a complete list, don't you?"

"Of course. I just don't want to look like an eager fool by calling. The houses might be stalling because they're losing the accounts. We've done the same thing when a client wants to switch."

"It's one o'clock, Arden. Make at least one call. Get the lay of the land. If you don't like what you hear, call the Markham woman."

"All right, as long as you think it's a good idea. Roland . . . would you like to come over for dinner? I was planning on making some Thai food. I know you like it. Just dinner, a few glasses of wine. Around seven-thirty. I'll have to stop at the market on the way home."

"Yeah, sure. Beats takeout or the Marriott café."

Arden left her partner staring into space. For some reason, she felt nervous and jittery. Something, somewhere, was wrong.

The house in Manassas was alive with activity as the Sisters prepared to make the trip back to Pinewood. Myra stood by the kitchen door talking to Annie.

"Annie, are you sure you can handle this? If you have any doubts, now is the time to voice them."

"Surely you jest, Myra. I can't wait for tomorrow morning when I go to the bank. I don't want you to worry one little bit. After I do the bank gig," she laughed using one of Kathryn's favorite words, "can I come out to Pinewood?"

"No, Annie. You have to stay here. All kinds of people are going to be visiting you. The SEC, the Feds, all those bank officers. Your staff is here and can attest to your recent arrival. Your two guards are on an extended vacation. You'll have to monitor the security gates on your own. Alexis typed up a set of instructions for you. She left it in your bedroom. Refer to it if things get muddled. Whatever you do, do not call any of us at Pinewood. You can, however, call Nikki at the firm since she is your new attorney. She will cover your tracks. Be careful what you say. In this high-tech age, everything can be tracked and traced. I learned this from Charles."

"It's all so exciting. I wish I had . . . oh, Myra, I wish so many things. It's not too late for me, is it?"

"It's never too late, my friend. You're back among the living. Stick with us, kid, and life will become even more interesting. Oh, Annie, don't you just love those girls?"

"I do, Myra, I do. I'm so glad you're allowing me to become a part of all this. When is Charles going to . . . to do the deed?"

Myra looked down at her watch. "He said he was going to transfer the money at two o'clock.

He's quite punctual. I imagine the bank will be calling you shortly afterward."

"We're ready, Myra," Alexis called from the kitchen door.

Annie stood in the doorway waving to all of her new best friends. She stood there for a long time before she turned around and walked over to the refrigerator. She made herself a ham sandwich and poured a cup of coffee. As she sipped and chewed, she kept her eyes on the digital clock on the stove as the numbers ticked off. When the red numerals hit two o'clock, Annie drew a deep breath and held it.

Now, according to Kathryn, the dark brown stuff was going to hit the fan. She was so excited she could hardly stand it.

The ladies of Pinewood clustered around Charles as he flexed his fingers dramatically. The clock readout on the computer read 1:59. Precisely at two o'clock, Charles's nimble fingers hit the keyboard. A blizzard of numbers raced across the screen for a full five minutes. When the screen turned black, the women gasped.

"What happened? What's wrong?" they chorused.

Charles whirled around, a huge smile on his face. "It's done! The money is gone. All of it. At this moment it is being transferred all over the world six times over. I have . . . ah . . . people who are seeing to the multiple transfers. It will take *years and years* for anyone to trace the transfers. Alexis, dear, your revenge is *almost* complete."

The women hugged and congratulated Alexis.

"When will Gillespie and Sullivan know something is wrong?" Nikki asked.

"Probably by the close of business today, possibly sooner. I'm a little surprised that it hasn't already happened, since Kathryn assured them the accounts would be transferred ASAP. It's my opinion they are playing it cool so as not to appear overeager. I'm also certain that by today they are starting to worry a little," Charles said.

"I'm starving," Kathryn said.

"You're always starving. You're like a bottomless pit," Alexis said, punching Kathryn lightly on the arm. "Isabelle promised to make crab cakes for lunch."

"Run along, ladies, I have work to do. Save me some of the crab cakes."

"We will, dear. Come along, girls, I'm rather hungry myself. We can chatter nonstop and not disturb Charles."

Lunch was a rousing affair, to Myra's delight, as the women insisted she sit and allow herself to be waited on. They giggled and laughed as they talked about everything and anything from Ted Robinson and Maggie Spritzer, to Yoko and her date the following day. All of them jumped in to plan Yoko's wardrobe until she said it was a martial arts exhibition and there was no need to dress up. "Undress," she giggled, "would be more like it."

"You naughty girl!" Myra smiled. Yoko tittered again as she placed silverware on the table.

"About tonight . . ." Nikki said.

"I have it covered." Alexis said. "I'm going to call Arden at the office around three. I plan on saying I understand she's been trying to locate me. I'll make arrangements to go to her apartment around eight or eight-thirty. I will take a bottle of doctored-up wine that will knock them out for several hours, thanks to Charles and his never ending supply of medicines. I'm going to pick up my friend at seven. He knows what to do and for a princely sum of money, thanks to Myra, he will do what I want. When he's finished, he will relocate to Miami, courtesy of Myra. Like I said, I have it covered. Who wants to go with me?" Alexis asked.

"Count me in. I wouldn't miss this for the world," Nikki said.

"Okay, but you can't come into the apartment until they're out cold."

"Gotcha. What about your friend?" Nikki asked.

"Well, he's a little flaky, loses track of time, things like that. You'd do me a big favor if you could pick him up. You'll enjoy his company. He's a real trip, if you know what I mean."

"Consider it done," Nikki said.

"Now what should we do?" Yoko asked.

Kathryn fixed Yoko with a keen stare. "You can tell us all what you have planned for this date you have tomorrow evening. In detail. Don't leave anything out. We'll vote to tell you if it's acceptable."

Yoko tossed her wadded up napkin at Kathryn who expertly dodged it. "Yes, Mama-san," she said giggling again.

"We really need to discuss it, kiddo. In case you get into a sticky spot, we'll bail you out."

Yoko's face puckered up as she tried to make sense out of what Kathryn said. "Forget it! I was teasing. But you don't know him well enough to go to bed with him yet. Do you hear me?"

Murphy reared up and barked loudly.

"Do not worry. I am playing hard to get. See," she said, pulling her cell phone out of her pocket. "Harry has called me thirty-seven times during the past few days and I did not return his calls. I am being . . . mysterious."

"Yeah, a real Mata Hari," Isabelle quipped.

As the women bantered back and forth, Myra let her thoughts drift to what Charles was doing in the war room. She finally excused herself to take a plate of food to him. The women were still giggling and laughing when she left the kitchen.

Myra sat at the round table with Charles while he ate his lunch. She waited until he was finished, then asked, "How long will it take before they arrest those awful people?"

"My best guess would be sometime tomorrow. That's why Alexis has to exact her personal revenge this evening. Everything is on target, my dear. Is there something in particular you're worried about?"

"I'm not exactly worried, Charles. I am . . . a bit apprehensive about Annie. This is all so new to her. She appears to have bounced back remarkably well. What's that expression? She did a 180 and ran with it."

"Annie is having the time of her life, thanks

to you, my dear. Don't jinx her now. I have no doubt that she will make us all proud of her. Lately, we all seem to be conversing in clichés but even so, I will risk another one. Annie is taking to the Sisterhood like a duck to water. I see her as being a definite asset to our little team."

"I just wanted a second opinion, dear."

"Well, now you have it. I must get back to my work to make sure we all stay safe and on this side of the law." Myra blinked and Charles laughed.

Myra sighed as she got up, picked up Charles's lunch plate and left the war room.

"Stop worrying, Mom. It's happening."

"Oh, darling girl, thank you. You know me, I'm not happy unless I'm worrying."

"You miss out on a lot when you do that. This revenge was flawless. Aunt Annie seems really happy. I'm so glad you were able to enlist her help. I hope you're relieved that the two thorns in your side, Maggie Spritzer and Ted Robinson, are gone."

"I am, dear. I did quite a bit of worrying about those two. I'm so glad Charles intervened. He wouldn't tell me what he said to them. I suppose it's better I don't know."

"The only important thing is they're gone. I am so proud of you. I wish I could hug you, Mom. I wish that more than anything."

Tears rolled down Myra's cheeks. "Darling girl, I wish that, too. More than you can ever know." She turned when she felt something brush her cheek. She literally swooned and almost dropped the plate in her hand. Gingerly, she brought up her fingertips to touch the spot on her cheek. She was stunned to find her tears had been wiped away. "If this is all that is allowed me, I'll take it," she whispered.

Arden Gillespie settled herself behind her desk. It was 2:30 pm. She took a deep breath before she fired up yet another cigarette. She looked down at the condensed file in front of her that listed all of Anna de Silva's accounts. She took a second deep breath before she dialed the private number of the broker in charge of the account at Smith Barney. She identified herself and said, "I was wondering, Mr. Gilbert, if you could give me some indication as to when you plan to transfer Anna de Silva's account to my firm. It was my understanding the account was to be transferred three days ago. Is there a problem?" There, she'd voiced her worst fear. She waited for what she expected to be some cockamamie excuse.

"I beg your pardon. Who did you say this was?"

Arden felt her heart flutter in her chest. "I *said* I was Arden Gillespie of Gillespie and Sullivan. I *asked* you when you would be transferring Mrs. de Silva's account to my firm as per our agreement. I hope you aren't going to tell me there's a problem. I don't like problems, Mr. Gilbert."

"I don't like problems either, Miss Gillespie, but I have no clue as to what you are talking about. I have had no instructions about transferring Mrs. de Silva's account."

"That's impossible. My partner and I had a meeting with Mrs. de Silva and her personal assistant, Ellen Markham, who assured us both that *ALL* of Mrs. de Silva's accounts were to be transferred to our firm. I can understand you don't want to part with such a lucrative moneymaker, but it is Mrs. de Silva's wish. Perhaps you should call her to confirm this. I'll be happy to provide you with the phone number. Mrs. de Silva is no longer in Spain, she's in Manassas."

"That I did not know. I'll call her immediately. I have the phone number in Manassas and I'll get back to you."

"See that you do, Mr. Gilbert. I am not a patient person."

Arden disconnected the call and immediately dialed the number of Goldman Sachs. She went through her spiel with exactly the same result. She started to panic as alarm spread through her. She fired up another cigarette as she pressed the button that would ring in Roland's office. "Come here immediately. We seem to have a problem. *Now*, Roland."

Sullivan collapsed, his eyes wild with fear when Arden brought him up to date. "Something's wrong," was all he could manage to say.

"You're damn right, something is wrong. I want you here when I make the next call. Maybe you should make it. While you're doing that, I'll call that ice witch to ask her what kind of game she's playing."

Forty minutes passed with both brokers getting sicker by the moment. Arden's hands were shaking so badly she had to clasp them together to stay calm. The phone rang. They looked at one another before Arden finally picked it up on the sixth ring. "Arden Gillespie," she said.

"What? Sara! Sara Whittier! Well, yes, Roland and I have been trying to find you. Why were we trying to find you? Because . . . because Roland would like to make amends to you for what you went through. I should have said, Roland and I want to make amends . . . How kind of you to say it isn't necessary but it is necessary . . . You want to come to my apartment this evening? Let me see if Roland is free." She looked over at Roland and widened her eyes. She mouthed the words, should I say yes? He nodded. "Roland said that would be fine. Then I guess we'll see you around nine or so. Oh, you're leaving tomorrow. How nice."

Arden leaned back in her chair and closed her eyes. "What's happening here, Roland? None of those brokers have called me back. Sara calls us *now*!"

"Then go straight to the source. Call Ellen Markham. Let's get this settled right now. Demand to speak to Mrs. de Silva."

Arden licked at her dry lips but she did as instructed. She frowned at the strange voice on the other end of the phone. Must be the housekeeper. "This is Arden Gillespie. I'd like to speak to Ellen Markham, please."

"I am sorry, madam, you must have the wrong number. There is no one here named Ellen Markham." Her eyes frantic, Arden looked down at the number on the file. In a voice she barely recognized as her own, she said, "Then I'd like to speak to Mrs. de Silva."

"Mrs. de Silva has gone into town. She won't return till later in the evening. Do you care to leave a message?"

"Damn right I care to leave a message. Where is the Oriental girl? I'll talk to her."

"There is no Oriental girl here, madam. Do you care to leave a message?"

Her voice trembling with fright, Arden said, "Ask Mrs. de Silva to call me please, either at home or at the office." She rattled off both numbers before she hung up.

Roland jumped off his chair. "What the hell was that all about?" His panic matched Arden's.

"The woman said no one named Ellen Markham lives there and there is no Oriental woman there either. De Silva has gone to town and won't be back till later tonight."

"Call one of the brokers back," Roland told her.

Arden made call after call to every broker on her list and was told the same thing. "Mrs. de Silva did not authorize any accounts to be transferred. Mrs. de Silva said she never heard of the firm of Gillespie and Sullivan. She said she is subjected to things like this all the time and it is just a nuisance someone like her has to put up with."

Arden could barely get the words out of her mouth to repeat the phone conversations to Roland. He looked like he would collapse any moment.

"Bring up the escrow account at Virginia State Trust," Roland croaked in a hoarse voice.

Arden was so nervous she kept hitting the wrong keys. It took her five tries before she was able to log onto the site that would give her the balance in the escrow account. She stared in disbelief at what she was seeing. "It's gone, Roland. The account is closed."

There was no mistaking the panic in Roland's voice now. It transferred itself to Arden who could barely stand erect. "Maybe you made a mistake. Try it again."

"Roland, I did not make a mistake. Look, it's the Gillespie/Sullivan/de Silva account. The account number is correct. It says right here the account was closed at two o'clock this afternoon when all the money was wired out of the account."

"My God, what are we going to do? We're on the hook for all that money." A vision of himself selling shoes in some discount store flashed in front of him. "We were set up!"

Arden started to cry.

"Shut up, Arden, this was all your idea. Now look what's happened. This is what your greed has gotten us into."

"You went along with it. No one is that smart. Think about it, Roland. Who has the smarts to set something like this up? I'll tell you who, that goddamn Sara Whittier, that's who. How very convenient that she called just an hour ago. How goddamn convenient. And you want to pay her off? When pigs fly." Arden was screeching now, her voice ricocheting around the luxurious office. "I'm going home," Arden said suddenly. "Are you coming?"

Roland thought about the question. He closed his eyes and nodded.

His shaky hand on the doorknob, Roland whirled around when the phone rang. He looked at Arden, stark fear in his eyes. Neither made a move to answer it. Finally, Arden retraced her steps and pressed a button. When she heard the voice of Hiram Peacher, she closed her eyes. "This is Arden Gillespie." She listened, her knuckles turning white on the edge of the desk. She didn't say good-bye, she simply clicked off the button and sank to her knees, her hands still clutching the edge of the desk.

"What? For Christ's sake, what?" Roland shouted.

"Our presence is required at the Virginia State Trust *immediately*. The bankers will keep the bank open until we get there. Mrs. de Silva is already there. He . . . he said . . . he would wait until tomorrow to . . . to . . . to call the SEC boys."

Roland ran his fingers through his already messy hair. He finally found his voice. "Then I guess we better be on our way and not keep the bankers at Virginia State Trust waiting. Get up, Arden, it's too late to cry."

"We could run away. We could . . ."

"Shut up. Go wash your face and comb your hair. The least we can do is look presentable." Roland's voice was almost calm when he said, "I wonder if this is how Sara Whittier felt when we brought her world crashing down around her when she hadn't done a thing to deserve it."

"Will you shut up about Sara Whittier already! I can't stand to hear her name!" Arden screamed at the top of her lungs.

"You better get used to it, my dear. I think we're both going to hear that name a lot from here on in."

Arden screamed again and again as she headed for the washroom where she splashed cold water on her face. She dried herself off with a paper towel and was stunned at the haggard-looking reflection glaring back at her from the mirror.

Chapter 25

Anna de Silva paced the confines of Hiram Peacher's office. She decided it didn't look all that much different from the old days. The draperies and the carpet were new but the furniture looked the same, possibly reupholstered. She knew it was the same because of the carved pineapples on the wooden arms. So long ago. She smiled at the bowl of all day suckers sitting on the old man's desk. Today they called them blow-pops. Hiram had explained that there was bubble gum in the middle of the suckers. Annie laughed again as she accepted the sucker Hiram handed to her. She unwrapped it and stuck it in her mouth. "Ah, grape, my favorite. You remembered?"

"I remember everything about my favorite

customers. I must say, Anna, you are taking this all rather well."

"I'm used to it, Hiram. People try to scam me all the time. Fortunately, I have very good people who watch over me. It will all be taken care of." Anna looked at her watch. "How long before they get here?"

"A half hour. It really depends on the traffic. The guard will bring them around to my private entrance."

Anna sucked on the lollipop, enjoying the sweet taste. "Have you given any thought to them skedaddling?"

The old banker roared with laughter. "Now that's an expression that dates us both, Anna. They'll be here because they simply can't believe this has happened.

"I remember the very first day you came in here with your daddy. I had just started working here. I was all of twenty years old and you were ten. I remember how our fathers talked about us like we weren't even there. And, here we are again. Amazing, when you stop to think about it."

Anna opted for a little fib and said, "I remember that day, too. You look to me, Hiram, like you want to smoke a cigar. It's a nice balmy evening; so why don't we go outside so you can fire up that stogie."

"Ah, a lady after my own heart. Yes, let's do that. Let me tell Jackson where we'll be when our *banditos* arrive."

* * *

Her body quivering, Arden looked around the bank's parking lot. Two shiny Mercedes Benzes were parked side by side. A nondescript Ford was parked at the far end of the lot. "I don't see any police cars," she whispered.

Roland snorted. "And I suppose you think that's a good thing." He looked up when he felt a raindrop hit his cheek. Rain was good for the spring flowers, he thought inanely. Patsy always used to say that in the spring when she planted the first flowers of the year. He wondered what she was doing right this minute. He wondered why he was so calm all of a sudden.

"Don't you?"

"No, Arden, I don't. This is a sort of come-to-Jesus meeting. They're going to give us a chance to put the funds back. Tomorrow is when the shit will hit the fan."

"We didn't take the money," Arden hissed.

"Prove it," Roland said, heading for the bank entrance. Arden had to run to catch up with him.

Jackson Petrie, the guard, watched the couple approach. He knew something serious was going on but it wasn't his business. His instructions were to allow them to enter and that's exactly what he was going to do. Before he opened the door, he buzzed Mr. Peacher's office. He asked for ID and scrutinized it carefully through the door before he opened it. Satisfied, he motioned the couple to walk across the lobby and down the hall. He kept his hand on the butt of the gun at his hip. Well, he would have something to tell his wife of twenty-five years over breakfast in the morning.

Hiram Peacher opened the door and nodded to Jackson. The door closed the moment Arden and Roland stepped over the threshold. He indicated two chairs flanking a square table filled with magazines. His voice colder than ice, he made the introductions. "Even though you know each other, allow me to make the introductions again. Anna de Silva, Arden Gillespie and Roland Sullivan."

Arden looked at Roland, not comprehending what she was hearing. Finally she was able to say, "Did you say this woman is Anna de Silva?"

Anna stood up. "I was Anna de Silva when I woke up this morning. As a matter of fact, I've been Anna Ryland de Silva most of my life."

"Then who was that woman we met at your house who said she was you?"

Anna reared back. "My dear woman, you and the gentleman with you were never at my house and there is no one in my house impersonating me. Who are you people?"

Arden struggled for words. "Then who was Ellen Markham and that Oriental girl named Sumi something or other?"

"I have no idea what you're talking about. Hiram, you really should have called the police."

"But you signed all the contracts. I have them right here," Arden said, making a clumsy attempt to open her briefcase. Her eyes pleaded with Roland to step in.

"You okayed everything, Mr. Peacher," Roland said. "We submitted everything you asked for. You said you verified everything. Obviously, if this is really Anna de Silva, you have some explaining to do, too. We acted in good faith. How could we know the woman we met at her home wasn't Mrs. de Silva?"

Anna stood up and looked across the desk at Hiram Peacher. "I want to prosecute. To the fullest extent the law allows. That is not my signature on those documents. I never set eyes on either one of you before this moment. I do not know anyone named Ellen Markham or Sumi something or other. Hiram, I expect you to make this right."

The old banker pierced Arden and Roland with a steely gaze. "This *IS* Anna de Silva. This is her current passport. This is her birth certificate. These are her fingerprints. Mrs. de Silva was still in Spain when you say you met with her. Her passport verifies this. I regret to say you were duped but that doesn't change the situation."

"Return the money and I might reconsider and drop the charges," Anna said. "If you don't return the money, you will be held accountable. I really must go, Hiram. I'm having dinner with my very good friend, Judge Cornelia Easter." She totally ignored the two brokers.

Arden and Roland sat in stupefied amazement while the two old people discussed Judge Easter and other pleasant memories while their own lives crumbled at their feet.

When the door closed behind Anna, the old banker looked at the two miserable people sitting across from where he was standing. "You weren't very clever, either one of you. Did you really think you could get away with this?"

"We didn't do anything," Arden cried. "We never touched the monies in that account. You have to prove we did. We're guilty of stupidity, but that's all we're guilty of. Someone framed us."

"And who might that person be, Miss Gillespie?"

"I don't know," Arden wailed. "Roland, for God's sake, say something. Make this man understand we did not do what he says we did."

Roland cleared his throat. "Mr. Peacher, neither my partner nor I had anything to do with the escrow account. She's right, the burden of proof is on you."

"This meeting is over," Peacher said. "I've already notified the proper authorities. You can tell your story to them tomorrow at nine in your offices. My advice to you is, do not attempt to flee the area. It will go that much harder on you if you try something so foolish. Good evening, Miss Gillespie, Mr. Sullivan."

As Jackson arrived to escort them from the bank, Arden was crying and screaming that she hadn't done anything wrong. Roland ignored her, his shoulders stiff as he made his way to the car. He didn't bother opening the door for Arden who was still wailing as she climbed into the passenger seat. Roland stomped on the gas pedal before her door was closed and she was buckled up.

"I want to kill someone," she screeched. She totally forgot that just hours ago she had been plotting Roland's death. "It's that damn Sara Whittier. I know it. I feel it. I can smell her goddamn smarmy perfume, that flower crap she used to wear. She's behind this. Well, I'll fix her ass when she comes to the apartment tonight. You better not weasel out on me either."

Arden continued to screech. "Are you *ever* going to say anything, Roland?"

"They have to prove we transferred the money. The bank, I'm thinking, is on the hook, too. We need to make some calls when we get to your place. I want a lawyer with me in the morning. You'll need one, too. I'm going to call Marcus Barclay. I have his home phone number. Who are you going to call?"

Arden wiped at her smeared tears. "That all-female law firm in Georgetown. The one who started the firm. I think her name is Quinn, not sure if it's her first or last name. I understand she's the rainmaker at the firm. I fucking hate this, Roland. We did nothing wrong. We have to fight this and I mean down and dirty fighting. I am not throwing in the towel. Some goddamn thief stole our money. Ours *and* the bank's. You're taking this very well, Roland. Are you sure you didn't have something to do with the wire transfer of that money?"

"I refuse to dignify that question with any kind of response. Let's just get home so we can decide what we do tomorrow when the SEC boys invade our office. I also think we should cancel our meeting with Sara Whittier. Call her."

Arden started screeching again until her face

turned an alarming beet color. "Are you out of your mind? She's at the bottom of this, mark my words. I can't cancel even if I want to. She didn't leave a number. We have to make two phone calls. How long is that going to take? Five minutes? I want to go over all those contracts again. I damn well want to see Anna de Silva's signature. The real one. How did the bogus signature pass muster the first time? A smart lawyer will have to deal with all that. I'm not going down without a fight. You better be standing at my side, Roland, and yes, that's a warning and a threat." She flopped back against the seat as her tears started flowing again.

"For God's sake, will you please shut up. I can't stand that infernal sniffling. You need to get your wits about you." *What did he ever see in this woman?*

The rest of the trip into the city was made in silence. Oddly enough, Roland's thoughts were on his family and what they would say and think tomorrow instead of what was going to happen to him when he got to the office. He was rapidly becoming resigned to the inevitable: going to prison. When he got out, he would be lucky if a discount shoe store would hire him. What did Sara Whittier do when she got out of prison? He wished he knew if she had been able to get a job.

Was Arden right that Sara was responsible for their present plight?

Roland slowed and made a right turn into Arden's apartment complex. He'd been here so often, he could make the trip with his eyes closed. "We're here, Arden, get your things together. If I see one more tear, if I hear you sniffling, I'm leaving."

"All right, all right. We forgot to stop at the store. That means I won't be doing any cooking."

"Food! You're thinking about food! My God, how can you even think about food? Will you open the damn door already?"

"You are one ugly person, Roland Sullivan. Sniping at me isn't going to do either one of us any good. We're in this together. Actually, I was thinking about you in regard to food because you're like a bear if you don't eat on time. Fine, I will stop thinking about food and ask me if I care if you starve."

She was right. He was a bear when he didn't eat by seven o'clock. His stomach was rumbling but he ignored it.

Inside, with the door double locked behind them, Roland headed for the bathroom where he called his attorney on his cell phone. He could tell he had interrupted the attorney's dinner but the man was still businesslike when he reacted to Roland's dilemma.

"I'll be there at nine. Do not speak to anyone and don't say a word. Not even to your partner. Are we clear on this, Roland?"

"Crystal." Roland clicked off the phone and sat down on the edge of the bathtub. He dropped his head into his hands. He wanted to cry so bad he could taste his tears. He fought them off.

More than anything in the world he wanted to call Patsy, to hear her tell him things would be all right and she would stand by him no matter what.

That would only happen the day pigs grew wings and flew. Still, he looked at his cell phone, daring himself to call his wife. It took all his willpower to shove the phone into his pocket.

Arden had a glass of wine ready for him along with some crackers and cheese set out on a tray in the living room. She looked up at him, her eyes questioning.

"Marcus will be at the office in the morning. How about you?"

"I'm waiting for a call back. The office was closed but there was a number to call for an emergency. I called that number and the message said I would be called back within two hours. I left a long message."

"What time is Sara due?"

Arden looked at her watch. "Soon. We'll deal with her when she gets here. Let's look over all this paperwork. We're going to need to know every single word backward and frontward by tomorrow morning."

The crackers, cheese and wine were gone when Roland removed his glasses. "If de Silva's signature is forged, the forger is one hell of an expert. Look, Arden, we were set up and framed. Accept that fact, okay? We fell into it like the greedy fools we are. There's not another thing we can do until tomorrow. Even then, our lawyers will be taking over and all we can do is stand by and watch our lives crumble about us."

Arden sucked in her breath. "Unless we can convince Sara to tell us what we want to know. There are two of us, Roland. She's just one skinny young woman. I could kill her with my bare hands."

Roland leaped to his feet. "Stop right there, Arden. I won't be a party to any foul play where Sara is concerned. I'll turn you in myself if you so much as look at her crossways. Be sure you understand that. Tell me you do?"

How hard could a double murder be to pull off? Arden sighed and curled up on the sofa. She wanted to go to sleep so she could wake up to find this was all a big bad dream. "All right, I understand," she mumbled.

Alexis stared at the door of Arden Gillespie's apartment. She was here. She was actually standing outside the woman's door. This was her moment and she was alone to savor it. She was excited but calm. She wondered how that could be. The only thing she carried with her was a bottle of doctored-up wine, the seal intact. Charles was a genius when it came to such things. Other than her heart beating a little faster than normal, she felt fine.

Alexis rang the bell and took two steps backward so that she could be seen clearly from the other side of the door. She almost gasped aloud when she saw Arden staring at her with such hatred, she blanched.

"Well, what are you standing there for? Come in. Roland is here. Now, tell us what you want."

"I don't want anything, Arden. I just wanted to tell you and Roland I forgive you. I'm leaving for Europe in a few days and I want to leave all my baggage behind. A marvelous opportunity has come my way. If I wasn't in the place I am right now, this new world wouldn't have opened up for me. Look, I brought a bottle of very good wine to show there are no hard feelings."

Arden's eyes were rife with suspicion. "And just why are you so forgiving, Sara?"

Alexis didn't miss a beat. She handed the bottle of wine to Roland. "Because hate is a killer. You have to move beyond it to function. Now, the past is just a bad memory that I try not to think about."

"Did you put poison in the wine? Why did you set us up with the Countess?"

Alexis laughed. "The bottle is sealed, Arden. What Countess are you talking about?"

"Don't play the innocent with me. How convenient that you should arrive today of all days. Cut the bullshit, Sara. I'll have more respect for you if you own up to how you managed to pull this off."

Alexis tried not to watch Roland take the foil off the bottle and uncork it. She could see him walking toward the china cabinet for a third wine flute. "If I knew what you were talking about, I might be able to answer you. Are you blaming me for something? If you are, please don't. Look, I have a very nice life now. There's no way I would jeopardize it for you or for Roland. If there's something wrong in your life,

I had nothing to do with it. However, what goes around, comes around. You did frame me; you and Roland were responsible for me going to prison. I said I forgive you. Forgiving you is important to me. It might not be important to you but I can't help that. So, are we going to make a toast to my good life or not? Otherwise, I have to leave."

Roland poured wine into three glasses. He looked up at Alexis and said, "I'm sorry, Sara, for everything that happened to you. I wish you a good life. Arden," he said, his voice cold and demanding, "drink a toast to Sara. She has nothing to do with our current problem." He hoped what he was saying was true.

Alexis thought she would gag at Roland's words. "I know you mean that, Roland. Bottoms up," she said sweetly. Arden and Roland drained their glasses.

"Why aren't you drinking the wine?" Arden asked suspiciously.

"Because it was drugged. I'm no fool, you bitch!"

"Damn you! Roland . . ."

Roland toppled over onto the couch. Arden simply crumpled and slid to the floor like a rag doll. Alexis immediately scooted to the front door and opened it. She whistled sharply. A moment later she heard the elevator door slide open.

Alexis clapped her hands in glee.

* * *

Nikki turned around when she heard her name called. She let loose a loud sigh of relief. This wasn't exactly the most desirable neighborhood to be in after dark. "I'm Nicole. And you must be . . . Snake?"

"Yeah. Let's get this show on the road, okay, counselor. I got things to do and places to go."

"Oh, well, yeah, sure. Hop in . . . Mr. Snake."

"Nah, Snake is my nickname. My real name is Melvin Goodwin."

Nikki drove as fast as she could. She was running late and hoped Alexis was on schedule. "It's not that far, Snake. So, how do you know Alexis?"

"Don't really know the lady but know someone who knows her. He turned me onto her. Said she was good for the green so I said okay. Plus, the vacation was a bonus. Not often I get to go away for six months. Sounds like I'm going to prison for an extended stay, eh?" he cackled. "Always wanted to go to Miami. Some of my idols live there. I'll be able to study their techniques. Might even decide to relocate. I'm looking forward to the trip. Ain't never been on an airplane before." He cackled again.

Snake was perpetual motion, shaking his legs, waving his arms and shaking his head from side to side as he babbled about his art. Nikki made grunting sounds to indicate she was listening to what he was saying. Later, she couldn't remember a thing he'd said.

"Okay, ah . . . Snake. This is our destination.

Please wait here until I see if Alexis is ready for us."

"Sure, no problem. Pretty fancy address. I ain't sure I'm going to fit in here."

"Don't you worry about a thing, Snake. We'll take the service elevator. Just have all your gear ready when I get back."

"You betcha. I'm ready now, counselor."

As Nikki made her way to the building and the lobby she wondered if it had been a mistake for Alexis to tell Snake she was an attorney. She'd said it was the one thing that had closed the deal—free legal representation for the rest of Snake's life. The good part was not having to actually give her name to Snake. Alexis had told him he would have to go through her to get to Nikki and he'd bought the whole deal. She couldn't worry about that now.

The plan was for her to wait in the hall by the elevator. Alexis would open the door when it was time for her and Snake to join her. All she could do now was wait.

The moment Nikki heard Alexis's whistle, she punched the elevator button. Five minutes later she accompanied Snake and all his gear into the service elevator to Arden Gillespie's floor.

Alexis held the door open. Snake scuttled through with all his gear, Nikki following him, rolling her eyes as she did so. Alexis laughed and couldn't stop. Nikki gave her a playful swat and then laughed herself. This was Alexis's moment. If she wanted to laugh, she should laugh.

"Okay, Alexis, baby, tell me what you want.

You were a little vague at our last meeting. Who do you want me to work on first?"

Alexis pretended to ponder the question. "Do him," she said pointing to Roland. "I'm going to shave her head and that might take a bit of time. You know what to do, right, Snake?"

Snake looked down at his tools. "I tattoo the name Sara on his left cheek and tattoo the name Whittier on his right cheek. On his forehead I do my trademark snake, a small one, and the word BASTARD in big letters. You said I could pick the colors. Do I have it down right?"

"You got it, Snake. Get going. Be as quick as possible and don't worry if he twitches. He'll be out for quite a while." She turned to Nikki. "Did you bring my shears?"

Nikki tossed a canvas bag at Alexis before she sat down on a deep green chair and swung her legs over the side. This was Alexis's gig. She was just here as an observer. She watched as Alexis shaved Arden Gillespie's beautiful luxurious blond hair. When she was finished she stood with her hands on her hips to survey her handiwork. "She's pretty ugly without all that hair. What do you think, Nikki?"

"Not pretty at all. I have to call her back and leave a message. Think about it, Alexis. What are the odds of that woman calling me to represent her and here I am sitting in her living room watching you shave her head?"

Nikki whipped out her cell phone and hit the return call button. When she heard Arden Gillespie's voice, she went right into her spiel.

"This is Nicole Quinn, Miss Gillespie. I received your call earlier but I'm afraid I won't be able to represent you. My calendar is full. I'm sure you won't have a problem finding a capable attorney. Thank you for considering me in your hour of need."

"Your hour of need!" Alexis doubled over laughing.

"What did you come up with for Arden's tattoo?"

"Nothing outrageous. My name on her face, too. I thought the word BITCH in big letters across her forehead. Yo, Snake, let's put the snake on Miss Gillespie's forehead because she is a snake. What do you think?"

"Works for me," Nikki said.

"Me, too," Snake said.

"Yeah, it works for me, too. They'll go through their stay in prison with those tattoos. That makes me happy. Really, really happy. You don't think they'll get out on bail, do you?"

"Not a chance."

It was eleven o'clock when Alexis packed up her clippers and shaver. She looked over at Nikki. "Our work here is done."

"Snake, you do good work. Do you need a ride to the airport?" Alexis asked.

Nikki watched as money changed hands.

"Would appreciate it. Anytime you want some work done, call me."

"I'll do that, Snake."

On the ride back to Pinewood, Nikki glanced across at her passenger. "You okay, Alexis?"

"Yeah, I am. Thanks for being there."

"That guy Snake. He kind of grows on you."

"Hey, anytime you want a work of art done, I bet he'd do it for free."

Both women laughed all the way back to Pinewood.

Epilogue

Myra paced and dithered in the kitchen, to Charles's amusement. He was tempted to say something to his lady love but decided against it. Sometimes Myra had to work things through on her own without any help from him. He busied himself at the stove, stirring things that didn't need to be stirred as he stared out the kitchen window at the young women on the terrace.

Today they were a lively bunch, giggling and laughing. That had to mean things in their world were right side up. He felt more than pleased with himself for his part in Alexis's revenge. She was happier than she'd ever been. A burst of raucous laughter invaded the kitchen by way of the open window. Myra stopped pacing to peer over his shoulder. "I hope they're still in a laughing mood when we adjourn to the war room."

Charles twinkled. "I think you can count on it, dear. It's time." He set about turning his pots and pans to simmer. He took one last look in the oven and decided he could be spared for an hour from his culinary duties.

"Fetch our guest, Myra, and I'll bring the girls. It's going to be all right. Trust me."

"I do, Charles, I do. But . . . but we did this on our own without consulting the others. That's not how we do things. What if . . . if . . . one of them . . . pitches a fit. Oh, I do love that saying."

"Then we'll deal with it. Run along, dear."

Myra headed for the living room where Annie de Silva was reading a NASCAR magazine. She looked up at Myra. "This is so interesting," she said, pointing to the glossy magazine. "I'm going to go to a race one of these days."

Myra laughed. Not at what Annie had said but at her attire. Today, Annie was dressed in baggy jeans and an oversize tee shirt that said: CHICK WITH BRAINS. "Kathryn gave it to me. It's quite comfortable. Kathryn said it is in-house attire which means I can't wear it to the grocery store or the bank."

"When was the last time you were in a grocery store, Annie?"

"A hundred years ago. I'm going to do that, too. I'm going to do everything I haven't done in years and years. Did you tell the others? Are they all right about me . . . you know, joining up?"

"No, I didn't tell them. We're going to surprise them. I don't anticipate a problem, Annie. They all adore you. You aren't worrying, are you?" Myra asked as she opened the secret panel that would take them to the war room.

"A little. I so want to be a part of all this. I mean actively. I want to participate, not just use my money. You don't think I'm too old, do you?"

"Hell no! If you're old, so am I. We can still contribute. Mightily. I forgot to ask in all the excitement, how did dinner go with Nellie?"

"It was wonderful. We talked for hours. Played catch-up. We didn't talk much about Jenny. That's for another day with a good supply of wine. I'm glad she's in the loop."

Myra whirled around. "Shhh. No one knows that, Annie."

"Oooh, sorry. Good Lord! This place looks like something you'd see in the White House. However did you do all this?" Annie asked, looking around in awe. "You were right, Myra, this definitely is not a Mickey Mouse operation. I cannot tell you how excited I am to be part of this."

"Today you observe and listen. When our meeting is over, you can ask all the questions you want. Ah, I hear Charles and the girls. Don't sit down yet, Annie," Myra whispered as she eyed Julia's chair in the corner.

The women filed into the room and stopped short when they saw Annie standing next to Myra. As one, their gaze swivelled to Julia's chair just as Charles stepped down from his dais with a chair on casters. He placed it next to Myra's chair. He pretended not to hear their sighs of relief.

Annie looked around at the women. "Is it all right for me to sit down? If you would rather I go upstairs, I can do that, too. I don't want to be here if you don't want me. But if that's the case, I'd like to stay in the background to help in any way I can."

"Just what I need, another mother," Yoko quipped, breaking the ice. The others held out their hands as they made welcoming sounds. No one mentioned Julia's empty chair that still faced the wall.

Myra called the meeting to order. "Is there any new business?" The women shook their heads. "Then let's get to the old business." She beckoned Charles to join them.

"I'm happy to report that Maggie Spritzer and Ted Robinson are enjoying their new life in the Big Apple. They are living together in an apartment on the West Side. They have adapted to their new jobs. I will update you as new reports come in."

"It's been ten days! What's going on with Gillespie and Sullivan?" Nikki asked.

Alexis sat up straighter as she waited for whatever it was Charles was going to say.

Charles placed a stack of newspapers in the center of the table. He smiled. The others laughed out loud.

"I like this one best," Alexis said, pointing to a picture that was above the fold of the *Post* that showed Arden Gillespie and Roland Sullivan being led from Arden's apartment in shackles.

Snake's art work appeared sharp and clear. The caption under the picture read: Who is Sara Whittier?

Charles continued to smile. "The couple is out on bail but hiding out in Miss Gillespie's apartment. Both have legal representation that is in no way superior. The firm of Gillespie and Sullivan is closed. Mrs. Sullivan has taken her children away on an extended vacation which means she will not be standing by her husband in his hour of need. An investigation into Sara's old case has been reopened.

"The monies we transferred out of the escrow account will be transferred later this week to Alexis's old clients along with a handsome return on their previous investments. Anonymously, of course. I took the liberty of transferring monies to Alexis's new brokerage account that Myra and Nikki have set up for her. Five years' salary, the cost of a new house and new car, five years of health-care premiums, and a rather large sum of money as compensation for the incarceration, pain and suffering she endured. The rest of the monies will be returned to the Virginia State Trust. Does this all meet with your approval?" A robust chorus of ayes boomed in Charles's ears.

Myra looked over at Alexis who had tears in her eyes. "Have you been avenged, dear?" Alexis nodded as she swiped at her tears.

"Are you going to take back your real name?" Nikki asked. "I can do all the paperwork if you want to do that. It's your call, Alexis."

"Not right now. Maybe sometime in the future. Alexis Thorne is who I am these days. I don't know if Sara Whittier could do what Alexis Thorne does. Thanks for the offer, though."

"Then it's settled. You are our Alexis. You're one of us," Myra said, then continued, "You all know Annie. She's also one of us now. I think she has proved that she belongs to our little group. She performed admirably in Alexis's revenge. We couldn't have done what we did without her help. Please welcome her to the Sisterhood."

The women pushed their chairs back and walked around to where Annie sat. They embraced her, kissed her on the cheek. Congratulations rang in the air.

Annie beamed as she reached across to squeeze Myra's hand.

"Welcome to the Sisterhood, Annie," Myra said.

"What's our next . . ." Annie struggled for the word she wanted, "gig?"

"Normally what we do is choose a name out of the shoe box but this time we don't have to choose. Our next adventure is on Yoko's behalf. We will adjourn now and reconvene in one month, at which time we will come up with a suitable solution for Yoko's revenge."

Kathryn clapped Yoko on the back. "That gives you a whole month to seduce old Harry. Feel free to call us at any time of the day or night."

"You're too late!" Yoko giggled.

"You did *the deed?*" Isabelle said, shock ringing in her voice.

"You bumped uglies in the night!" Alexis drawled. "Well, damn. When?"

"Just you never mind," Yoko said.

"And how was it?" Nikki weighed in.

"How many words do you want?" Yoko said, smiling from ear to ear.

"One will do, dear," Myra said.

"Spectacular!"

"Spectacular is good," Annie said.

Charles could feel his ears heating up. He tried not to laugh but a small sound escaped him. Yoko looked up at him and winked. He gave her a thumbs-up.

"I think this meeting is adjourned. I'll see you all one month from today. Run along, girls!" Myra said, making shooing motions with her hands.

When the door to the war room closed behind the young women, Myra turned to Annie. "What do you think, Annie?"

"I love them all. I can't wait till the next meeting."

"The time will go quickly since you're going to go cross-country with Kathryn. Trust me, you are going to have the time of your life."

"How can I ever thank you, old friend?"

"Just be happy, Annie, just be happy."

Charles stepped down and hugged Annie. "Welcome to the Sisterhood, Annie."

More by Best-selling Author

Fern Michaels

__About Face	0-8217-7020-9	$7.99US/$10.99CAN
__Kentucky Sunrise	0-8217-7462-X	$7.99US/$10.99CAN
__Kentucky Rich	0-8217-7234-1	$7.99US/$10.99CAN
__Kentucky Heat	0-8217-7368-2	$7.99US/$10.99CAN
__Plain Jane	0-8217-6927-8	$7.99US/$10.99CAN
__Wish List	0-8217-7363-1	$7.50US/$10.50CAN
__Yesterday	0-8217-6785-2	$7.50US/$10.50CAN
__The Guest List	0-8217-6657-0	$7.50US/$10.50CAN
__Finders Keepers	0-8217-7364-X	$7.50US/$10.50CAN
__Annie's Rainbow	0-8217-7366-6	$7.50US/$10.50CAN
__Dear Emily	0-8217-7316-X	$7.50US/$10.50CAN
__Sara's Song	0-8217-7480-8	$7.50US/$10.50CAN
__Celebration	0-8217-7434-4	$7.50US/$10.50CAN
__Vegas Heat	0-8217-7207-4	$7.50US/$10.50CAN
__Vegas Rich	0-8217-7206-6	$7.50US/$10.50CAN
__Vegas Sunrise	0-8217-7208-2	$7.50US/$10.50CAN
__What You Wish For	0-8217-6828-X	$7.99US/$10.99CAN
__Charming Lily	0-8217-7019-5	$7.99US/$10.99CAN

Available Wherever Books Are Sold!

Visit our website at **www.kensingtonbooks.com.**